THE TICKER

A Novel

Meredithe

Robert M. Davis

Robert M. Davis

THE TICKER

ISBN: 978-1-61170-135-7

Cover designed and illustrated by Bob Archibald

Printed in the USA and UK on acid-free paper.

Robertson Publishing™
www.RobertsonPublishing.com

To purchase additional copies of this book go to:
amazon.com
barnesandnoble.com
www.rp–author.com/robertdavis

DEDICATION

For Joanne, Brian, and Kelli

"EVERY GREAT DREAM
BEGINS WITH A DREAMER"
—Harriet Tubman

CHAPTER ONE

The diagram of a human heart with colored parts was now etched in my brain. A healthy heart. White sanitary paper covering the examination table scrunched underneath my slacks when I shifted my weight. On the opposite wall, backlit lighting illuminated my latest chest x-ray, reminding me of a dark cloud formation blocking the sun.

Two sharp knocks on the door made me flinch. Dr. Louis Titelman re-entered the examination room with a handful of printouts and closed the door. The silver stethoscope dangling from his neck shone like an expensive piece of millennium jewelry. How different he looked in a white doctor's smock instead of the usual Hawaiian shirt covering his ever-expanding paunch.

Louis ignored my inquisitive stare. He sat down on a mobile metal stool and scooted to a small desk. His face was cheerless as he compared my latest EKG and blood work to previous tests. As my closest friend of thirty-six years, he could disregard my presence anytime he damn well pleased. But as my cardiologist, I felt snubbed by his inattention. Perhaps Louis' behavior was payback for my being a recluse since the funerals.

My open, starched, white shirt exposed an ugly red scar embedded in my chest like a flaw in a painting's canvas. Shortness of breath was a common occurrence, along with biting pokes of pain, dizziness, nausea, and bouts of fatigue. Even the task at hand, maneuvering buttons through buttonholes, had been upgraded to major chore.

The wall clock with the twitching second hand showed 9:52 a.m. I'd been sitting here the better part of an hour. They say the minutes tick faster as the years mount up, a saying that didn't prove true in my case.

A large September calendar hung underneath the clock. The first nine days were x'd out in heavy black ink. Monday the tenth

1

stood conspicuous as the first open square.

"Huh," escaped me. September tenth, my birthday. A justifiable oversight. Louis and I had other things occupying our minds today.

Several filing cabinets were positioned to the right of the calendar. A framed photo of Louis and my family stood prominently on the middle cabinet's top, taking me back twelve years to 1989. A happy time. Helen was still alive and well, looking as beautiful as ever. Our daughter Katie, the spitting image of her mother except for my blue eyes, had just started high school. I towered over Louis' squat five-foot-five-inch form by a good eight inches. Other than a fuller face, his features hadn't changed much in twelve years, but mine had. I was forty-five years old then, without a hint of silver in my dark hair.

"Hey, Louis." My scratchy voice sounded like a squeaky gate in need of lubrication. I cleared my throat. "Remember me? The patient?"

"Another minute, please." Louis had a finger pointed at one chart while his eyes studied a set of numbers on his computer screen.

I might as well have been talking to the EKG machine. After my operation Louis had made me promise to scale down my involvement at Proffitt Advertising. I had done him one better. I quit going into the agency. I even followed his strict health program that included a diet of leafy, dark-skinned, tasteless food and excluded fine cigars, Grey Goose vodka, and rib-eye steaks. My karate regime, softball, golf, and high-stakes poker became former pastimes. I was a good patient, more for Louis' sake than my own. Yet there had been another indefinable reason that drove me to stay alive.

A double knock again. Louis didn't react. Nor did he notice the door opening. Nurse Sally stuck her brunette head inside, offering a sweet smile.

"I'm sorry to interrupt your examination, Mr. Proffitt." She inched further into the room. "Dr. Titelman, your 9:15, 9:30, and 9:45 appointments are in the waiting room. What should I tell them?"

"There's no definitive time when I can see anyone," Louis

2

snapped, without lifting his gaze from the computer screen. "Ask if they want to reschedule. Best I can do."

Louis' words came out cold and edgy, unlike his usual Teflon personality. Sally backpedaled out of the room and closed the door. His shoulders slumped. He rubbed his forehead. Then his face creased into a big wrinkle. That bad, huh?

"What's going on, Louis? I'd rather be enlightened by you instead of some aloof, snot-nosed cardiologist who'd remember my cardiogram before recognizing my face."

Louis inhaled a deep breath. He stared out the window, then at me. Both hands slid his glasses away from the bridge of his pronounced nose. He chewed the end of an ear piece. Another sure sign he was troubled.

"Morgan," he said in a low tone, "there are some discrepancies."

Morgan? Louis had just called me Morgan, my formal, hold-you-at-a-distance, first name. All my life, to family, friends, and business associates, my name had been Mo. What the hell was this about?

"I want you to see another heart specialist," he continued, after finding his doctor's voice. "Get a second opinion. Francis Sawyer is considered the best in the San Francisco Bay Area."

Louis removed the phone receiver from the wall. He punched one button. His Adam's apple jutted in and out.

"Sally, get Mr. Proffitt an immediate appointment with Dr. Sawyer. You'll find his number—"

"Whoa." My hands waved like a desperate man flagging down a ride from the side of the road. "Hold on, Louis. You're my cardiologist. I know I haven't been very sociable for awhile, but we've been the best of friends since our days at Stanford. Don't saccharin coat anything. Give it to me straight."

Louis returned the phone to the wall and sniffed for air. This man had always been a rock during times of crisis. He helped me through my wife's failed bout with cancer, then six months later, Katie's death in a car accident near Yale University where she was a student. The hair on my arms stood at attention. I didn't need to be a heart surgeon to understand why he was avoiding giving me his medical conclusion.

"How long do I have, Louis?"

"I don't know for sure." He affixed the glasses back onto his nose. "But another operation is out of the question. Even if your condition was operable . . ."

The stool that had seemed attached to Louis' ass slid away when he stood. His eyebrows stitched together. The lower portion of his face quivered.

"Heart failure could happen anytime, Mo," Louis said, "with or without warning. An hour. A few days. If you drift with the current, meaning lie in bed, you could possibly survive a week or two. In other words, the more you exert yourself, the less time you'll have." Louis took a squeaky breath. "You may encounter dizziness that could bring on fainting, nausea, shortness of breath, fatigue, and pain in your chest and arms. Or your heart will just stop. Use the nitroglycerin tablets you always carry with you, but keep in mind that overdosing on nitro in a twenty-four-hour period could be coun-terproductive due to your blood pressure and current medications."

A sense of relief freed years of amassed burden, opening the floodgates to my adrenaline. How ironic. Louis' diagnosis has given me newfound strength and a temporary lease on life. Ever since Katie was killed – goddamn it, murdered – I'd been an emo-tional cripple. God knows I'm not a religious man, but deep down I believed there was a Supreme CEO up there. I had often wondered why He hadn't taken me sooner, rather than making me endure such a senseless existence. Now I was getting the sign I'd been waiting for.

I hugged Louis like he was my brother and affectionately pat-ted his shoulders. His body shook with emotion. Wish I could do or say something that would make him feel better.

"You've lived well, Mo," he whispered, "at least before tragedy and disease corrupted your heart. You're a wealthy man. Is there anything you've regretted not doing in your life? If so, in the time you have left, please let me help you make it happen."

Time, once a commodity of little value, was now precious and limited. Louis' diagnosis and offer of help inspired something lying dormant inside me ever since Katie's death. Before I could take on a final endeavor, however, I would need assistance to compensate a select few for their bestowed loving-kindness.

I released Louis and reached into my suit jacket pocket lying at the foot of the examination table. A clipping from this morning's *San Francisco Chronicle* came out with my folded silk tie. A grainy black and white photo of Oliver Kane attached to the article stared back at me. An article about a miscreant driver set free to maim and kill again because of Kane's proficiency in court. God willing, I was going to kill the bastard responsible for the death of my daughter.

Was I out of my mind? Morgan Proffitt, a revenge-crazed vigilante? Revenge, however, wasn't my motivation. Taking another person's life was against every fiber of my moral code. And it wouldn't bring Katie back. But if I eliminated Oliver Kane, other sons and daughters would be saved. Was it worth an eternity of burning in hell? Hell yes.

"I don't have any regrets, Louis," I said, looking up at him.

I just lied to the best friend a man could ever have. Yet deceit was necessary. If I revealed my scheme to Louis, he could be implicated. Or he'd try to stop me.

I replaced the *Chronicle* article in my jacket pocket and knotted my tie with vigor. Now I understood why I'd been forced to hang around this long. I was back in the game, even though I'd just been given life's two-minute warning. My heart pulsed stronger than it had in years. Were there enough ticks left to carry out my mission?

Chapter Two

A thick layer of gray overcast constituted San Francisco's mid-morning sky. For the first time, I noticed how rough the light green exterior appeared on the multi-storied medical building housing Louis' practice. Even the street traffic seemed louder than usual. Luscious scents from a nearby bakery flirted with my nose. I was hungry, but not for food. Instead, I was eager to create a scheme that would put Oliver Kane out of business, permanently.

I hitched up my suit-coat collar and inhaled a mouthful of crisp air. How many more breaths did I have left? A pragmatic rather than maudlin thought. I didn't dread the idea of death. However I did have a fear of dying before I could complete my mission.

I glanced up and down the street, first east then west. The cabdriver I often used to transport me to my appointments with Louis was parked somewhere in the vicinity. I punched one button on my cell phone. The driver picked up after two rings.

"Henry," I said in a voice more robust than normal, "you'll find me on the sidewalk in front of the Geary Boulevard main entrance."

"Be right there, Mr. P. I'll have you home in no time."

"There's been a change in plans. We have several more stops to make before returning to my house."

"No problem." He chuckled. "My time, and the meter's time, is your time. See you in a minute or so."

I verified a phone number in my address book that I hadn't dialed in years and pressed eleven numbers. After three rings there was still no answer. It wouldn't surprise me if the number was no longer in service.

"This is Bruno Santiago from S.O.S. Investigations," a familiar, recorded voice announced over the line. "Please leave your name, number, and. . ."

"Damn," I muttered under my breath. Agita, the medical term

for heartburn that I learned from Louis, invaded my chest and throat.

After the beep, I left Bruno a succinct, yet adamant, message to call me back ASAP. Priceless seconds were turning into wasted minutes. In my head I could hear the tick, tick, ticking of a clock.

Still no sign of Henry's yellow cab. An elderly woman wearing an oversized, blue overcoat that almost touched the sidewalk hurried towards me, pushing a small metal basket on wheels. Hunched shoulders made her tilt forward. All of her worldly goods were probably stored in that basket. At first glance her chiseled features stretched over a weathered complexion. A second look made me realize the beauty in her face. I'd seen her before but couldn't place where.

She stopped three feet away then inched closer. The cart provided a shield between us. Her intense, gray eyes questioned me.

"Please accept my apologies for staring," I said. "For the life of me, I can't remember where we've met."

"I walked as fast as I could when I first saw you, Mr. Proffitt, hoping you'd still be here." Her lips spread into a gummy smile. "I never forget kind people. For years, you, your wife, and your daughter helped serve us Thanksgiving dinner at Saint Joanne's Kitchen like we was guests in your home. Haven't seen you in a long time, though."

"Yes, it's been years. Forgive me, but I can't recall your name. I believe it begins with the letter B."

Two quick horn blasts directed my attention to the street. Henry's idling cab was double-parked. I held up one finger. He nodded then activated flashing hazard taillights. My gaze returned to the woman.

"Your memory ain't so bad after all, Mr. Proffitt. My name is Bonnie."

"Bonnie. Of course." I withdrew my fingers from my pants pocket and shook her rough hand. "You liked the turkey wing. And my wife's special bread dressing. You made Helen feel like she was the greatest chef in San Francisco."

Tears gathered in her eyes. Bonnie examined the green bills

I'd left in her hand. She squeezed the money tight then shook her head.

"Thank you." She pushed the money back to me. "Like always, you've given me way too much."

"Please accept the gift, Bonnie. It will do my heart good."

"God bless you, Mr. Proffitt. Will you and your family be going to the food kitchen this Thanksgiving?"

Her question stopped me cold. Thanksgiving was less than two months away. Louis' prognosis replayed in my head. Weeks and months were no longer in my future.

"We'll be there," I said, moving towards the cab, "if not in person, definitely in spirit."

CHAPTER THREE

My attorney, Robert Schecter, tapped the tip of his pen against a note pad and squinted at me from across his office desk as if I'd just run for a ninety-yard touchdown – the wrong way. Hell, if I had earned the diplomas displayed on the wall behind him, I'd be thinking the same thing.

"What's going on, Morgan?" Robert combed a hand through a white skunk-like stripe of hair in the middle of his head. "I haven't seen or talked to you since you won that karate tournament. When was it? Six years ago? Then you barge into my office this morning without an appointment, like a racehorse on steroids, wanting to make significant changes to your personal estate and to Proffitt Advertising. May I remind you, after the passing of Helen, then your daughter Katherine, you never returned my calls or letters to update the disbursement of your holdings? Why the urgency now?"

A legitimate question. I had no desire to tell Robert, or anyone else, I didn't have long to live. In Robert's case, the last thing I wanted was sanctimonious words from an insincere person. Or for him to spend time that I didn't have trying to talk me into something I didn't want. For those few people who counted, I would say goodbye in my own way while all my faculties were still intact. Not when I was curled up in a bed surrounded by somber faces waiting for fate to do its number.

"I didn't realize that my coming here unannounced would throw Tabasco on your ulcer, Robert." I leaned forward in the chair and placed a hand flat on his glass desk. "Here's what's pertinent. I'm paying you four hundred dollars an hour to perform a service that accommodates my wishes. That's all you should be concerned about."

I removed my hand from the glass leaving a palm print behind. Robert eyeballed the smudge and wrinkled his nose. To my knowledge, no law said a client had to like his attorney. Robert's ego could fill the Goodyear blimp, but he was a hell of good lawyer, one of San Francisco's finest. His first-class finagling had saved me from paying for things I had and hadn't done. But now, like him or not, I needed Robert to perform one last, accelerated service for me with as little of his time-consuming counsel as possible.

"Again, what's your hurry, Morgan?" Robert pointed a manicured fingernail at his notes on a yellow legal pad. "It's a relevant request based on your history and the information you've provided."

After I had buried Katie, the clock seemed to move in slow motion or not at all. Time had been my most useless asset then. That was before this morning's appointment with Louis. Now time was more valuable than anything I owned. Yes, I was in a hell of a big hurry.

"If you're challenging my competence, Robert, forget it. I've never been more lucid in my life. You might say I've had an epiphany. To that end, I want the revisions to my living trust executed immediately."

I looked at Robert's contemporary clock. He'd paid a zillion dollars for a mass of metal rods and big ball bearings enclosed in a glass frame. I never could decipher how to tell time on that sucker. But the relevance of time kept jabbing at me. Bruno, the private investigator, still hadn't returned my call.

"I'd be remiss if I didn't provide counsel here." Robert underlined two words on his pad. "It's understandable why you'd want to give half of your investment portfolio to cancer research, and the other half to create a trust for Dr. Louis Titleman's free medical clinic. However, two of your amendments still concern me: bequeathing your five-point-two-million-dollar house and furnishings plus $5,000 a month from a trust account to your maid Lucille Green, and leaving Proffitt Advertising to Virginia Webb, an employee."

My purpose was to create quick-fix restitution. Too late in the game to verbally express my gratitude to the three people who had looked after me with blind loyalty. Louis, my ignored friend, Mrs. Green, my housekeeper and devoted family caregiver. And Virginia, my protégé who ran the agency after Katie died. Better to mend the neglectful wrongs by showing my appreciation in a tangible way. Then, I was free to focus on Oliver Kane. Robert would drop his briefs if he knew I was planning to eliminate a member of his lawyer brethren.

"We're not talking chump change here, you know?" Robert continued.

"Good point." My eyebrows arched up. "You have concerns about how much I'm leaving to my two trusted employees. Why? Do you think I should leave them more?"

"More!" Robert's light complexion took on a red hue. "My God. Do you realize these two women will never have to work another day in their life when you die?"

"I believe that was the point, Robert."

"Perhaps you should take some time to mull over how you want your assets passed on." Robert stood up and smoothed invisible thigh creases in his pinstriped wool slacks. "Remember, if something happens to you after we incorporate these revisions, they're set in Super Glue. Call me in a few days. But make an appointment, will you?"

"Sit down, Robert." I waited until his butt touched the seat again. "I've always been under the impression that one's will is designed to dispose of one's belongings and assets as one wishes. My wishes are Windex clear, even if they don't meet with your approval. Quite frankly, I plead guilty about being inattentive. You were absolutely right. These changes should have been made years ago. Your firm's paralegal should have no   problem incorporating the amendments in a timely manner – meaning this afternoon."

Robert aimed a finger at me, obviously to make a point. A cell phone chimed. We reached into our respective pockets. My phone was the one with a party on the line.

"Yes, this is Morgan Proffitt."

"Mr. Proffitt," a deep voice replied. "Bruno Santiago returning your call. I got back to you as quickly as I could. It's been a long time since I've had the pleasure of talking to you. Thought maybe you'd found yourself another East Coast private investigator."

"Not a chance," I said, eyeing my watch. It was 11:27 a.m. I'd left Bruno a voicemail almost an hour and half ago. But if I threw some big league attitude his way, I could lose him. "Thank you for getting back to me so quickly. I have an urgent matter that needs your attention."

"That's what I'm here for, Mr. Proffitt."

Robert's eyes questioned me as if I was on the witness stand. I rose from the chair. My dialogue with Bruno needed to be relocated to a more private venue.

"Listen, the reception in here isn't very good," I said to Bruno while staring at Robert. "Please hold the line until I can find a better spot."

I nodded to Robert then moved to his private exit door. My hand reached for the doorknob but stopped in midair. I turned and pointed at his ludicrous clock.

"I'll be back no later than four o'clock this afternoon to sign all the necessary papers, Robert. Everything had better be in order."

I swung the door open with gusto and headed for the windowed stairwell, anxious to resume my conversation with Bruno. The Boston private detective represented step one in eliminating Oliver Kane. Now I was getting somewhere.

Chapter Four

I scowled at the tiny cell phone in my hand as if it was the guilty party. "Damn it, Bruno." The acoustics on the cement stairway landing bounced my words back at me. Bruno had put me on hold while I left Robert's office. Didn't anyone respect my time, or lack of it?

More than ever, I needed to be mindful that the damaged part in my chest was irreplaceable, unfixable, and could stop operating at anytime. Puffing short breaths in and out didn't relieve the tension brewing in me.

11:49 a.m. by my watch. Minutes were speeding around the clock. I had no way of calculating if the time I had left was sufficient enough to kill Oliver Kane. But that wasn't going to stop me from playing the hand I'd been dealt. Conflicted thinking for a moral man who abhors violence. Before today if someone had come to me with a scheme to commit cold-blooded murder, I would have stopped him. Yet the righteousness of my plot to rid a societal evil like Kane seemed more than justified.

The three green metal safety bars I leaned against protected me from plunging down twenty-two floors while I waited for Bruno to come on the line. Proffitt Advertising had used Bruno for East Coast investigations with great results. Hell, I'd never even met the man in person. From his voice alone, I had him pictured as tough looking, heavy, maybe 250 pounds or more. Short brown hair. Wide, mashed-in nose. And big hands. But it wouldn't matter if he looked like Don Knotts. I trusted Bruno Santiago. He was a pro's pro who could dig up the kind of intelligence I needed to expose the vulnerable cracks in Oliver Kane's life. What makes that bastard Kane tick?

"Mr. Proffitt." Bruno sounded out of breath like he was talking and running the Boston Marathon at the same time. Background wind some three thousand miles away muffled the line's quality. "Sorry about putting you on hold like that. One of my sources was relaying some time-critical information. How can I help you?"

"Do you know who Oliver Kane is?" My stomach soured at the sound of the name.

"You pulling on my Jockeys, Mr. Proffitt?" Bruno said. "Everyone in these parts knows about Oliver Kane. He's a muck-a-muck celebrity now in the New England area. The man loves the limelight. If you're thinking. . ."

A whistle sounded from the phone, followed by a cranking engine whine.

"Bruno! Bruno!" What the hell was happening?

"Watch it, asshole," Bruno bellowed. "Sorry, Mr. Proffitt. I almost got run over by some kind of big construction vehicle. Boston sport. It's not even safe to walk on the sidewalks here. If you're thinking about hiring Kane's services, I gotta tell ya, the guy's an all time shit-heel. He makes ambulance chasers look like social workers."

"Then we're talking about the same Oliver Kane," I said, moving across the cement landing to the wall. "I want to retain your services. The assignment I'm giving you this time is for me personally, not Proffitt Advertising. Make this your highest priority. In other words, stop everything you're working on."

"You know I've always been there to accommodate you," he said in a softer voice. "But my caseload is beyond full. I've been turning down jobs for weeks. If I were to drop everything just to work on your case, you'd have to beef up your ante."

I expelled a sigh of relief. For a moment, I'd thought Bruno was refusing to take me on as a client. His supply and demand hustle wasn't a concern. On the contrary, Bruno was being upfront about panhandling me for more money. In all likelihood, his caseload was full. A private detective of any distinction charged more when he was fat with work, especially when an anxious caller wanted immediate action.

"I have no problem paying for an exclusive, Bruno."

However, I was in a quandary as to how much money to offer Bruno. If I doubled his rate, would that be enough to sway him to drop his other clients? Conversely, if my money offer knocked

Bruno's sox off, would he get suspicious and barefoot away?

"I'm heading to Western Union to wire you five thousand dollars," I said. "In cash. You'll receive another five thousand once you've completed the assignment. Should I keep walking? Or should I turn around and redeposit the money into my account?"

A sound that resembled an animal's growl gushed through the phone's tiny speaker. He was considering my offer. We both knew the key word in this negotiation was "cash," a form of insulation that could keep his pockets warm, reputation clean, and wife in the dark – if he was married.

"How can S.O.S. Investigations assist you in regards to Oliver Kane, Mr. Proffitt?"

"You're familiar with the drill, Bruno." A flood of energy surged through my body. "I need to know Kane's exact whereabouts right now. And his schedule for the rest of the week. Get me as much information as you can on Kane's background and how to contact him. Specifically, I want his phone numbers, including private, cell, and fax. Send me photos, addresses, and Boston area maps showing the places he frequents most in his daily work and social routine." I took a needed breath. "Obviously that would include more than his office and home. I'm talking about gyms, restaurants, bars, racetracks, houses of ill repute, anywhere he goes on a regular basis."

"The basics," Bruno said. "What else?"

"Does he have a big entourage around him? How many partners in his firm? What do his employee's and ex-employees say about him? He just got married for the fourth time. Does he cheat on his new wife? How many kids does he have from previous marriages?"

My daughter's beautiful face flashed in my mind. Get a grip, Mo. This was for all the unsuspecting Katies still in harm's way. Focus on the task at hand.

"What's Kane's financial status?" I continued. "Is he as flush as he appears to be? Get a credit report if you can." A maddening car alarm sounded on Bruno's end. I waited for Bruno to distance himself from the noise. "How dirty is Kane? Has he ever been in trouble with the Bar Association? And what are Kane's quirks?"

"Gotcha.   The good stuff: unethical deals, porn, gambling, broads, booze, drugs.   Does Kane spit on the sidewalk, play pocket pool, and what brand of fu-fu juice does he use?"

"You've got it, Bruno.   I'll wire you the money—"

"Shouldn't be a problem," he said.   "'Cept I've got a couple questions for you, Mr. Proffitt.   But I gotta get my car out of a parking garage or I won't have enough dough on me to pay the fee.   From past experience, I know my cell phone's gonna fade in and out.   It should only take a couple of minutes.   Can you hang on?"

"I'll hold," I grumbled.   He had no way of knowing I'd taken out a second mortgage on borrowed time.   "But hurry, Bruno.   The clock is against us on this one."

I retrieved a *Wall Street Journal* article from my inside coat pocket.   The paper shook in my hand like I was traveling over a bumpy road.   Yet another piece about a prominent client being rescued in court by Oliver Kane.   But the article didn't give any of the details I'd asked Bruno to provide.   The storyline then shifted to why Kane was regarded as a rainmaker; an attorney who brings in big business by coddling wealthy, high-profile politicians, movie stars, business executives, and athletes.   Kane had saved these special clients from the consequences of driving under the influence of alcohol and drugs, prescribed or otherwise.   The article ended by referring to Oliver Kane as the "DUI Doctor."   A sick, but fitting description.

Bruno's phone emitted disjointed noises.   He'd been right.   Conversation under these conditions would have been frustrating.   I gawked at Kane's picture.   Only this time I saw a photo of two mangled cars.   Adam Harding, the spoiled son of a rich politician had killed Katie with his car, but he made it seem like she'd killed herself.   I had visualized that mental picture every day of my life since the accident.

Harding had been under the influence when their cars had smashed together.   His blood alcohol concentration had been .09, the equivalent of four beers.   At that time, Connecticut's blood alcohol content limit for driving intoxicated was .10.   One tenth of a point had saved Harding from being charged with a DUI or anything else.

My attempt to put Adam Harding in jail had failed.   At the

preliminary hearing Oliver Kane's plea to have the case thrown out of court for lack of evidence had been granted. Kane then had the balls to sue Proffitt Advertising on Harding's behalf because Katie's car had been registered to my firm. As the only witness, Harding claimed Katie had been driving recklessly fast for the rainy conditions, causing her to spin out of control into Harding's car. My insurance company had settled with them for a quarter of a million dollars, paying off the killer-*cum*-witness. What a sham. Commit a murder and get paid for it.

I jammed the cell phone hard against my ear. In my eyes, Oliver Kane was just as responsible for Katie's death as Adam Harding. How many other Oliver Kane clients were still behind a steering wheel because of Kane?

"Hey, buddy," Bruno barked. An eardrum-busting whistle blasted through the speaker. "I need a friggin' receipt for the twenty-three bucks I just gave you to park my car for an hour and five minutes. You guys should be picked up for prostitution." A loud tire squeal came next. "Can you hear me, Mr. Proffitt?"

"Loud and clear, Bruno." I switched the phone to my undamaged ear.

"I can get you all the information you need and more." Bruno hummed to himself. "It'll take four, maybe five days."

"Unacceptable," I said. "At the latest, I need the information on Kane by 10 a.m. tomorrow morning San Francisco time. You have twenty-two hours, Bruno, and the clock's ticking." Faster than he'd ever know. "Ten thousand dollars in cash for less than one day's work."

"What's this about, Mr. Proffitt? You never squeezed my balls like this before. And the amount of money you're offering flies red-flag high. But I'm supposed to overlook the amount you're waving at me 'cause it's in cash." He snorted. "You know I run an above-board operation. Let's be honest with each other here. Are you requesting info on Oliver Kane because you want him to represent you or someone you know? Or is this regarding some other agenda that I don't want to know about?"

A pain in my chest said hello. "I'm not going to BS you, Bruno. Your assumption's a hundred percent correct."

"Okay, now we're on the same page," he said. "I'm aware of your daughter Katherine's accident with Kane's client, Harding,"

"Then you know the Adam Hardings of this world will continue to hurt and kill innocent people as long as Oliver Kane is allowed to keep practicing. Kane and his clients literally get away with murder."

"Yeah, you're preaching to the preacher," Bruno said. "That wasn't even the first time for the Kane/Harding team. Under Kane's counsel, Harding was acquitted of an earlier vehicular manslaughter charge when he ran over a pedestrian a year before he killed your daughter. In reality, Oliver Kane got the kid off so he could murder again."

"I'm not familiar with the prior accident," I said.

"Kane convinced the jury that Harding wasn't negligent," Bruno said. "The incident took place at night, no moon. Vandals had broken the streetlight and the pedestrian wore dark clothing. The only witness was a woman who had first reported Harding driving over the speed limit without headlights on. Later she inexplicably recanted her original statement. She said Harding wasn't speeding, both headlights worked fine, and the pedestrian was nowhere near the crosswalk." Bruno emitted a sharp laugh. "How much memory reduction payola do you think the woman got from Harding's rich daddy?"

"My thought exactly, Bruno. You know, if Harding had been incarcerated after that first manslaughter offense, Katie would be alive today. And so would Adam Harding. Not even the great Oliver Kane could save Harding from his last accident. The kid wrapped his car around a snowplow after sideswiping another vehicle, killing two other people. His blood alcohol concentration was three times the legal limit." Acid burn singed the walls of my stomach. "We've got one hell of a screwed-up legal system when Kane and his clients have more rights than the people they kill."

"No need to do a sell-job on me, Mr. Proffitt. I've been following Kane for years. He's the type of man who'd cheat on an ethics test."

What did Bruno mean about following Oliver Kane for years? That he'd investigated Kane before? If that was the case, Bruno had most of the information I needed on file.

A door opened below me. The click-clack sound of fast-paced high heels resonated. Was she going up or down? I shifted to the railing and lowered my gaze to the network of stairs. This was one conversation I wanted to keep private.

"Are you still there, Mr. Proffitt?"

"Wait," I whispered.

High Heels was moving down. I caught the tail end of a green skirt and crimped red hair. Maybe she had the same problem with elevators as I did. The up and down motion often made me dizzy. A door slammed shut. I was alone and safe again.

"I'm here, Bruno. My apologies. Someone was within listening range."

"Due to the nature of our conversation," he said, "I can understand your concern. But think about it, Mr. Proffitt. If I can figure out what you're up to, so can the police. You're going to get yourself and me into some big-time trouble."

"Trust me, Bruno, that's not going to be a problem. I wasn't trying to impugn your integrity with my offer of cash. I simply want to dissolve any business connection between us for your protection."

"Appreciate that," he said, "but what about you? And why the big hurry?"

"To answer your question, I've waited until the last minute."

"What does that mean, specifically?"

"Health issue on my part," I said.

"How bad?"

"I won't be buying any green bananas."

An annoying beep sounded from Bruno's phone, interrupting his meaningful silence. I paced the stairway landing. Was he digesting the significance of my last statement? Accepting death was often more difficult for the other person.

"Jesus, I'm sorry, Mr. Proffitt." Bruno exhaled a sigh after his phone beeped again. "Look, I want to help you. But I need a little time to consider if my single reason for providing you with data on Kane overshadows a shitload of logic why I shouldn't. Plus my cell's battery is crapping out on me. I'll call you back from my office landline."

"Bruno, don't . . ."

He rang off before I could offer a rebuttal. Damn it. A smart move on his part. He didn't want to hear any hard-sell persuasion from an ex-advertising exec. My supply of patience had drained lower than Bruno's cell phone battery. What the hell was Bruno considering? The ethics of abetting me in a moral or legal wrong? Or could he be weighing the large dollar reward I'd offered him versus the risk of losing his license and livelihood? I rubbed the back of the phone against my cheek. What was the single justification for Bruno to come on board?

I slipped the phone back into my coat pocket. Perhaps Bruno's involvement might come down to how sympathetic he was to my cause. Or how strapped he was for cash. Another thought made me grind my teeth. What were my chances of getting to Oliver Kane if Bruno turned me down? Probably similar to the prognosis Louis had given me in his office. Too late for me to find another New England private detective I could trust. Nor did I have time to track down Kane myself. If Bruno didn't join Team Mo, I'd have to fly to Boston without knowledge or a plan, like a blind man devoid of his other physical senses and his white cane.

The stairs looked inviting. I felt strong enough to walk down twenty-one flights to the first floor. Instead, I opened the stairway door and headed to the elevator. I had to keep reminding myself to be vigilant about my strength and energy. Then again, Louis' prognosis could have been wrong. Aside from the dizziness, shortness of breath, and erratic pain in my chest, I hadn't felt this energized in years. Maybe I had a month. Or even a year.

The heel of my hand pressed against my temple. No, Louis wouldn't steer me wrong. I had to play this smart and assume that the time estimate he had given me was correct.

The hallway path to the elevator was vacant. When it came to crunch time, would I be capable of taking the life of another human being, even if that life belonged to a despicable person like Oliver Kane? The photo of the two mangled cars flashed before me again. Given the opportunity, I'd kill Kane.

12:03 p.m. by my watch. I stepped up my pace. Bruno's indecision would give me time to withdraw cash from one of my banks to finance the mission.

The elevator door slid open, exposing an empty car. Instrumental music pitched from ceiling speakers. A heavy pressure invaded my chest two steps into the elevator. Breathing was difficult. I could hear and feel my heartbeat. The floor shifted under me. Waves of dizziness threw me off balance. The door clanked shut, sealing me inside.

"Not now," I choked out.

I grabbed the security of the handrail. Metal walls closed in on me, consuming most of the car's treasured air. My finger stabbed at the "Open" button and missed twice before hitting it. I tasted salt from sweat on my lips. Was this a prelude for the final heart attack? Or was I experiencing my first claustrophobic panic attack after fifty-seven years?

I touched the outside of my coat pocket that housed a small glass vial of nitro tabs. Louis had said too much nitroglycerin in my system could be counterproductive. The last time I'd ingested nitro was a couple of days ago. But I still hadn't felt major pain yet. If I placed a tablet under my tongue now would it prevent a heart attack? Or induce one?

The door slithered open. I pushed away from the handrail. My wet shirt clung to my skin as if I'd been playing racquetball for an hour. Hallway air found my nostrils. The additional oxygen was precious. I chanced a deeper breath and waited for a strike of pain. Instead, the chest pressure ebbed. A sense of calm settled back into my limbs. Breathing through my nose was a luxury that made me giddy. I was still dizzy, but not as bad.

I moved back into the elevator and punched button number twenty-one. My slow journey out of this building would be one floor at a time. How much more would my heart endure?

Chapter Five

T he interior of the bank had gone through a major facelift. I didn't recognize any of the employees, including the young male teller who accepted my signed withdrawal slip. He scrutinized my face like I was 2001's version of John Dillinger. Granted, $50,000 was a large sum of cash to withdraw, but my account housed four times that amount. The teller abandoned his window with my slip to seek approval from his supervisor. There used to be a time when the branch manager would stop whatever she was doing to greet me. And I could withdraw any quantity of cash without getting the third degree.

My body flinched when the cell phone in my coat pocket chimed alive. An odd reaction since I was waiting for Bruno's call. The number on the tiny screen was from my home. I was disappointed as well as grateful. Mrs. Green must be concerned about me, but I don't want to tie up the line. Once I made my cash transaction I would return her call from Henry's cab parked in front of the bank.

1:28 p.m. on the wall clock. Three and a half hours since I left Louis' office. In that span of seconds my life had gone from turtle-time to turbo-time.

The cell rang again. My wonderful, care-giving housekeeper was persistent. Except this time the caller was Bruno. I answered trying not to sound too anxious.

"Back at ya again, Mr. Proffitt. I'll take your case."

"Good deal!" I pumped a victory fist.

A young man wearing a brown sweater stopped working his pen at a center island table. He peered at my undignified actions, adjusted his glasses, and lowered his head to his work on the counter.

"You're in luck," Bruno said. "I don't have anyone to go home to at night. So the next nineteen hours are yours. I can't promise all the information you've requested in that time frame. But I think you'll be more than satisfied with the data I send you."

"Thanks, Bruno. Same routine we've used in the past. But this time send the information to me using my personal phone, email, and fax. If you deem anything essential for my immediate attention, call me on my cell phone."

"Gotcha, Mr. Proffitt. It's a pleasure doing business with you again."

"Likewise," I said, before ringing off. And likely the last time we'll be doing business.

"Mr. Proffitt," an unfamiliar female voice called out. A short brunette wearing a gray pantsuit with thin blue pinstripes approached my side of the counter with my withdrawal slip in her hand. Her features were youthful enough to belong on a college campus. "I'm Margie, the branch manager."

"What happened to Connie?" I said, shaking her free hand.

"Oh. Connie retired three years ago." Margie nodded to the teller. He rotated his computer screen for her to view. "It's been quite awhile since you last made a transaction. Banking regulations have changed. I'm sorry, but we don't have fifty thousand in cash at our disposal."

I turned my head to measure the effect Margie's last statement had on the other customers. The waiting line consisted of a priest and an older lady who leaned on a walker. To their left, the young man in the brown sweater didn't look up.

"Normal procedure for a cash withdrawal of this amount," Margie continued, "would be to order the money ahead of time. It takes three working days. Would you like us to place an order, Mr. Proffitt?"

I understood Margie was just doing her job. But Connie would have bent the rules. Hell. Connie would have borrowed money from another branch to accommodate me.

"Margie, I can't wait three days." My eyes fixed on the bank's wall clock again, especially the speedy second hand. "How much of my money can I have today?" How inane did that sound?

"As luck would have it, we just received a shipment. I can let you have twenty thousand."

"Twenty thousand," I repeated.

She smiled as if this was my lucky day. My dilemma wasn't just about money. I could probably cajole a greater amount from her, at the expense of wasted time. The remaining uncertain hours were more valuable than money. I did some quick mental math while Margie waited for my answer. Counting the cash I had stashed away in my desk at home and in my money clip, I could add several thousand to the total. If I had to fly to the New England area, the cost of airline tickets, a car rental, and hotel accommodations could be covered by a credit card. But I wanted to pay Bruno's fee in cash via Western Union to avoid a trail, leaving the rest of my cash as bargaining chips for Kane's demise.

"I'd like to withdraw twenty thousand, Margie. And thank you."

"We'll need to see identification, a driver's license, bank card, and social security. And we'll have to fill out a CTR form."

"A what?" I said. How many other new banking practices and procedures was I ignorant about?

"That would be a Currency Transaction Report form for the government."

Margie studied my identification cards while the teller completed a one-page form. At least she didn't require me to produce fingerprints or DNA. When the teller finally slid the form across the counter for my signature, Margie returned my cards to me.

"Thank you, Mr. Proffitt." Margie offered her hand again. "I apologize if you've been inconvenienced. On your next trip in, please call us ahead of time. Or maybe you should try our online banking. All you have to do is log into our—"

"Thanks, Margie. I'll consider doing just that the next time."

"How would you like your money?" She glanced at the teller.

"Hundreds, please."

"For that many hundreds," the teller said, "I'll have to go to the vault."

Margie departed. The teller locked his drawer and sauntered towards a doorway in the back wall. I shook my head. My double-parked cabdriver had his meter running. The engine in my chest was sputtering on spit, but racing at redline. And the teller's cruise control was set at laid back.

A monitor high up on the side wall displayed a camera shot of the bank's interior. From that angle, the back of my suit jacket was wrinkled, something that wouldn't have bothered me before my appointment with Louis. Different story now. The old Morgan Proffitt persona had kicked in. Look sharp, be quick on the uptake, and always be ready to perform a song and dance routine.

The teller returned with a handful of bills. He counted aloud the hundreds in a slow, careful manner. The timer in my head ticked with each motion. When he reached a hundred, he pushed the green stack of bills aside, rubbed his hands together, and started the procedure over again with the next bundle.

"Twenty thousand," the teller finally announced, gathering the money together like a deck of cards. He slid white paper bands over Benjamin Franklin's faces and handed me the packets. "Anything else I can do for you, sir?"

"You could keep your voice down," I said. "And I could use an envelope."

"Right." The teller stooped to open a drawer underneath the counter. His fingers came up empty. He peered at an unoccupied window next to him and scratched his head.

"Never mind." I stuffed the bundles into my inside coat pocket. The two hundred C-notes felt weighty. Would the bills feel this heavy if they were minus two zeros? I looked for a telltale bulge. There was none. My money was traveling incognito.

The priest took my place at the teller's window as I headed for the front door. I passed the young man in the brown sweater at the center island table. His black-framed glasses and short-cropped, dark hair gave him the appearance of a law school student. Or a computer geek. Yet something was different about this guy. I shook my head. There was a good chance I was just being spiteful. He was about the same age as my Katie would have been, except he still had his whole life ahead him.

CHAPTER SIX

I pushed open the bank's door. A hawk-like wind, a city of Chicago term, blew the door closed until I exerted more strength. My tie flew up, slapping me across the chin. The overcast had given way to blue skies, with the sun darting between patches of white clouds. An opposite picture from when I'd first arrived. Had I been in the bank that long?

The yellow cab waited for me at the curb. Henry sat behind the steering wheel studying this morning's *San Francisco Chronicle* sporting green with a pen in hand. He was either charting baseball pitchers for today's games, or picking potential horse winners for the track. When Louis first discovered my heart trouble, he advised me to quit anything that involved wagering. In a sense, my last minute attempt to eliminate Oliver Kane was the biggest gamble I would ever make. And one I didn't want to lose.

When he noticed me coming, Henry tucked the paper above his visor with care. He was short, maybe a cigar ash above five feet tall. His seat cushion elevated his eyes higher than the steering wheel by the length of the half-smoked, unlit stogie protruding from his mouth. He wore an outdated black San Francisco Giants warm-up jacket and a Greek fisherman's hat with the Giants' orange insignia. I jerked open the back door and slid onto the seat.

"Thanks for waiting, Henry." A silly thing to have said since the meter was running. "I'm more familiar with the inside of a cab now than the Mercedes parked in my garage. I stopped driving after my heart operation, more for your protection than mine."

"Where to next, Mr. P.?" Henry asked, grinning up at his rear-view mirror. His cigar fit between missing bottom teeth.

"Western Union on Market Street. And please hurry."

I yanked on the handle to close the door. But the door didn't move. A leather-gloved hand held the door open. The young man in the brown sweater from the bank leaned in with a friendly smile.

"Mind if I share the cab with you, sir?" Brown Sweater said in a pleasant voice.

His black-framed glasses were missing. In the daylight, I could see that his short, cropped hair was a wig and the dark skin tone was makeup. The son of bitch had followed me out of the bank. He knew exactly how much money I'd withdrawn from my account. And where the bills were stored.

"Yeah, I do mind sharing the cab," I fired back. My fingers established a better grip on the handle.

"Hey, buddy," Henry barked. "This cab's taken. You'll have to grab another ride."

Any doubt I had about Brown Sweater's intentions disappeared. Henry's anxious expression and tight lips told me his thoughts were similar to mine. I tried to pull the door from Brown Sweater's grasp, with no success. This was not a drill.

Before Henry could get the cab in gear and pull away, Brown Sweater jumped onto the back seat, pushing me to the side like I was a featherweight. Click! A switchblade in his left hand popped open, inches from my neck. He smiled again, a fuck-you smile. He slammed the door shut.

My heartbeat shifted into a faster gear. I kept reminding myself to stay calm and take short breathes. This guy obviously wanted my $20,000 in cash. Would the money be enough to satisfy him? Or was he also after something else? Kidnapping? Had he cased my house and me, waiting for the right moment? Or maybe he got off on the thrill of hurting people after he got what he was after?

Henry's eyebrows flinched up when he saw the knife. His body dipped down. I could only hope my cabdriver wouldn't attempt something foolish. Too late. With his left hand he raised a rusty tire iron above his head. Bad move, Henry.

"Don't even think about being a hero, grandpa." Brown Sweater pressed the knife's blade to the side of my neck, penetrating the skin. "I'll cut this dude then do you."

Blood trickled down my neck. If Brown Sweater had dug the blade point a little deeper, there would be no tomorrow. Or the rest of today. How ironic. Yesterday I would have welcomed this guy to finish the job. But not now. If I volunteered the money to Brown Sweater, would he leave the cab with the two of us still intact?

Brown Sweater's glassy eyes told me all I needed to know. He was going to stick me whether or not I turned over the money. It was just a matter of when. And after he killed me, he'd go after Henry. Why leave a witness?

"Listen, punk," Henry's voice boomed inside the cab. "This gentleman has a bum ticker. I'll give you all of my fares, just leave us alone. Deal?"

Brown Sweater sliced through the Giants' warm-up jacket sleeve with a lightning quick jab, puncturing Henry's forearm. Henry screamed in pain. The tire iron fell and clattered to the floorboard. The bloody knife blade returned to my neck.

Henry just discovered that negotiating with a terrorist was useless. Brown sweater was way beyond the typical San Francisco street-tough mugger. He was most likely crazy high on drugs and desperate. Heavy tightness spread throughout my chest.

"Oh, shit," I groaned.

My heart felt like it had been gored. I had to get a pill into my system as quickly as possible. One hand covered my chest. The other dug into my coat pocket for the bottle. I held my breath, fearing the pain would escalate if I breathed.

"I make the rules here," Brown Sweater growled, his eyes narrowed at Henry. He knocked the pill bottle from my hand before I had a chance to remove the top. "Drive the fucking cab around the block and cross both Market and Mission Streets heading towards the Giants' new stadium." He quick-stabbed the front-seat headrest twice to get Henry's attention. "Do as I say and your backseat friend here might live. Make a false move, use the radio, signal a cop, or don't turn when I tell you to, and I'll start carving."

More intense pain rocked me. My watery eyes blinked at a furious pace. I nodded to Henry to follow the hood's orders. Henry grimaced, turned forward and shifted into drive. Traveling to a destination could buy us some time. But how much time?

Streetcars, buildings, traffic lights, and a herd of other objects blurred past us making me dizzy. Henry cornered too fast. A pack of pedestrians scattered for safety. Brown Sweater scowled at Henry and inhaled through his nose several times. He elevated the knife, aiming the tip close to the corner of my eye. Too close.

"The money, man." Brown Sweater angled the blade to touch my eyebrow. He sniffed again. "Inside your coat. I want the Franklins. Now."

My fingertips touched the money packets. Henry braked erratically for a red light, landing the taxi halfway into the cross-walk. The pill bottle rolled at my feet. Brown Sweater glared at Henry again. I launched an elbow. A sudden strike, but not with the velocity or strength I'd intended. The point of my elbow connected with Brown Sweater's Adam's apple. His eyes enlarged. Then his jaw dropped open. The knife plunged to the floor. He raised both hands to his neck gagging for air, stunned.

"Sweet mother of Jesus," Henry shouted.

The car behind us honked. Another hit of pain struck my chest. My fingertips curled up tight. The heel of my hand landed a blow to Brown Sweater's nose. I didn't hit him square, yet I could feel and hear bone crack. The side of his face hit the door. He slumped forward. The wig toppled from his head. Brown Sweater was a blond.

"Drive to the closest police department, Henry," I ordered through clenched teeth. "But stop a block away from the station."

The pain hadn't let up. Stay calm, Mo. Short breaths. My shoe searched for the pill bottle. Where the hell did it go?

"Jesus H Christ, Mr. P." Henry's head bobbed up and down. "Where in God's name did you learn that kung fu jujitsu stuff?"

My foot connected with the bottle. On the second attempt, I snatched the glass vial from the floor. But the safety top wouldn't come off. I never could get the hang of the damn tops. Too much pressure. Not enough.

Damn it. Concentrate. My closed eyes visualized the cap's directional arrows. A press then a twist on the top failed. Shit. I tried again. This time the top came off. I shoved a tiny white pill under my tongue and waited for it to dissolve into my system. The effects were immediate. My veins felt like they were on the outside of my skin. A good sign.

"Are you okay, Mr. P.? Jesus Christ. Is the guy dead? Jesus Christ."

Most of Brown Sweater's crumpled body lay prone on the seat. I placed two fingers on his blood-stained neck. A pulse. He was alive. His nose flowed blood. First time I ever had to defend myself using my martial arts training.

A flush of heat attached to my cheeks and ears. I felt another poke in my chest. But the pain had downgraded to discomfort.

"I'm all right, Henry." I secured the cap on the bottle and returned the pills to my pocket. "How about you? Have you lost a lot of blood?"

"Nah," Henry said, scrunching the tires against a curb. He opened a small first-aid kit and handed me an antiseptic packet and a bandage. "The cut just stings like a bitch 'cause I'm sweatin' like a pig in heat. Reminds me of the time...You were really something back there, Mr. P."

Police cars were parked in front of a building down the street. Two uniformed cops traveled down cement steps to the sidewalk. Henry and I would part ways here.

"Henry, the son of bitch lying at my feet is going to be out cold for awhile. Bring him to the police station. Tell the police what happened, but don't use my name. As far as they're concerned, you dropped a stranger off at the Fairmont Hotel. I don't have time to answer their questions."

"Buh-buh-but, Mr. P., what possible reason do I give to the police for not taking you straight to the station? Or for not calling them from the cab at the Fairmont?"

"You're full of stories, Henry. Pick a good one."

I pushed open the door with an effort, causing a smack of pain. The City breeze stuck to my clammy skin. I stuffed ten crisp one-hundred-dollar bills into Henry's sweaty palm. Creative story money. The last thing I wanted to do was explain to the police why I was carrying over $20,000 in cash on me.

"You should have a chunk of change left over from my fare, Henry." I pointed to the green sports page protruding from the visor. "Why don't you make the bet of your life? Put it all on the

Giants to win tonight. I've got a good feeling."

Henry's lips moved as he counted then recounted the hundreds. Another story he could add to his collection of tales. People would have to take Henry's word for it. Neither Brown Sweater nor I would be available to verify the details. My raised hand flagged another cab.

A Blue Cab slid in behind Henry's bumper. The driver's head was covered by a turban – no team insignia on the front. My eyes lifted to a brilliant blue sky to talk to a man I'd neglected most of my life. I hadn't asked God for anything since Katie died, except for an answer to my question why.

"We both know I'm operating on borrowed time with no means of paying You back," I whispered. "More than ever, I believe You're keeping me alive for a reason. I just need a little more time."

I opened the Blue Cab's backseat door and slid into the middle. Was I being guided through this last experience? Or maybe it was luck. Perhaps a combination of both. Keep those miracles coming.

CHAPTER SEVEN

I stood at the foot of the walkway to my Seacliff home. The Blue Cab's exhaust gathered around my tired legs like ground fog until I closed the rear door and the driver sped away from the curb as if he was racing towards a checkered flag.

Late afternoon sun fired its rays into my squinting eyes. A hand went to my forehead to cut a glare that morphed the view. My divot-free lawn sloped upward and doglegged to the right around the corner lot like a lustrous San Francisco Olympic Club fairway. Some people go home to get away from it all. I was anxious to get back inside my recluse resort, not to get away from people, but to fire up my computer. How soon would Bruno deliver on his end of the deal by emailing me the Oliver Kane information?

It was 4:41 p.m., almost seven hours since I left Louis' office. For the first time in years, I was physically paying the price for a full day's worth of activity. I transferred the Western Union receipt from my coat pocket to my wallet. $220 to wire $5,000, the first half of Bruno's money installment. But time, not money, was my concern.

The mahogany front door with beveled glass inserts opened before I could jam my key into the lock. A woman with wild white hair like Barbara Bush stood before me, her hand squeezing a portable phone. The frumpy housedress and flower-print apron covered a squat, sturdy frame. Her face was etched with concern. She was a foot shorter than me. At this moment, however, I was the smaller person.

"Thank God you're home." Mrs. Green's eyes zeroed in on my neck and the dried blood on my collar. She gasped and reached for the bandage Henry had handed me. "Goodness gracious, Mr. Proffitt. What in the Lord's name happened to you?"

I flinched away from her probing fingers. Her normal rosy-cheeked complexion turned the shade of a Golden Delicious apple.

Poor Mrs. Green. If I confessed to my ultra-serious caregiver that a drug-crazed hoodlum attacked me, I'd probably have to perform CPR on her. That would be one hell of a role reversal.

"Nothing to fret about." I smiled to back up my statement then pivoted past her into the house. "Just a small cut. Brushed up against something sharp."

"I've been so worried about you." She darted back into the entryway and braked in front of me with both hands poised on her wide hips. Her hazel eyes narrowed, going back and forth from my neck to my face. "You rarely go out. And when you do, you never come home this late. I tried reaching you on your cell phone, but you didn't answer. I called Virginia at your office. She hadn't talked to you since she delivered your birthday present on Saturday. I even called Dr. Titelman. His nurse Sally said you left a little past ten this morning. Where in tarnation have you been? I was ready to send the police and National Guard after you."

She was right, of course. In my haste to make final arrangements, I forgot to call her back. I had avoided a crazed robber, but there was no escaping this one-woman, butt- chewing posse. Hell, Mrs. Green was as much a part of this family as I was, and the only family I had left. My hands ascended into the air to a surrender gesture.

"Please accept my apologies, Mrs. Green. I should have returned your calls. Got kind of busy and lost track of time."

Her right eyebrow flexed up. Nice move, Mo. The word "busy" caught her attention like blinking hazard lights. I took two strides towards my study. Mrs. Green countered my move and blocked me again.

"You look awfully pale," she declared, reaching again for my neck. "I want to take a look at that so-called small cut."

"Please, Mrs. Green." I blocked her hand with my palm. "It's not worth bothering with. Besides, I need your help. Would you please pack a small bag? Allow for two, make that three, days' worth of clothes. And make sure my navy blue, pinstripe suit is clean and pressed."

"Pack?" she repeated. "Why would you need a packed bag, Mr. Proffitt?"

"I'm going to the East Coast." My eyes shifted to the study again. "It could be on a moment's notice."

Her breathing came out in loud spurts. Mrs. Green didn't budge. Her calm demeanor was bypassing "storm" and going straight to "hurricane." She looked at me as if I was an imposter. In a sense, I was.

"Now, Mr. Proffitt," she said, "you know the doctor gave you strict orders about not flying." She touched my forehead with the back of her hand. "You're not running a fever, but you look tired. I'll brew you some green tea. Why don't you relax for a spell in your study? Better yet, lie down on the couch. I'll bring you a pillow and a blanket."

"I am a bit fatigued," I admitted, "but this morning the good doctor removed the reins and gave me his blessings to do whatever I so desire." Damn, it pained me to stretch the truth to Mrs. Green. "The trip is a top priority. Something I wish I had done a long time ago. Besides, this way I'll be giving both of us a vacation of sorts. I bet you'll be glad to get rid of me for a while."

Mrs. Green caressed my arm the same way Katie had. I could still feel Katie's fingertips when she had said goodbye to me at the San Francisco Airport. The last time I ever saw my daughter alive. Now I faced Mrs. Green who didn't know the score, yet could experience the same outcome if I didn't return.

"I don't care what Dr. Titleman said, Mr. Proffitt. You shouldn't be flying." Mrs. Green wrung her apron with both hands. "And I don't give a hoot about a vacation. I only care about you." She released the apron leaving a knot of wrinkles. "Please don't take this trip. Build up your strength, first."

"I've never been more eager to travel."

"So you say." She folded her arms under her ample bosom. "Then I'm going to travel with you. I will pay my own way, thank you."

Mrs. Green had assumed many roles with the Proffitts. Katie's super nanny. Helen's nurse. And a tireless caregiver to me, the lost soul. She knew us all so well. Not once had I heard her complain. At least Mrs. Green would always have a place to live. Or she could sell the house and have enough money to do anything she wanted, including hiring her own housekeeper.

"A wonderful offer, Mrs. Green." Swallowing was difficult. I stepped back from her, fearing I'd give myself away. "I'm sorry. Traveling with me isn't possible. I need to be alone on this trip." My stomach rumbled loud enough for both of us to hear – a reminder that I hadn't eaten anything today. "Hey, what's for dinner? I'm famished."

"Oh my gosh." Fingertips went to her cheeks. "I baked you a birthday cake this morning. Then I became so worried about you being away, I completely forgot about dinner." She glanced towards the kitchen. "How about a big tossed green salad, some steamed vegetables, and—"

"How about steak?" I said. "Rib eye, charred rare. The thicker the better."

"A steak?"

"Mashed potatoes piled with butter. And broccoli smothered in cheese."

"Yes, Mr. Proffitt." Her features crouched into a puzzled expression. "That used to be your favorite meal. I'll have the market deliver the thickest steak they have." Her lips parted into a smile. "Perhaps you are ready to go on a trip after all."

"Now, in the meantime, I have some work to do in my study."

"Yes, sir."

But Mrs. Green remained in the same spot clutching her apron again. Her eyes were fixed in a blank stare on the hallway wall. I couldn't blame her for being stunned.

"Hello?" My hand waved in her face. "Earth to Mrs. Green. Hello?"

"Sorry, sir," she said, shaking her head. "It's just that . . . This is all so remarkable."

"Yes, I agree." I removed a fat money clip from my pocket and handed her six thousand dollars, along with a slip of paper. "Please do a small favor for me, Mrs. Green. After I leave for the airport, go to the nearest Western Union and send five thousand dollars to the person listed on the paper. From there, I want you to do something frivolous with the leftover money. Go get a manicure, pedicure, and any other kind of cure you so desire. Just do something for yourself."

"Mr. Proffitt," she said, flapping the hundreds. "You've given me way too much money to spend on pure self-indulgence. I can't accept this."

"Yes, you can. Furthermore, to ensure that you'll actually pamper yourself for once, I want to see the receipts from your San Francisco experience when I return. I hope you won't disappoint me."

"But, Mr. Proffitt—"

"I won't take no for an answer, Mrs. Green." I turned and pointed to the front door. Every time I moved my head, the bandaged skin on my neck felt stretched. "One more thing. A packet of legal documents from my attorney will be delivered here sometime tomorrow. The envelope will be addressed to you. Just a formality. Please keep the package in your possession until I get back."

Mrs. Green nodded her understanding. Virginia at the office would be receiving a similar packet. My stomach growled again, but something besides hunger gnawed at my insides. What would Mrs. Green and Virginia think of me if I was accused of premeditated murder? Not the way I wanted to be remembered. Perhaps I could shield the truth from them and still succeed with the mission. Once I received Bruno's information, I'd figure out a way to pull off that maneuver.

"Oh, one last command, Mrs. Green." I folded her fingertips over the cash and smiled. "While I'm gone, treat this place like it's your own."

CHAPTER EIGHT

The thick, half-eaten steak on my plate lay nestled between the broccoli and mashed potatoes. I pushed the plate towards the center of the kitchen table, next to the beautiful un-sliced chocolate birthday cake Mrs. Green had baked for me. My desire for forbidden food had proven to be much larger than my stomach.

Before dinner, a soothing shower and shave had re-energized me. But fatigue was creeping back into my limbs. With both hands on the table, I pushed to rise from the chair. The new bandage on my neck concealed a cut that could have used a few stitches, followed by a tetanus shot. But then, why bother?

On the way to my study I glanced at the grandfather clock in the hallway. Almost 6:11 p.m. That would be 9:11 Bruno time. The study's overhead lights and desk computer had been purposely left on. I punched into my email account and scrolled down lines of spam-gram topics. Nothing from Bruno, yet. Nor had he called my cell phone. Disappointing, but not surprising. He still had almost sixteen hours before the deadline.

I sent an email to myself to satisfy my paranoia. While waiting for the message to pop up, I ogled an oil rendition of Boston's Fenway Park on the wall, an early birthday present from Virginia. The new owner of Proffitt Advertising had remembered Fenway was the only major league ballpark I hadn't experienced in person. Perhaps the painting was her way of trying to motivate me to get out of my funk and go there.

My email message popped up. I was dressed, ready to depart for the airport. Every minute saved, hell every second, would allot me a greater chance of nailing Oliver Kane. What were Kane's strengths? Even more important, what were his weaknesses? Every man has vulnerabilities. How many did Kane have? And how could I exploit them?

I drummed a pen on the desk. The round-trip tickets and seat assignments I'd purchased earlier on the Internet were good to go, with the exception of tonight's 8:37 flight. Standby status had been the best I could get on that one. But the 5:00 a.m. flight was my most realistic first chance of flying to Logan Airport in Boston.

Something heavy dropped upstairs. It sounded like it came from my bedroom. Most likely Mrs. Green was packing for my trip.

I headed for the stairs. My journey up each step was long and slow. I was out of breath when my foot planted on the upstairs landing. The door to Katie's darkened bedroom was always open. I entered her room and turned on the light. Her purple hippo clock, with eyes that moved side to side, said 6:23. Her white, antique furniture and frilly, lilac curtains were still in place. One of the stuffed hippos fell to the carpet when I sat on the purple-and-green-patterned bedspread. The mattress was soft, comfortable. Her subtle, blossom smell lingered. I never lost the feeling that Katie had just stepped out for a few minutes and would be returning soon. And I'd be here to greet her.

On the dresser, a photo of the three Proffitts brought on a smile, albeit brief. Helen's striking beauty and elegance made my heart thump. Always did. Katie was smiling, happy. Every strand of her long, straight, auburn hair was in place. Freckles and all, she was so darn cute.

That photo was taken in Katie's high school senior year. I had the look of a contented man. Katie often said I resembled Michael Douglas. Her mother argued that I looked more like Cary Grant. The two women in my life flattered me. And I loved it.

Katie's softball mitt and cleats hung from the closet door. She liked going to Giant's games at Candlestick Park. My precious daughter would con me by saying, "You need to relax, Dad. Get your mind away from work, and smell the garlic fries."

Maybe the Giants were playing now. I scooted across the bed and switched on the radio atop her headboard bookcase. Horrible rap-crap blasted from the speaker. I flipped off FM and made several quick turns to the left, landing the dial on 680 AM. The booming radio voice of Giants announcer Jon Miller filled the room.

"Stay tuned for the Giants-Astros game totals and post game wrap," Miller announced. "We'll be right back after these messages from our sponsors."

"Come on, Jon," I said, staring at the radio. Did Henry place a bet on the Giants like I suggested? "Who won?"

A familiar commercial followed. Virginia had written the catchy lyrics to the jingle. I stifled a yawn. My head fell back onto a pillow covered by the bedspread. I had to stay awake, ready to move once Bruno communicated with me. My fingers touched the cell phone through the material of my pants' pocket.

My eyes closed. If I fell asleep, I might never wake up again. Dying in my sleep, especially in Katie's room would have been my chosen way to go out. But not now. Not yet. I forced my weighted eyelids open.

Then again, exhaustion could also do me in. Another commercial came on. Keeping my eyes closed for just a bit could be beneficial, as long as I didn't fall asleep.

CHAPTER NINE

The room trembled like I was in the midst of an earthquake. The shaking ceased when my eyes crept open. A pink hippo smiled at me. What the hell was he so happy about? My eyelids closed again. The quake returned.

"Mr. Proffitt," Mrs. Green said with urgency. "Please wake up. You have a phone call."

I held up a hand as a signal for Mrs. Green to stop shaking the mattress and squinted up at her. My throat felt like sandpaper. Several hard swallows did little to lubricate the tightening tissue. I wasn't even sure my voice was in working order.

"Mr. Proffitt. There's a Mr. Bruno Santiago on the phone in the study. He says it's vitally important that he speak to you."

Holy shit. My hand touched the phone in my pocket. If something was urgent, why hadn't Bruno called me on my cell phone as instructed instead of using my private landline?

"Are you all right, Mr. Proffitt?" Mrs. Green frowned.

"Just a little muddleheaded." I sat up. Attempting to get to a standing position wasn't going to be easy with a spinning brain. "Tell Mr. Santiago I'll be with him shortly."

6:52 by Katie's clock. I moved towards the bathroom. My, God. Had I slept all night and missed the 5:00 a.m. plane? At least Bruno was getting back to me before the 10:00 a.m. deadline. When was the next flight I had booked?

A splash of cold water on my face jolted life back into my system. I removed the cell phone from my pocket. The time was 6:53 p.m., not a.m. I frowned into the mirror at the dumbshit shaking his head at me. No wonder my brain felt so fuzzy. I had less than an hour's sleep. Bruno had left three messages. Obviously, something had gone wrong if he was requiring my immediate attention.

My legs proved unsteady going down the stairs. I used the handrail as a crutch. As soon as both shoes touched down on the floor, I sped as fast as I could into the den and picked up the phone. Damn music filled my ear. Bruno had put me on hold just like this morning.

I opened Bruno's email while waiting for him to come back on the line. Page one was a list of Oliver Kane's phone numbers and addresses. The second page was a map of downtown Boston and Logan Airport. Pages three through five were other maps locating Kane's home, office, preferred restaurants, gaming rooms, and gym. Gaming rooms jumped out at me. Kane was a gambler. Maybe gambling would be his downfall.

The printer spewed out hard copies, while I scrolled through the information. A traditional brick house filled the screen. Kane's home. Two stories like mine, but larger and more secluded. The lavish grounds were protected by a metal fence and gate. Was the security barrier in place to protect a vast array of extravagant valuables? Or did Kane fear for his own safety?

In the next picture, Kane wore a black overcoat and stood next to a limousine parked in the circular driveway in front of his house. He could afford the luxury of a limo, at the expense of his rich clients and the misery they inflicted upon others. What kind of expensive car did Kane drive when he wasn't being chauffeured?

Christmas lights hung from his house and bushes. Patches of snow decorated the grounds. This photo wasn't recent. My earlier suspicions were correct. Bruno had investigated Kane before. Was this picture from a one-time inquiry or was he involved in an ongoing investigation? As long as the information was up to date, I didn't have a problem with Bruno using previously accumulated material. Easier for him and saved both of us time.

Mrs. Green glanced at me when she passed the den doorway. I closed the door and went back to my desk. No doubt in my mind, if she knew what I was attempting to do she'd call the police, National Guard, and County Mental Health Department.

My eyes traveled back to the computer screen. Bruno had sent a photo of Kane's office, a prestigious downtown Boston stone-and-glass exterior with "Kane Tower" in big metal gold letters embedded above the entrance. A hand-written notation indicated the whole seventh floor was dedicated to the Oliver Kane Law firm.

Next a photo popped up of Rhonda Kane, wife number four. She was an attractive brunette, in her middle to late thirties. Whoa. The face of a longhaired blonde named Tammy Jo Moore followed the picture of his wife. Tammy Jo was bring-the-dead-back-to-life gorgeous. According to Bruno, she was a movie star wannabe, Los Angeles Clipper cheerleader, and Oliver Kane's mistress.

The subsequent picture stopped me cold. I stared at a close-up photo of the man, bringing back memories of seeing Oliver Kane in a New England courtroom at Adam Harding's preliminary hearing. I doubt Kane had even known I was there. In the photo his black hair was slicked straight back *à la* Pat Riley of NBA basketball coaching fame. Intelligent dark blue eyes. Kane looked to be in his late thirties or early forties and was Hollywood handsome. A line of white skin split through his thick left eyebrow. The menacing scar counterbalanced his comely features.

Kane's vital statistics came next after his photo. Born in 1954, making him forty-seven years old, only ten years younger than me. I hadn't been close when I guessed his age. Five-foot eleven and a hundred and seventy pounds. Aside from the scar, Kane looked like a pillar of the community. Too bad the contents didn't match the appearance.

"Mr. Proffitt." Bruno's deep voice replaced the music. "Did you get my email?"

"Yes, I'm reviewing it now, Bruno. From the data I've scanned so far, it looks like you've done a terrific job. But am I missing something? Why are you calling me?"

"Hold on, Mr. Proffitt. I'm getting a report here as we speak."

Electronic sounds belched in the background on his end of the line. My eyes shifted to the screen while I waited for Bruno to get back to me. He sent a bevy of magazine, newspaper, and Internet articles on Kane, many of which I hadn't seen before. I would read them after he finished his telephone report.

"Sorry about the interruption," Bruno said. "It's the nature of my business. But you'll be interested in the data that was just faxed to me."

"I don't understand the urgency of you wanting to speak to me, Bruno."

"Please bear with me, Mr. Proffitt. Before I explain the importance of this call, allow me to first cover some of the background information you requested. You'll understand why after I break the big news to you."

We were going to play this Bruno's way whether I approved or not. I poised a pen at a pad of lined paper, eager to fill the page with pertinent notes.

"Go ahead." I didn't try to hide the frustration in my voice.

"To date," Bruno said, "Oliver Kane has fourteen employees in his law firm, but no partners. He did have a partner once, but Kane screwed him royally. Historically, the firm has huge turnover. Most of Kane's employees don't last longer than a year, two years max. Kane's in debt all the way up to his gonads. Spends his money faster than he can produce it. He has three ex wives and no children. It costs him a friggin' fortune for alimony." Bruno grunted out a laugh. "You'd think a high-priced mouthpiece would be smart enough to have a decent prenup. The man obviously has a soft spot for women."

"Got it, Bruno." On the pad I underlined weaknesses and scribbled the words "women" and "debt" underneath. "What else?"

"You get a peek at Kane's ball-busting blonde mistress?" Bruno said. "The scumbag cheats on her too. High living, broads on the side, gambling, drugs – rumor has it Kane is hooked on the white powder – all keep him deep in the red. But it doesn't stop him from maintaining a counterfeit front of prosperity both personally and professionally."

"What's Kane's preferred choice of gambling?" I asked listing "gambling" and "drugs."

"He likes the ponies, but he loves playing poker, especially high-stake Texas Hold'em. Kane also belongs to the area's most exclusive country clubs. Eats at the finest restaurants. Wears $6,000 Italian suits. Drinks the most expensive Scotch whiskey money can buy. And he reeks nice from Clive Christian cologne that probably costs ten bucks a dab."

Jesus. What brand of underwear does Kane wear? I doubt the answer would be Fruit of the Loom. But it wouldn't surprise me if Bruno had that information too.

"I got it from a reliable source," Bruno continued, "that they're close to foreclosing on Kane's house. Bottom line, Kane's broke, stretched to the max, and strapped for cash." Bruno hummed off key. "There's more. Hang in there for a sec, Mr. Proffitt."

Paper rustled in the distance. I circled five powerful words that formed a seed of a plan: women, debt, gambling, drugs, and cash. The knowledge Bruno had relayed was important, especially that Kane was deep in debt, needed cash, and had an addictive nature. All false fronts. Kane seemed like a man who would do anything to continue his flamboyant lifestyle and stay in the public's eye.

"Okay, here we go," Bruno said. "Kane doesn't drive. He uses a limo service and cabs. No one knows why for sure, but it's thought the scar on his face has something to do with his reluctance to get behind the wheel."

"Nice work, Bruno." I added "doesn't drive" to the list. "Hell, if I were Kane, I wouldn't drive either given the contemptible people he lets loose on the streets. What other quirks does Kane have in his psyche closet?"

"I had a long conversation with a former Oliver Kane employee," Bruno said. "Kane fired him over philosophical differences five years ago."

Fired five years ago? That would be 1996. The year Katie was killed. A coincidence?

"What exactly does 'philosophical differences' mean?" I asked.

"We're not talking about Plato and Socrates here," Bruno said. "If it's not done the Oliver Kane way, there's no other way but the doorway. This guy's ego is as huge as the Boston Garden. He revels in his notoriety. Kane sees himself as a media darling. Even got a publicist, for chrissakes. The publicity brings him more big ticket clients." A bell sounded, followed by beeping. "I'm sure this won't surprise you. Kane prioritizes his case list by how much a client is willing to pay him upfront. In cash."

Bruno had raised his voice. An image of a pissed-off Kodiak bear with razor claws and glistening fangs floated in my head. This man was my ally now – or maybe even before.

"The more blatant the circumstances," Bruno said, "the more money Kane can demand. He feels no shame whatsoever about helping clients escape hard punishment even if they've been in trouble before. There's more, Mr. Proffitt." Bruno had lowered his volume. "I don't know if you want to hear it. It's about your daughter Katherine."

The knot in my stomach jumped to my chest. Was I up to hearing information about Katie that would hurt me? I drew in a deep breath. What choice did I have? No matter how bad the news, I needed to know.

"Go on, Bruno."

"That former employee told me Kane had a big victory party after Adam Harding's settlement against Proffitt Advertising." The words hissed from Bruno's mouth. "Harding was at the party, drunk. He boasted how he got even with the cold ass bitch from California. The one who wanted nothing to do with him. Harding admitted following Katherine from a dorm party to her car. Then he played what he called a little harmless game of bumper tag with her when she drove away. She panicked, lost control of her car, and smashed into him. He said nothing would've happened to Katherine had she been more receptive to him in the first place."

"For God's sake, Bruno." Jesus. How much more would my broken heart take? "I don't want to hear any more."

"I'm sorry, Mr. Proffitt, but maybe you do. Here's the punch line. Kane raised his glass of scotch at the party and said, 'Here's to all the ice queens and the big paydays they represent.'"

"Oh my God." I was about to lose my birthday dinner.

"I'm not trying to hurt you, Mr. Proffitt. Honest, I'm not. I can only imagine what you want to do to Kane. In truth, from a legal standpoint, I don't want to know. But for what it's worth, I sure as hell hope you succeed. Hence the urgency of my call tonight."

"I don't understand, Bruno." My hand pressed against my chest.

"You've shared with me why time is of the essence," Bruno said. "You have less time than you think. Kane's leaving for Los Angeles tomorrow morning at 7:45 a.m. Eastern time from Boston's Logan Airport. Less than ten hours from now. I'm faxing you his Logan itinerary, including his flight number. Sorry, but I lose Kane once he lands in L.A." Bruno cleared his throat. "I can tell you he's planning on taking Tammy Jo Moore to Hawaii, but I don't know when. From a strategic standpoint, you need to come to Boston. Now. The best shot you've got at isolating Kane would be at his home or office before he leaves."

I had an hour and a half to get to the San Francisco Airport and catch the 8:37 p.m. flight to Boston. If I failed to make that plane, I'd miss my best and perhaps only opportunity to kill Oliver Kane.

CHAPTER TEN

The Mercedes engine purred like a catnip-enhanced kitten. Bright headlights shone a path down the driveway. I set the driver's seat back to accommodate my long legs and adjusted the rearview mirror. All systems were go with the exception of a driver who hadn't been behind a steering wheel for almost five years.

"Look out, San Francisco."

My overeager right foot punched down on the gas pedal after I shifted into drive. The Mercedes streaked down the driveway. The power of having a live steering wheel in my hands again was a familiar, yet uneasy, sensation. Operating a moving vehicle was sheer madness on my part, but a necessary evil if I wanted to make the 8:37 p.m. flight to Boston. I could have asked Mrs. Green to drive, but she'd ask too many questions. Questions I didn't want to answer. Plus, she drove like she was taking a driver's license test. I considered calling a cab, but if they were late or didn't show up, I'd miss the plane. My best option was to roll the dice and chauffeur myself to the airport.

I turned onto our tranquil, tree-lined street like an unrestrained, white mustang chasing the wind. My seatbelt flap-talked at me until I buckled up. The time, 7:36 p.m., glowed on the digital dashboard. I could be at the airport in less than twenty minutes. Then again, I was one traffic jam away from watching the flight soar over my head from a freeway parking lot.

"Oh, shit." I had acquired tickets for every flight in the next twenty-four hours, with the exception of tonight's overbooked 8:37 p.m. flight leaving me on standby. My only hope would be last minute cancellations, or passengers arriving too late, or not at all. Perhaps I could upgrade to first class or pay off a passenger to scalp his or her ticket. Hell, I could afford to buy every seat on the plane and the fuel too. Bottom line, I was getting on that flight even if I had to fly the damn plane myself.

The gas pedal inched closer to the floor. I cut a left turn too sharply. My leather briefcase idling on the passenger seat crashed into the door. The Benz's back end drifted into a slide. Calm down, Mo. Concentrate. Smashing into a vehicle or running off the road would eliminate any chance I had of making the flight.

A right turn headed me towards Nineteenth Avenue, beyond that, the 280 freeway, the 380 ramp then a straight shot to the airport. Park the Benz, check my luggage . . .

"Luggage? What the hell was I thinking, or not thinking?"

In my haste, I'd left without the suitcase. Mrs. Green would be in a panic when she discovered the satchel lying on my bed. What else had I forgotten? I patted down my pockets. My cell phone was where it should be, along with my wallet, money clip, and pills. The essentials.

The briefcase holding Bruno's printouts slid back to the middle of the seat. My fingers caressed the soft brown surface. I'd brought the right case, but was I doing the wrong thing? If a man came to me with the same lunatic scheme I was about to attempt, especially a man who could keel over dead at any time, I'd tell the poor son of a bitch he was demented. Yeah, crazy. Maybe I was crazy. Nothing had ever seemed right after Katie was killed. But what if six or seven years ago, someone just like me had eliminated Oliver Kane and his legal lunacy? Katie along with a host of other victims would be alive today. The gray area between right versus wrong balanced on a fine line.

Remnants of a plan formed, but it had more holes in it than a Whiffle Ball. What was the missing piece that would tie everything together? Right now, I was leaving a rendezvous with Oliver Kane up to chance. Too optimistic. Somehow I had to develop a way for Kane to be interested in me. For Kane to want to meet with me. I used to excel in these situations back when my creative gene was functioning on all cylinders.

"Whoa!" The back of a white Volkswagen Jetta convertible with the top down suddenly appeared just ahead of me. My shoe hit the brake pedal hard. The Benz's radials grabbed enough asphalt to avoid a collision. That was close. Had I been concentrating so hard on Kane's demise that I wasn't paying attention to my driving?

A glance at the speedometer answered my question. The Jetta driver was traveling fifteen miles under the speed limit with a cell phone pinned to her ear. I flicked the headlights on and off. If anything, she slowed down even more. I still hadn't reached Nineteenth Avenue yet. My senses came alive from anger. Had we collided, the accident would have been my fault in spite of her malicious driving. Our legal system often didn't take into account the immorality of wrong and the righteousness of fair.

I eased my foot back onto the gas pedal. The night's periphery had become brighter, moved faster, and sounded louder. Driving alone in the early dark served as a perfect think tank opportunity for me to zero in on an effective plan. But first I had to rid myself of the Jetta girl.

I pulled out around her but an onslaught of cars sped towards me. I swerved back behind the Jetta and honked the horn. She turned her head and raised her middle finger. Unless this gal maneuvered the steering wheel with elbows or knees, her car was operating on automatic pilot.

My hands choked the steering wheel as if it was the Jetta girl's neck. How self-centered could she be? She didn't give a holy crap about anybody but herself. Just like Oliver Kane, except Kane didn't drive.

The words I'd circled during my conversation with Bruno appeared before me like an illuminated billboard: ego, debt, gambling, cash, women, and doesn't drive. I could offer Kane a ride. Then what? A sigh of disgust flew from my mouth. Why would Oliver Kane accept a ride from a total stranger? What if I offered him my services? But what services of mine would he need? Kane already received the best media advertising of all, free publicity from winning big cases. Yet people in trouble, strangers, sought out the DUI Doctor for his legal expertise. What if I were to seek Kane's counsel regarding an illicit situation?

"Bingo!" I slapped the steering wheel. "That works!"

I pulled the Mercedes into the other lane again. An oncoming vehicle blasted its horn. My car and I were now invincible. I pulled back in ahead of the Volkswagen. Jetta Girl's hand rose in the windshield and formed a one-finger salute again. I waved a thank you back to her for inspiring me.

* * * * *

I turned the Mercedes onto the ramp leading to the airport. A low-flying jet with its nose tilted upward crossed my windshield. Auto traffic merged together from numerous directions. An army of red taillights appeared to the left for airport parking. Something had slowed down the process. Maybe the automated ticket machine needed manual assistance. Or all the parking spaces were filled. I wasn't about to wait in that line to find out what the problem was.

The Benz drifted into one of the departing-flight lanes. A taxi cut in front of me like my car didn't exist. The whole damn scene was intimidating, but that wasn't going to stop me. We were all fighting for the same thing, but I had so much more to lose.

Traffic in the departure section slowed. At least here the cars were moving. A United Airlines sign came into view. Cars, passengers, skycaps, and luggage filled the curbs. A San Francisco airport traffic cop blew a whistle and waved for me to keep moving. Sorry, pal, but this was my stop. I jammed the gearshift into park and removed the key from the ignition. I was triple-parked. Not being concerned about consequences had some advantages.

I stepped out onto the street with my briefcase in hand. The scene was eerie. Horns blared from behind. Every eye, including the eye of a camera, seemed zeroed in on me.

"Your attention please," a recorded female voice announced from overhead speakers, "unattended vehicles left at the curb will be cited and towed at the owner's expense."

"Good deal, Valet Parking." I shimmied between cars heading to the curb.

"Hey, you can't park there," the cop yelled. "Move your car now or I'll have it towed."

I stopped and turned around midway on the sidewalk. The man in blue was only performing his job. Why should I make it more difficult for him? I removed the Benz's thick key from a silver hippo keychain Katie had given to me one Father's Day. Like a softball pitcher I underhand flipped the car key to the cop. His eyes widened as he cupped his hands attempting a Willie Mays basket catch.

"A donation to the Policeman's Ball," I hollered, then entered the airport.

I breezed past the baggage check-in, saving energy and minutes. Added time to insure I got a seat on the plane. Departure signs led me across patterned gray carpet to a high powered x-ray machine and metal detector. My briefcase moved on the conveyor belt as I walked through the archway. The alarm went off. I had to go back, empty my pockets onto the conveyer, and go through again. This time the archway was silent. I collected my things and hurried to the departure area. If the x-ray machine had provided an in-depth image of my damaged heart, would I have been allowed to continue my journey?

Chapter Eleven

The gate area was filled close to capacity. A line of passengers waited to conduct business with the boarding agent. I stared at the agent from my waiting-area chair as if she was the focal point of my frustration. She wasn't. Getting in touch with Oliver Kane had become my immediate concern. I'd fight my ticket battle with the agent after I made contact with Kane. 7:58 by my watch. Time wise, I was still in good shape here in San Francisco. But it was 10:58 p.m. in Boston. Rather late to be calling someone personally or professionally.

The first three Oliver Kane phone numbers from Bruno's list got me only as far as Kane's voicemail. Leaving a pitch to Kane on a recorded message would be as fruitless as trying to roll a seven on one die.

I punched in the last digit of the fourth number and leaned back into the vinyl seat. I was primed, ready to perform to my one-man audience, yet he was nowhere to be found. Ring number one. My heart pounded with nervous excitement the way it used to before I made a major presentation. Come on, Kane. Answer your damn phone. Ring number two.

I was on the fifth ring, yet voicemail hadn't kicked in. What if I couldn't speak to Kane before the 8:37 take off? Talk about rolling the dice. A quick glance at the last phone number on Bruno's page added more acid to my queasy stomach. In hindsight, maybe I should have pulled the car over from the freeway and called. . .

"Yes," a male voice answered.

"Oliver Kane," I blurted, sitting up straight.

My thumping heart felt like it was going to jump out of my chest. Background voices and cards being shuffled filtered through the line. Was Kane playing poker?

"Who is this?" Kane shot back. "And how the fuck did you get this number?"

I'd heard that deep, southern, nasal voice on TV and in a court-room before. By Kane's words and tone, I was off to a poor start. Were my persuasion skills still sharp enough to make a sale?

"Obtaining your phone number wasn't a problem for me, Mr. Kane. I have many connections. My name is Morgan. And I need your services."

"Listen, pal, you're calling me at eleven o'clock at night on my private line. If you're not a member of the Kennedy family, I don't want to talk to you right now. *Capice?*"

"Mr. Kane, there's a very good chance you'll covet my wealth and power as much as a Kennedy. I've been following you for a long time. I'm a man who's used to the very best. Therefore, I want you to represent me."

Kane exhaled a melody of breaths into the phone. Plastic poker chips splashed together. He sniffed hard like he had a cold.

"Call," Kane said, followed by the clamor of more chips.

"I fold," a background voice grumbled.

I'd be willing to bet the value of the chips Kane just threw into the pot was more than what the average person made in a day. Was he on a roll and flush with chips? Or was he deeper in debt? The outcome of our negotiation could depend on Kane's chip count.

"What did you say your name was?" Kane asked.

"Morgan."

"Well, Morgan. As you can probably tell, I'm busy at the moment. Tomorrow I'm going out of town. On business. So call my office for an appointment."

I rubbed a hand through my hair. Nice blow off, Kane. I wouldn't consider a liaison with Tammy Jo Moore in Hawaii to be business. Then again, he might have to labor keeping up with the youthful Miss Moore, as well as shielding the truth from wife number four.

"Making an appointment two weeks from now isn't possible, Mr. Kane. I'm assuming that you're flying tomorrow from Logan Airport, departure at 7:45 a.m., making your arrival in Los Angeles at about 9:30 a.m. Pacific Standard Time?"

Kane growled something that I couldn't make out. Good. I had his attention.

"Don't you just love flying from the East Coast to the West Coast and gaining three hours?" I said. "Gives you more time. For business."

"You've got my private line. My itinerary. What else do you have?"

"Money," I shot back.

"Hold that thought."

Strange muffled noises came across the line. Kane's voice sounded distant and distorted then came in clearer. His hand must have been covering the phone.

"Time," another voice boomed. "I need time." A heavy New England accent.

"For chrissakes, Stanley," Kane barked. "Make a goddamned decision, will you? This isn't advanced calculus. The frigging pips and numbers on the cards aren't going to change. Fold, call, or raise."

I added "impatient" to the list of words describing Oliver Kane. He sounded like a man who was losing and on tilt. Kane was accustomed to winning at all costs in court, but that didn't make him a good poker player. I could offer him an opportunity to get out of the hole, where he could ultimately fall into a deeper, permanent one.

"I don't know how you got my number or travel plans," Kane said in his courtroom voice. "But I'm impressed with the way you've done your homework. Odds are you've gone to a great deal of trouble and expense to obtain your information. Why don't you cut to the short strokes? What do you want?"

"I want you, Mr. Kane."

"For what?"

"Here's the deal," I said. "It's essential that I meet with you before you leave Boston. Therefore, tomorrow morning I'll provide your transportation to Logan Airport. It will afford us a perfect, albeit short, opportunity to converse."

"Are you out of your fucking mind?" Kane added a long sniff. "You're either one ballsy son of a bitch or simply nutso. Either way, your reasoning is flawed and you've wasted enough of my time."

"I can provide twenty-five thousand good reasons," I said in low, confident tone. "For the privilege of having you as my passenger,

I'll give you a nonrefundable twenty-five-thousand-dollar cash retainer. What time should I pick you up, Mr. Kane?"

"Goddamn it," he hollered. "The jerk-off sucked out on the river card. How are you supposed to beat dumb fucking luck? He had no business even being in the hand in the first place. No wonder I'm losing."

"Mr. Kane? Mr. Kane?" Damn it. Did he even hear that I just offered him twenty-five thousand in cash? Where the hell did he go? "Mr. Kane?"

A number of voices came across the cell phone line. None of them sounded like Oliver Kane. It was past eight o'clock on the west coast. I glanced at the line of people waiting to confer with the gate agent. Time was becoming more critical with each passing second. How deep in arrears was he? Would $25,000 even cover his loses?

"Are you still there, Morgan?" Kane asked in a softer voice.

"Yes, Mr. Kane." Thank God he came back on the line.

"Did you say twenty-five thou? Followed by the C word?"

"That's exactly what I said. A hell of a good offer just to ascertain your opinion on my situation, don't you think?"

"At least you've got your priorities straight, Morgan. I'm considering your proposal."

At this point in most negotiations, I usually turn as quiet as a monk on silent retreat. But with Kane, I needed to crank up the pressure to near overload to make him commit.

"Think of it this way," I said. "If, after we meet, you decide not to take me on as a client, you're still cashing out twenty-five thousand. Unlike poker, this is one hand you can't lose."

"Deal me out," Kane said. "Hold on, Morgan."

Kane puffed into the phone like he was extinguishing a series of candles. Lack of background noise from his line indicated he'd walked away from the poker table. His silence told me he was mulling over my offer. The God of Poker may have dumped all over Kane and at the same time blessed me.

"You're pretty damned sure of yourself," Kane said, "if you're offering a nonrefundable cash retainer just to speak to me." He made a smacking sound. "Who knows, you might have a pretty good case. In any event, I want you to wire me ten thousand now. Then I'll know you're for real."

"Not a chance," I said. My teeth mashed together. The son of a bitch could back out on me at any time and still be ten thousand dollars richer. "Let me make myself real clear here. Wiring you upfront money isn't going to happen. My cash and I are a package deal. The twenty-five thousand is just for our initial consultation. Should we proceed further, you'll not only be compensated with a much greater cash payday, but you also may be blessed with a case that could bring you more fame and notoriety than you've ever imagined."

More silence. Most clients would do anything Kane said to have the DUI Doctor make their trouble go away. Yet, if I was too agreeable, it could be a deal breaker.

"You've got all the answers, don't you?" Kane said.

"If I had all the answers, Mr. Kane, I wouldn't need you."

"Good point," he said. "Okay, here's the way this will work. I'm throwing in a slight irrevocable goodwill codicil. You need to up your ante by an extra twenty-five grand. Again, in cash. This isn't negotiable. Do we have an agreement?"

Holy shit. I had him. Before I jumped at Kane's counterproposal with a counter of my own, I wanted to make him sweat for a few beats. Ironically, fifty-thousand dollars had been the amount I tried to withdraw from the bank earlier today. Based on Bruno's information, Kane was in a desperate situation. He didn't want to lose the opportunity of a quick, cash turnaround. Nor would his narcissistic personality allow him to lose our negotiation. Holy lawyer shit. I've got him.

"My original offer of twenty-five thousand is more than fair, Mr. Kane. That, you're guaranteed. I'll pay you in full when we meet. However, if I like what I hear from you, in essence that you've convinced me my problem is going to be eliminated, I'll kick in the extra twenty-five thousand. That's how serious I am about meeting with you."

"Fifty thou if I'm good, huh?" Kane said. "That's a lock, as sure as betting against the Red Sox to win a World Series. Pick me up outside my office building at 6:00 a.m. If you're late I won't wait.

I'm assuming you already have the address."

"Yes, Mr. Kane. I'll be waiting for you at 6:00 a.m. sharp."

"One last thing, Morgan. Your research should have impressed upon you that I'm not a man to fuck with. Don't ever forget that. And don't bother with any lame last-minute phone-call excuses. I don't like disappointments. You get one chance with me, and one chance only. Is all of that understood?"

"Understood and noted, Mr. Kane. I look forward to our meeting."

Kane clicked off. My shoulders slammed back into the airport chair. I didn't even realize the fingers on my left hand had been clenched into a fist during our conversation. This result was satisfying beyond belief, but the performance had zapped much of my energy. There had been a time in my life when it would have taken me hours to come down from an act like this. Now I needed to garner enough strength to stand in line and charm my way into getting a boarding pass for tonight's Boston flight.

8:08 p.m. by the wall clock. I was on a roll. Too bad my meeting with Kane wasn't at Fenway Park. Then I could kill two wishes with one stone.

CHAPTER TWELVE

The gate agent slid my computer printout indicating standby back to me. She twirled a shiny brown curl around her finger without changing expression. Her dark eyes, shielded by narrow, black-framed glasses, didn't show a hint of sympathy. Somehow I needed to trip the compassion switch hiding behind this agent's tough exterior.

"I'm sorry, Mr. Proffitt," the gate agent said. "This flight to Boston is overbooked. You're on standby. I can't assign you a seat."

"Miss, there must be a way for me to secure a seat on this plane."

"No guarantees, sir. You'll have to wait for availability. That is the best I can do for you right now." She peered at the woman behind me. "How may I help you, ma'am?"

"Hold on, please." I raised a palm in the air. My eyes shifted from her face to a metal, winged nametag pinned to her blazer jacket. "Patricia. I don't think you understand. It's imperative that I be on this flight."

"Yes, sir. I do understand. And I advise you to sit down and wait."

Ouch. Volleys of distressed grumbling erupted from behind me. The line dwellers were restless. Who could blame them? There was always one person trying to screw with the system. Tonight I was that guy. Sorry folks, even if I have to delay the takeoff, I would be on this plane.

"May I please speak to the gate agent supervisor, Patricia?"

"Sir, I am the gate agent supervisor." She glanced at her computer screen. "Just so you know, we automatically put your name on a standby waiting list in case we have VDB's or no-shows."

"And a VDB is?"

"Voluntarily denied boarding," she said. "We ask for volunteers who are willing to give up their seats in exchange for compensation and a confirmed seat on a later flight."

"Okay, I understand the process. However—"

"Sir, if you understood the process, I'd be helping the next passenger."

She clapped her hands together and looked past me again. I moved to block her view.

"My apologies for taking up so much of your time. I promise you that this isn't a ploy to circumvent my position at the expense of other passengers."

A man sidled up next to me and laid a hairy, balled fist on the counter. His ivory-colored cowboy hat and pointed, black boots still left him a good seven inches shorter than my six-foot-one. He glared at me like we were about to have a shootout at the OK Counter. Then he pointed to the pocket watch in his now-open hand.

"Dadgummit, lady," the man drawled. "There's gonna be a line revolt if you don't do something right quick. And I'm going to be headin' the charge."

"Sir," she said.

"I don't know what this fella's problem is," the cowboy said, "but we're runnin' out'a time. You know, partner," he said to me, "where I come from, if there's a' accident, drivers go to the side of the road so the other folk can keep moving."

"With all due respect to your southern-fried wisdom," I said, "this isn't your—"

"I'll handle this, Mr. Proffitt." Patricia eyed me while pointing a red fingernail at the cowboy. "Sir, I'm well aware of the time and your concerns. This gentleman was in line before you. You're interfering presence isn't helping the situation." She held up a cell phone. "You have two choices. Please take your place back in line or I'll call security."

The cowboy tilted his hat back, exposing a creased forehead, and glared at me. His shoulders straightened. Patricia raised the phone to her lips. He turned around and shuffled back to his place in the line. Her features softened, a look that suited her better.

"Thank you, Patricia. For what it's worth, I find myself in a life and death situation."

"You and everyone else, sir." She emitted an emphatic sigh.

"Wish I could plead over-dramatics here," I said, placing a hand over my heart. "But I can't. It's crucial I make this flight."

"Sir, can you please verify your emergency situation for me?"

I could tell her the truth. I need to be on this flight in order to arrive in Boston by early tomorrow morning to murder a man before he departs for L.A. Did that fit into the emergency classification? In contrast, I could lie to her, but everything I've said so far had been factual. Besides, this lady would likely see through any falsehood.

"No, ma'am, I can't substantiate anything." My tone was matter of fact, not apologetic. "You'll just have to take my word for it."

"Perhaps I can get you on another flight." Her fingers attacked the computer keyboard as if she was playing the piano. "Let me see, the next flight to Boston is—"

"12:05 a.m.," I said. "You'll find I have a reservation on that flight. And the 5:00 a.m. flight also. But circumstance has made the ETA for those flights too late for me. It's imperative that I arrive in Boston by early morning, Eastern Standard Time. This flight lands at Logan Airport at 4:57 a.m." I rubbed a hand across my cheek. "What will it take for me to get a seat on this flight without getting you into trouble?"

"Patience, sir. Just wait and see what happens."

"I understand it's your duty to follow the rules." I smiled. "And you're doing one heck of a good job." I was still the only one smiling. "Could you at least tell me where I am on the standby list?"

"You're standby passenger number nine," she said.

"Nine! I'll never make it."

"Sir," she offered in a hushed tone. "I've already confirmed the first four standbys – one couple and two individuals." She glanced back at the screen. "I can bump you up to the fifth position. That's the best I can do."

"Thank you." A gnawing feeling in my stomach warned me not to push her any harder. "I wasn't lying to you. It's vital I get to Boston by tomorrow morning."

"I know." The smile she'd been hiding emerged. "After working for the airlines all these years, you get to read people pretty well. I sincerely wish you good luck getting a seat on this flight." She focused on the lady behind me. "How may I help you, ma'am?"

I walked away. Patricia's smile had vanished by the time I sat down. The chair felt less comfortable than before. What had I gained from our negotiation? Four places on a waiting list. There had to be another way.

My briefcase rested on the vacant seat to my right. I flipped it open. Was there a plan B if I lost my one chance to meet Kane in Boston? I still had plenty of time to fly to L.A. and wait for him at that airport. Without my interference, he'd board his 7:45 a.m. plane from Logan Airport tomorrow and land in Los Angeles five and a half hours later. But then what? Even if I managed to make contact with Kane in L.A., metal detectors precluded me from bringing a weapon to the boarding gate. Nor could I count on my depleting strength to land a deadly karate blow. Every bit of my leverage was based on getting to Kane before he departed for Logan airport. Plan B wasn't an option.

Night's mysterious shadow played through the windows overlooking the tarmac. Rows of chairs intermingled with carry-on luggage and travelers with vapid expressions. Hundreds of people around, but a sinking feeling of isolation enveloped me.

How many passengers did the plane hold? Sounded like a lead-in to a joke, but there was nothing funny about the situation I was in. The more important number now was how many of the waiting passengers had boarding passes to claim their seats.

A man limped towards me with his face buried in an out-of-town newspaper. A series of sneezes made him stop. The photo of the assassinated Afghan Northern Alliance leader appeared on the page facing me. My God, there was unrest everywhere, particularly in that area of the world. Seldom did I read the front page of a newspaper or watch broadcast news anymore. Even if the news wasn't so bad, by the time they sensationalized the headline, blue skies developed a black hole. The man sneezed one last time and moved on.

Hell, if the dead Afghan leader had been one of the four people ahead of me on the standby list, I'd be a step closer to getting on the plane. How cold and unfeeling I'd become. Had my right-from-wrong morals been erased from my psyche? Or perhaps my conscience simply rationalized that killing Oliver Kane was no worse than executing a person guilty of transgressions against humanity.

A baby's shrill cry sent a shiver down my neck into my shoulders. My nerves were on edge, exposed and tender. But I'd welcome sitting next to a finicky set of infant twins or even Saddam Hussein if I could procure a boarding pass for this flight.

A young man handed over the struggling infant in his arms to a younger-looking girl. Maybe the baby was sick and the airlines wouldn't allow the three of them to board the plane. No such luck. The newborn's fussing ceased when the mother introduced her breast, as if they were alone in their living room.

Next to the nursing mother, a man wearing a light blue suit sat slumped with his eyes closed. His red face tilted away from the girl. He was breathing through his mouth. His black loafers rested under the chair. Did he know or care that part of his big toe was exposed through a hole in his sock? Perhaps jet lag had gotten the best of him. If he could sleep through that baby's cry, he could sleep through anything. Even a boarding call.

My heartbeat quickened. A young woman sitting two chairs away from the sleeping man caught my attention and kept it. She was attractive. Not as pretty as my Katie, but the likeness of their faces were quite remarkable. I couldn't help but stare at her. Auburn had been Katie's color, too, but the young woman sported a shorter hairstyle. Her figure was thinner and she was a few inches taller than Katie's five-four. From this distance I couldn't tell if she had a tiny patch of freckles around her nose. What I could see was that she wore a black sweater, black slacks, and by the scowl on her face, a dark mood.

She gazed at me with swollen eyes, focused on a land only she could see. Someone or something had upset her, and she wasn't trying to hide it. Her fingers folded together on her lap, concealing what she was holding.

A sailor wearing dress blues stopped to talk to the young woman. She didn't respond. He stooped and leaned closer to her. If she knocked him out with a hard right cross to the chin, I could take his seat on the plane. Instead, she threw him a sneer vicious enough to make his head rock back. The sailor shrugged his shoulders and slinked away like a ship with a leaky hull. Maybe she was too upset to board the plane.

"Your attention please," Patricia announced. "Flight number one five seven to Boston is full. We're asking for volunteers willing to give up their seats in exchange for compensation and a confirmed ticket on a later flight."

My body tilted forward in the chair, zeroing in on the boarding station. No one was coming forward. Damn it. Maybe they didn't hear Patricia's announcement.

"Your attention please," Patricia said. "Will passengers holding first class tickets or needing special assistance please line up at the boarding gate."

A line formed by a closed door that led to the plane. I used to travel first class and now I qualified for special assistance. But without a seat assignment, it didn't matter.

In what seemed like seconds, most of the special passengers disappeared through the boarding gate doorway. No one had approached Patricia. She raised the microphone to her lips again.

"All remaining passengers with boarding passes please line up at the gate."

Patricia watched a flurry of passenger movement to the boarding area. My eyes shifted to the sleeping man. He could be sleeping his way off the plane.

The waiting area was nearly empty. All the goodbye kisses and hugs had been exchanged. A tearful girl propped herself at the window for a lonely last look at the jet outside. Only a few people remained seated, including the sleeping man. The young lady who reminded me of Katie also remained seated. She stuffed whatever she'd been holding into an oversized purse and stood up. Another one of my options just got in line.

Chapter Thirteen

A handful of passenger wannabes remained in the waiting area, none more anxious than I. Any margin of minutes once in my favor had now ticked away. It was 8:21 p.m. San Francisco time, 11:21 Boston time, and crunch time in reality.

A young couple nodded and smiled to each other as if they had come to an agreement. They rose from their chairs as one and marched to the boarding station, leaving their blue carry-on luggage behind. Patricia processed the paperwork in less than a minute. The couple returned to gather their bags and departed the waiting area holding hands. Two places down on the standby list. Three more to go. Come on, people. This wasn't the army, for God's sake. The airline was offering compensation and another flight.

"Your attention please," Patricia announced into the microphone. "Will passengers Mr. and Mrs. Buhl please come to the boarding station?"

A platinum blonde woman tugged her older partner from his chair. Her skintight pants and blouse had long surrendered to middle age spread. She headed towards the gate area with her man in tow. No doubt the fortunate Buhls. Perhaps I could create my own luck.

"Pardon me, folks." I said, stepping into their path.

Whoa. Her strong perfume attacked my nose, leaving a smell that would linger in my nostrils for awhile. I locked eyes with the woman. The husband or boyfriend stood a few feet away, gazing at the floor. He had the look of a man wanting to fly solo. She tugged on her earlobe, displaying a sparkler on her finger the size of a doorknob. If the ring had the same dollar value as a door handle, perhaps she'd be receptive to my proposal.

"We're in a hurry," she said in a testy tone. "What do you want?"

"I'm sorry to bother you. I need to be on this flight. To that end, I'd like to offer you a considerable amount of compensation – in cash – for your plane seats."

"How much?" the man asked, after lifting his head. His eyes sparkled with interest.

"Two thousand dollars for each ticket," I said.

"Fred, are you out of your mind?" She placed a hand on her hip and glared her indignation. "They aren't for sale, mister."

"Three thousand," I offered.

"What you're asking us to do is illegal, you know?" she said. "The answer's still no."

"Name your price, then."

"Not interested." She grabbed Fred's arm and headed to the gate. "They should really do something about airport hustlers. If we had the time, I'd report this creep to security."

The Buhls stopped at the agent's desk. I waited for incriminating fingers to be pointed at me then returned to my seat when they rushed through the doorway without incident. A familiar face on the TV screen caught my eye. Oliver Kane on CNN news. He posed on cement steps outside a city government building. Sunlight reflected from his sunglasses. Was this a recent news clip or footage from an earlier case? A young, thin, black man wearing a crooked baseball hat stood a foot taller next to the attorney, most likely a wealthy basketball player in trouble. The young man yawned and looked anything but remorseful. Truly an archetype Kane defendant.

Kane removed his sunglasses, squinted into the camera, and ended the interview by pointing a finger the same way Bill Clinton did while denying having sex with "that woman." A female reporter's closed-captioned words read, "The charge is manslaughter. Will the DUI Doctor cure another star athlete ailing from legal trouble?"

Pressure mounted in my chest. Dizziness made me grip the arms of the chair for stability. Sweat accumulated on my face and neck. I puffed out short breaths.

Two passengers emerged from the jetway into to the terminal building carrying their ticket packets. They stopped at Patricia's station. If one more passenger volunteered his or her seat, the boarding pass was mine.

Patricia called for Passenger Swenson. No one budged. Perhaps Passenger Swenson was in the bathroom or. . .Shit. A tall woman with hair the color of light toast stood up listening intently to a cell phone. Her shoulders slumped as if she was self-conscious of her height. She was probably in her late thirties, old enough to be understanding about my situation, but maybe not too old to be set in her ways. Her face creased into a horrified expression. She put a hand over her mouth.

Vertigo hit me as I rushed to intercept the woman. She had hitched a nylon satchel over her shoulder. Her eyes were filled with tears when I approached her.

"Excuse me, miss. It's imperative I get on this flight." My palm unveiled a full money clip. "I can provide generous compensation beyond what the airline is giving for your standby place and any inconvenience I may cause you."

"Sir, I also need to be on this flight," she said in a shaky voice. "My brother is in critical condition at a Boston hospital. I can only hope to make it to him in time. Sorry."

The back of her hand wiped her wet cheeks. I recalled the night of Katie's accident, rushing to the airport with a disbelieving mind. What would I have done if someone had approached me and asked for my boarding pass? Would I have been as nice and respectful as this poor woman?

"My sincere apologies for bothering you. I hope you get to your brother in time."

Moments later, the lady disappeared through the gate entryway with a boarding pass.

I teetered off balance on the way back to my chair and briefcase. One person was ahead of me on the waiting list. And one seat was available on the plane. I removed my cell phone from my suitcoat pocket, just in case I had to make the call I'd been avoiding.

The area was almost deserted. Seven strangers waited for that last boarding pass. The only traveler who didn't look concerned was the sleeping man in the blue suit. I glanced at Patricia. Her eyes were still fixed on the computer screen. Perhaps, in a moment of compassion, the gate agent supervisor would jump me one place on the standby list. She shrugged her shoulders as if she was trying to decide who to call. Come on, Patricia. . .

A strike of pain hit my chest and traveled down my arm. The cell phone slipped from my hand and broke apart in two pieces on the floor. My stomach bubbled nausea. The burning acid taste in my mouth could have melted a Tums container. I'd ingested my quota of meds earlier today in the cab. Would another pill accelerate heart failure? Louis wouldn't have cautioned about overdosing as a scare tactic. A second pain hit. What could be more harmful than a fatal heart attack?

The vial's cap popped off on the first try. Several pills tumbled into my palm. I picked up a round white tablet and held it between a thumb and forefinger. The drug was small in size, but dynamite in potency. A hard thumbnail pinch proved ineffective in breaking the pill in two. I bit through the surface with front teeth, leaving half in my mouth. The jagged-edged piece slid under my tongue.

The hurt and heaviness in my chest continued. I should have taken a whole pill. Patricia's voice blared from the speakers. Did she announce my name? She wasn't looking in my direction. Come on, meds. Work your magic. One more time. I leaned back into the chair and closed my eyes. The lining in my throat was as dry as a sauna room. I visualized Oliver Kane's smug expression. My fingers squeezed the side of the chair as if I was riding out a rollercoaster sway. Just give me a little more time.

An electric-like surge flowed through my veins. Pain was still present in my chest and arm, but not as sharp. Fatigue gripped me, a familiar, after-the-pill reaction. Damp clothes clung to me. None of that mattered. I was still in the game.

"Your attention please," Patricia called out, looking in my direction.

"Call passenger Proffitt," I whispered, trying not to show the discomfort I was in. "Call passenger Proffitt."

"Last call for passenger Lemon. Would passenger Lemon please come to the gate?"

No one made a move. I still had a chance. Six people looked at each other. Either passenger Lemon wasn't here or he was the guy sleeping. Either way, the next person on the list to get a seat on the 8:37 flight to Boston was passenger Proffitt.

I kneeled to the floor and reassembled my cell phone. Was it still in working order? On the way to a standing position, I saw a woman shake the sleeping man's shoulder.

"No," I grunted out. "No. No. Please don't do that."

She shook him again. The sleeping man awakened with a frightened expression. His eyes blinked like a coded message. He got to his feet then fell back into the chair.

"Hey, I'm here." His voice was loud enough to carry across the bay to the Oakland Airport. He struggled to rise again, grabbing the back of the chair for balance. His stocking foot stabbed at a shoe and missed. "I'm Thomas Lemon."

My legs felt wobbly, almost boneless. I willed my lethargic body to move as fast it could to Lemon, which wasn't fast at all. My plight was hinged on a man who had the last boarding pass and a big toe sticking through the hole in his sock.

"Mr. Lemon." My head jerked back. Good God. The man reeked of whiskey. "I'm in an emergency situation. I need a boarding pass for this flight. You're my last hope." I flashed a handful of hundreds. "Please. I'll pay you ten times the value of your ticket."

"Piss off, buddy." He pushed my hand away. "You can't buy me."

"Mr. Lemon, please. It's vital that I make this flight."

"Well, that's tough shit," he said, breathing alcohol fumes in my face. "If the airport has a chaplain, bargain with him. Me, I'm not interested in you or your sappy story."

Lemon weaved his way to Patricia. She peered in my direction then lowered her gaze. How close had Patricia been to calling the name of Proffitt instead of Lemon?

The remaining standby people were spread out like dots on a map. I didn't have the heart to tell them passenger Lemon, not Proffitt, was taking the last available seat on the plane. Maybe they could wait for the next flight. I couldn't.

I was panting by the time I neared my briefcase. Wait. What if I chartered a plane? Why hadn't I thought of that before? How long would it take me to process a flight? An hour? Two hours? Hell, Kane would be long gone by the time I landed.

I sat down before I fell down. Only one way to find out if my cell phone was still operational: Call Oliver Kane and ask a question

I had been forewarned not to ask. To Kane, missing a flight would more than qualify as a lame excuse, unless I recaptured his attention.

I stared at Kane's private phone number. Every square millimeter of my heart had believed I was destined to be on this flight to Boston. I hit the cell's On button. The screen lit up, answering my question regarding its working condition. My finger inched to Redial, then stopped. I still had a ticket for the 12:00 a.m. flight. What if I explained my situation to Kane and doubled the money by offering a hundred thousand dollars? Call the extra fifty thousand his disappointment bonus in lieu of his catching the next flight to Los Angeles? Fifty thousand additional dollars to wait four hours. Was that enough money to make a man deep in the red think twice?

Loud shouts made me turn toward the boarding area. Patricia was talking into her portable phone. Thomas Lemon stood at the counter with arms and mouth moving in different directions. He screamed out again. She turned her back to him.

"Could I have your attention please," Patricia announced.

In all probability, she was giving the airline declaration that the flight was full. Sticky patches of sweat broke out on my face and neck as I zeroed in again on Redial.

"Will passenger Proffitt please come to the boarding gate?"

Whoa. Hearing my name stopped me cold. Or was I hearing internal wishful thinking? Patricia stared at me with a glorious smile.

Thomas Lemon's mouth flapped up and down like a puppet. He was waving his ticket packet at two burly security officers. The shorter officer wrinkled his nose when he sniffed Mr. Lemon's black-leather-encased liquor flask. Lemon was too inebriated to be allowed onto the flight. I'd been given another chance to finish my mission.

Miracles do happen. And the heavenly boarding gate awaited me. If I'd had a glass in my hand, I'd toast Thomas Lemon and the Man looking down on me.

CHAPTER FOURTEEN

I was greeted with, "Welcome aboard, sir," and a complimentary smile. The petite flight attendant was attractive in a perky-cute sort of way. Short red hair parted at one side, arched narrow eyebrows, and commercially-bright teeth. She power-gripped my hand while her greenish brown eyes examined my ticket packet. I wished I had her energy.

"Patricia called and gave me a heads up," she said, releasing my hand. "I understand we almost went into overtime getting you a seat on this flight."

"Patricia wasn't exaggerating," I said, glad the flight attendant used the term overtime rather than sudden death.

"Sir, you seem out of breath and your face is flushed. Are you feeling all right?"

Thomas Lemon had been kicked off this flight for too much alcohol in his system. If the airline people knew the condition of my heart, they'd never allow me to fly.

"I have a dizziness disorder," I said. "Comes and goes. It's not a big deal."

"Oh, my daddy has the same thing," she said, touching my elbow. "Mariner's Disease. Or it's something like that."

"You were close," I said, with a smile. "I believe it's called Ménière's disease – a life-altering malady, but certainly not life threatening."

"We'll do our best to make your flight as comfortable as possible." She tilted her head towards the cabin. "Your aisle seat is on the left near the back of the plane. Happens to be my section. I'll be there in a few minutes."

The metal door crunched shut behind me. I turned to face twin aisles dividing three sections of coach seating. First class was at my back. My dizzy brain soared off in the clouds, though the plane remained on the tarmac. At least I wasn't experiencing a whirling spin-a-thon.

I chanced a deeper-than-normal breath. A hot sensation lit up inside my chest like Vicks VapoRub. My heart had given me more than a warning shot in the airport waiting area. Louis' words of caution echoed in my head. The more I exerted myself, the less time I'd have.

I veered to the left. All the passengers were seated, cramped together like a full pack of cigarettes. My heavy limbs left me with a sense of walking uphill against traffic.

That awful perfume scent found my nose again. There she sat, the cold-hearted, blonde woman. She jabbed an elbow into her older partner's arm when she saw me approach. Blondie continued to glare at me from her center section seat like I could be the next D. B. Cooper. This lady was fortunate I wasn't a skyjacker like D. B. I'd kick her large butt off the plane with no remorse. A lighter load would get me to Boston faster and the awful odor would be eliminated.

I cleared my throat in disgust. How callous I'd become. The blonde woman had every right to wear any perfume of her choice. Nor did she have to sell her waiting-list place to me or any other person. Yet I wasn't here to make friends or influence people, Dale Carnegie be damned. I just couldn't allow anyone to distract me from my mission.

An empty aisle seat several rows ahead came into view. My strength continued its rapid decline. The prospect of sitting down enticed me to keep moving.

"No wonder we ain't in the air yet," a man drawled.

The accented voice came from the miniature cowboy who had tried to bully me in line. Without his hat, he was as bald as a sheared ewe and probably several inches shorter bootless. Was he now emboldened because this wasn't Patricia's territory to marshal?

"I should've known it was you," he said. "You're like a human flight delay."

To acknowledge him wasn't worth my energy. But this guy had no reason to gripe. Patricia had made good her promise to get everyone boarded on time. No one wanted this plane in the air more than I did. Good thing he and I weren't seated next to each other.

I approached the back of the plane. The outer rows in coach had only two seats instead of three. One less person to bother me. Except the person occupying the window seat happened to be the dispirited young woman who looked so much like my Katie. She had a cell phone pressed to her ear with, if possible, a more sullen expression on her face. The last thing I needed was to experience five and a half hours of her pent-up problems.

My fingers choked the briefcase handle in anger. Someone so young and attractive had no right to be this unhappy. She was too selfish to appreciate what she had. Unlike Katie, this lady had a lifetime of dreams yet to fulfill. How could she... Jeez, Mo, get a grip? This wasn't the first time I'd silently vented my frustrations at someone. Her woes weren't my problem. I didn't know anything about her. Nor did I care to find out.

The young woman returned the cell to her purse. Her eyes fixed on the back of the seat in front of her as if she was watching TV. I inserted the pill bottle inside the briefcase and placed my folded suit jacket into the overhead storage compartment. Perhaps my silent bitching had been premature. In fact, I may have caught a lucky break. She was no more interested in me than I was in her.

The briefcase rested on my lap when I sat down. My head jerked upward when something pulled on my shirtsleeve. The flight attendant who had greeted me stood smiling and holding a folded blanket. She knelt down until we were at equal eye level.

"How're you doing?" the female steward asked. "I thought it would be best to bring you a blanket before they're all gone."

"Thank you, miss. But I'm fine for the moment."

"Let's keep the blanket up here then," she said, rising up to open the storage bin, "just in case you get cold later on."

The attendant banged the door shut then leaned in close. She gave the young woman a long, hard look. Her features squinted into annoyance. Obviously, I wasn't the only person curious about my young neighbor's behavior.

"Please buckle your seatbelts. We'll be taxiing soon. And, sir, would you please put your attaché case underneath the seat before we take off?"

I guided the briefcase to the floor, upright next to my right foot to have quick access to my pills. Then I grabbed both seatbelt ends. For several seconds my mind blanked on how the damn thing worked. I finally snap-clicked the two parts together.

A sudden memory of my last flight made swallowing difficult. The trip back to San Francisco from New England with Katie in a coffin. Perhaps the young woman next to me was suffering a similar ordeal?

"Miss, would you please fasten your seatbelt?" the flight attendant asked raising the volume of her voice.

No response. The young woman's eyes still focused on the seat back. The attendant reached past me and patted the woman on the shoulder. Then she tapped her again. The young woman's head twitched in surprise, breaking her trance. Her blinking blue eyes settled in on me as if I was the one who had touched her.

She wore a heavy layer of makeup on her cheeks and around her eyes. Her features didn't need the enhancement. The beauty overload made her look cheap. She could be trying to cover up a bad complexion. More likely, she was just hiding behind a cosmetic mask. Katie never would have worn that much makeup.

The young woman continued to stare at me. Perhaps I reminded her of someone she knew. Or maybe she didn't understand English.

"Would you please fasten your seatbelt, miss?" the attendant repeated more firmly.

Again, the young woman didn't respond. The flight attendant sighed. She gave me a questioning look. I answered with a shoulder shrug. She tilted her body forward, connected the young woman's seatbelt the way a mother would for a child, then moved on to the next row.

I turned my head away from the young woman next to me to discourage any involvement. Better to concentrate on eliminating one sleazebag attorney than to engage in conversation with this troubled individual. She could simply be the type of person who went through life with her glass half empty, and cracked, too.

A bell sounded in the cabin.

"This is Captain Donald Rupp speaking. There's going to be a slight delay in our scheduled takeoff due to ground fog. Although we've been informed by air traffic control that the fog has lifted enough for takeoffs to resume, there's a bit of a logjam on the runway. Please keep your seatbelts fastened. We're going to taxi our way into the lineup. The delay shouldn't be long."

The captain made slight delay sound as if it was no big deal. Maybe not to him, but I couldn't afford any loss of time. My watch said 8:42 p.m. If the delay was twenty minutes, we'd be landing at Logan Airport around 5:12 a.m. Boston time. Providing no further obstacles, that would leave me forty-eight minutes to get off the plane, pick up my rental car, and drive to the Kane Tower office complex in Boston's financial district. A place I'd never been to before. That would be cutting it way too close. What if I had a taxi or a limo waiting for me? No, that wouldn't work. I had to be in the driver's seat.

Bells rang inside the cabin again. The plane jerked backwards, prompting my head to bounce into the headrest. My foot fished for my briefcase. Where the hell was it? Looking down, I could only see my shoes and the carpet right around them. My pills and the information on Oliver Kane were suddenly missing. Pulse points quickened throughout my body until I noticed the briefcase had slid towards the window into my neighbor's floor area. Either she didn't mind or she wasn't aware of the case's presence. I retrieved the briefcase and, this time, fenced it lying flat between my shoes.

The plane came to a complete stop then taxied forward towards the runway. Nothing I could do would propel this baby off the ground any faster. Pressure built in my chest again. A panic-induced heart attack wouldn't get me to Boston any faster either. Just the opposite. Any medical emergency, whether it was mine or someone else's, would kill my chance of my meeting with Kane.

The perky flight attendant spoke into a microphone giving passenger instructions. The speakers muffled her voice, making it difficult for me to understand what she was saying. Didn't matter. I had to concentrate on a final strategy. Once the plane landed, I wouldn't have time to develop a plan. The only advantage I had on Oliver Kane was surprise – he wasn't aware I was Katherine Proffitt's father. The man would probably shit a law book when he discovered there was no payday of $50,000 from our face to face. An event I was looking forward to.

The flight attendant stood near one of the TV screens. Her topic had switched to floatation devices. My eyelids tumbled down like collapsing venation blinds, bringing on a stinging protest from my eyes having been open too long. I could picture Kane and a string-bikini-clad Tammy Jo Moore floating in Hawaiian waters on a luxury raft with Mai Tais in their hands. My eyelids jumped open with a sense of urgency. My task at hand was to make sure Kane never got to the airport to board the L.A. bound plane.

Lights from the two planes ahead of us filled our small window patch. I had no idea if there were more elsewhere. Or how much time they allotted between takeoffs. From behind, a baby's cry knifed right through me. It didn't seem possible that something so small and fragile could be so damn loud. Whoa, and potent too. No secret about what was bothering the kid.

The young woman sitting next to me gazed straight ahead, unaffected. Her body shivered like someone coming out of a swimming pool into cold air.

"Are you okay?" I asked. "Are you ill?"

Again, no response. Even if she didn't understand what I'd just said, she must have known I was speaking to her. Why had I bothered, especially when I didn't care?

But I did care. If this young woman drew attention to her issue, whatever it may be, the delay could be longer. More lost time. And what if Katie had been sitting alone trembling on a plane? I would have been grateful had someone provided a helping hand.

I launched myself from the chair. Dizziness threw me off balance. My hand reached for my headrest while I waited for the spinning sensation to dissipate. The flight attendant's face contorted into a frown when she saw me standing. My free hand pointed to the upper storage compartment. She smiled and nodded.

When I released the back of the seat, both my arms extended out like I was hanging ten on a surfboard. My bearings were still off.

The unrest in my head brought on nausea. If I fell to the floor, my chances of landing in Boston would be nil. Most likely they'd throw me off the plane no matter what story I came up with. My left hand stabbed at the storage door and missed. I managed to grab the door handle on my next attempt and removed the blanket. The young woman flinched when I draped the cover over her.

"Do you need assistance back here?" the attendant asked.

"The young lady seemed chilly, that's all." I re-buckled my seatbelt. "How much longer will we have to wait before takeoff?"

"Oh, I'd say five minutes," the attendant answered. She surveyed the young woman's face then peered at the window. "Ten at the most."

Our attendant gave the woman another once-over before leaving. She was suspicious, probably of both of us. The sooner the pilot got the plane in the air, the better.

"Thank you for the blanket," the young woman offered in a frail voice, without looking at me. "That was kind of you. But you should mind your own damn business."

Where the hell did that come from? My row partner spoke and obviously understood English. I had no idea what her problem could be. But I now had a feeling that my act of kindness may have opened up a can of complications.

CHAPTER FIFTEEN

I leaned back into the headrest to take a break from reviewing the information Bruno had sent. It was 9:06 p.m. by my watch, but that was San Francisco time. I set the hands to 12:06 a.m. The date jumped from the tenth to the eleventh. Tuesday morning Boston time.

Sitting within the womb of a plane's cabin, listening to the cathartic hum used to relax me, often inspiring streams of creative and profitable thoughts. Yet I'd never bothered to learn the laws of aeronautics. I was always amazed how a large piece of metal could rise, float, then descend to the ground. Tonight's flight, however, was simply a means to propel me to an end – Logan International Airport – then to Kane Tower by six a.m.

The science of flying had nothing on the strange young woman sitting next to me. She was on a different plane, at least mentally. Her trance-like focus had switched from the chair back to the window's ebony screen. She hadn't said a word since I'd covered her with the blanket. Whatever her problem, mute was a good option for her.

The tiny overhead light beamed down on the Boston maps. To test my memory, I looked away from the diagram on top and visualized the streets leading from the airport to Oliver Kane's downtown office. Not a difficult task. I had a choice of taking one of two routes from the airport. The distance was about five or six miles, not nearly as far as I'd thought it would be. Traffic shouldn't be a problem that early in the morning. Getting to Kane Tower was still doable within the time frame, but I'd lost my margin of extra minutes due to the delay in San Francisco. And I still had a car to rent.

I peered down at the map again. An imaginary bank of stadium lights lit a familiar name several inches to the left of my destination. Fenway Park wasn't far from Kane Tower. To experience Fenway in person would be a thrill. Even seeing the historic ballpark from the outside would be a dream come true. Were the Red Sox in town? My eyes measured three inches. The distance was close enough to get a whiff of a stadium dog, yet the conditions of my journey put me out of tasting range, the ultimate tease.

"Ladies and gentlemen, this is Captain Rupp again. In order to make better time and to avoid turbulence, we've been granted permission to fly at a lower altitude than usual. We should pick up fifteen to twenty minutes of flight time, making our arrival at Logan Airport around 4:50 a.m. Eastern Standard Time. Enjoy the ride."

Yes. A break for team Mo. Pressure eased from my body. Those precious minutes we gained would loom large as a buffer. My plan was back on track again.

The flight attendant pulling a wheeled, metal serving cart that looked like a miniature armored truck stopped by my side. She hadn't lost her glorious smile. Katie had a similar smile that made everyone around her feel good. And an infectious giggle. . .

"What would you like for a complimentary soft drink, sir?" the attendant asked. "Also, you'll find in the pouch in front of you a menu of snack options."

"A cup of hot water, please." Mrs. Green's dinner was still weighing on me. Coffee or tea would keep me awake, but caffeine could throw my heart into overdrive.

The flight attendant poured steamy water from a metal pitcher into a paper cup. She put the cup and a napkin the size of a large cracker onto my tray along with a packet of mixed munchies. Her smile faded when she focused on the young woman's auburn hair.

"Miss, would you like something to eat or drink?"

The young woman's hand snaked out from underneath the blanket. She gripped the armrest then faced the attendant. She had a vacant expression, like a person with a concussion or on drugs.

"I-I'd like some water," the young woman said in a weak voice. Her head moved up and down, slowly. "Yes. Bottled water."

"Would you like something to eat to go along with the water?" the flight attendant queried, leaning towards the woman for a closer look. "Miss, is something wrong?"

"I just need some bottled water," the young woman snapped. "That's all I need."

The attendant's eyes widened. Could she figure out this woman's behavior any more than I could? Something was bothering my row mate, a glitch that could have an effect on this flight. Several years ago when I was on a business trip, the captain made an emergency landing at the nearest airport to attend to a passenger's problem. If this woman would just fall asleep until we landed, we'd all be better off.

The attendant glanced at the cockpit door. Was she considering warning the captain? If the plane detoured to another location to remove the young woman from the plane, it wouldn't matter how low the pilot flew, we could never make up the time. Why did this woman have to be on my flight?

"Miss," I whispered, pulling the flight attendant's sleeve to make her tilt towards me. "Don't worry about the young lady. I believe she's just anxious about flying." My tone came out calm, but the turbulence inside me was rough. "You probably see this all the time. She seems to be a bit traumatized. I'll keep an eye on her."

"Thank you." The attendant combed her short hair with her fingers. "You may be right. Sometimes it's difficult to tell what's going on with a passenger." She handed the young woman a plastic bottle of water and shifted back to her cart. "If you're a psychologist, there's a heavily-perfumed passenger several rows forward who could also use your services."

"Sorry, miss. I'm not a shrink. But I have watched Dr. Phil on Oprah."

The smiling flight attendant pulled the cart away. I had no idea if the young woman next to me had a fear of flying. For all I knew, her dog could have just died. Or she could be burdened with any number of psychological disorders. For the time being, we had avoided a shakedown from the air Gestapo.

The young woman managed to lower her tray. She turned her attention to the bottle of water. Her fingers lacked the strength to twist off the top. I leaned over, gripped the bottle with one hand, and broke the white plastic seal with a snap and a twist.

She eyed the bottle in her hand and sighed. Her fingers trembled like they belonged to a feeble person. Water jiggled out onto her tray and blanket. At this rate, she was going to get soaked. I reached for the bottle again.

"Don't," she fired out. The young woman pushed the bottle down onto the tray in defiance, splashing more liquid dots onto the surface. She scowled at me, then clamped her other hand onto the bottle's neck as if she was holding holy water.

She had every right to react the way she did. I had trespassed into her territory without permission. Yet, by countering my unsolicited help, she'd done me a great favor. I had far more important things on my mind than to concern myself with her problems. As long as she kept her Dr. Strangelove act away from the crew, she was on her own.

I rubbed my chin. This young woman and I made quite a dysfunctional duo. My heart could quit ticking at any time, and she was like a hair-trigger bomb ready to go off.

My eyes refocused on my tray desk. I removed an article about Oliver Kane from underneath the maps. The headline read: "THE MAN YOU LOVE TO HATE – UNLESS YOU NEED HIM."

Do the crime – pay the time, but not if you have Oliver Kane as your attorney. To date, not one of Kane's DUI clients has served a prison sentence. Kane is legendary for finding loopholes in the law and using state regulations to his advantage. The majority of Kane's cases are thrown out of court or settled before going to trial. That doesn't mean his clients aren't responsible for community service hours or paying restitution, but those are small prices to pay in lieu of being incarcerated behind iron bars.

Kane has become as wealthy as some of the rich Who's Who *clients he represents.*

My head lifted in surprise. According to Bruno, Kane was strapped with a multitude of debts, the reason he accepted my cash proposal and a meeting with me. Yet to Joe Citizen and the press, Kane had managed to keep his affluent public image intact. I resumed reading.

Kane's drive for power has made him a celebrity and in demand, the antithesis of a childhood marked with poverty and abandonment. In 1959, five-year-old Oliver Kane's life changed forever when his inebriated father smashed into another car head-on, causing three deaths. Jack Kane was convicted of vehicular manslaughter and sentenced to thirty years in prison. Shortly thereafter, Oliver's mother,

Yolanda Kane committed suicide. Without a legal guardian, Oliver bounced in and out of orphanages and foster homes for the next thirteen years.

I ran a finger along the edge of the page. Nice work, Bruno. This was the first article I'd seen on Kane's early years. Had young Oliver been in the car with his drunken father when the fatal crash occurred? That would explain why Kane didn't drive. And why he specialized in defending miscreant drivers.

Much has been written about Kane's courtroom antics and personal life. In 1999, Rhonda Chapman, a former Miss Maine runner-up, became Kane's fourth wife. True to course, the rocky two-year marriage has proved steady fodder for East Coast tabloids.

In the court of public opinion, Kane would have a difficult time convincing a jury of his peers he's nothing more than a legal predator. Like him or not, when a rich VIP is arrested for DUI with one phone call to make, Oliver Kane is probably the first name that comes to mind.

The article slipped from my hands as if it was on fire. The man literally made me sick. Oliver Kane had no more empathy for a victim demolished in a head-on accident than he did for the wrecked car. Nor did he care about the innocent lives he influenced with his courtroom antics. His drive for money, fame, and power blinded him to moral rights and wrongs.

What would Katie be doing right now if Oliver Kane hadn't been an attorney for the defense? My shoe heel stomped into the carpet. She'd be alive. Breathing. Happy. Why was an emotionally corrupt man like Kane allowed to influence the legal system?

I reached for my cup of hot water. A pain hit my chest. I panted through tight lips, afraid to induce greater hurt or another attack by breathing too hard. If I allowed my thoughts to keep running amok, I could expect more heart pain or worse.

I ventured a soft blow over the cup's rim before taking a sip. The next clipping was dated 1993. Eight years ago. Helen had been healthy. Katie was in her first year of high school. A period of my life that had been blessed. The article dealt with the aftereffects of losing a family member. The cause of the death was a wealthy young debutante's negligence. An attached picture showed a despondent family, including the dead woman's fiancé, leaving the courtroom. I could identify with their expressions, especially the tall, thin dark-haired fiancé in the center of the photo. He had the look of a man who wanted to murder someone after suffering the ultimate hurt and indignity of losing a courtroom decision to Oliver Kane. Wait. I'd seen that man's face before. At Adam Harding's preliminary trial. He had sat behind me grumbling under his breath.

The auburn-haired woman next to me coughed, producing a spastic arm movement that smashed into my elbow. Hot water spilled from my cup, burning the top of my hand.

"Damn it," I grunted aloud without thinking.

The cup fell from my fingers onto the tray, creating a flood of destruction. The printer ink on most of my articles and maps was smeared useless. The woman's clumsiness might have ruined everything for me.

"I-I'm so sorry," the young woman cried out.

A pain struck me in the chest. I covered my heart with a smarting hand. My shoe kicked the briefcase holding the Nitro bottle.

"No," I choked out.

The woman's finger's gripped my arm. Her face puckered as if she might cry. My teeth clenched together in anticipation of the next chest pain. She poured cold water over the tender skin on my hand, wetting my shirt and pants and hurting me even more.

"Stop," I growled, pushing the bottle away. "You're not helping."

The woman cowered towards the window. She lowered her eyes as if she was the injured party. Water continued to saturate my materials. The information Bruno had sent was soaked. This woman had no idea the harm she'd caused.

Another spasm hit me, but not as intense. I took in short, easy breaths. The back of my hand stung more than the hurt in my chest, a good sign. I waited for the pain to ebb then performed a damage inspection. Bleeding colors commingled into inky rivers. The papers stuck together then ripped when I attempted to separate them. An assessment wasn't difficult. The maps and articles were terminal. I crumbled the mess into a soggy ball and stuffed it into the seat pocket in front of me.

Kane's addresses and phone numbers were still in my brief-case. Unless my memory faltered, I had no need for the maps any-more. Perhaps the destroyed information wasn't as critical as I'd originally thought.

The pain subsided, at least for me. But hurt was still fixed on the young woman's sad face. She kept shaking her head. Had I somehow injured her without knowing it?

"Look, miss," I said, rubbing the top of my hand. "I don't intend to keep asking you this question, but are you all right?"

She refused to lock eyes with me or acknowledge my question. Her teeth bit hard into her lower lip. She was off in another world, just as she had been when I first spotted her at the airport.

"Oops." Our flight attendant stopped short in the aisle. "Looks like we've had a little accident. I'll be right back with a towel."

The young woman's body trembled again. Sounds came from her mouth, but I couldn't make out what she was saying. Her bizarre actions could send our flight attendant straight to the captain.

"I'll have this mess taken care of in a second," the attendant said, attacking the spill with a cloth towel. "Water's so much easier to clean up than coffee or liquor. Soft drinks are the worst." She straightened and pointed to a TV screen hanging from the ceiling. "Sir, did you want to watch our movie, *Pearl Harbor?*

A movie could be just the ticket to take my neighbor's mind off whatever was bothering her. If the young woman could somehow allow herself to get involved in the story, she was less likely to draw the crew's attention. I pulled out my money clip.

"Yes, I'd like to see the movie," I answered, handing our flight attendant a twenty. "This should cover the earphone fees for the two of us. The rest is for you."

"Our earphones are free, sir," the attendant replied, pushing the twenty back to me. "And we can't accept tips. Thank you for the thought, though."

The attendant snatched black plastic earphones from the seat-backs and placed them on our trays. The young woman stared at the headset lying next to her water bottle. You could lead a mare to a stream, only to find she had the tendencies of a mule.

My shoulders slumped back into the seat after the attendant left. Exhaustion had overtaken my mind and body. My eyelids tumbled down. How strange, to crave sleep when I didn't have much awake time. Yet a little rest, not sleep, might prove beneficial.

* * * * *

My eyes opened with a start. Cabin lights had been dimmed. Japanese planes flew in formation on the overhead screens. I hadn't seen this version of *Pearl Harbor* before. Title and words flashed on the screen. I couldn't have been out for more than ten or fifteen minutes.

Movement from the young woman made me turn to her. She was staring at a black ink sketch on white drawing paper. A drawing of a smiling dark-haired girl. She placed the sketch on the tray next to the earphones. The child, with her two front teeth missing, looked to be four or five years old. The girl resembled the young woman. Could be a younger sister. Or her daughter? But the woman looked too young to have a daughter that age.

She traced a finger along the water bottle's plastic grooves. Tears dripped from her eyes, but she was silent. She placed the bottle on her tray and removed a prescription vial of pills from her purse. Her eyes squinted to read the label's small print instructions. I could offer educated guesses as to what the medication was for. Being antisocial. Depression. Personality disorder.

The young woman struggled with the child-resistant top, just like me. The damn things were resistant to any age. A click sounded after several twists. The lid popped off. She tipped a yellow pill into her palm and studied it like a shopper inspecting a prospective lemon. Satisfied, she emptied the vial and reached for the water bottle. Then she raised her hand to her mouth as if the yellow contents were candy.

Chapter Sixteen

I seized the young woman's fist, full of pills, before she could release them into her mouth. Her eyes broadened in surprise, then narrowed in determination. Guttural groans escaped her throat. She struggled to liberate the pills by digging the nails of her free hand into my grip. I squeezed tighter until she removed the attacking hand. For the time being, I had strength and leverage over her.

"Let me go," she hissed, baring her teeth. "You have no right to stop me."

Another strike of pain hit my chest. My head craned into the darkened aisle. Where were the flight attendants? Taking a break somewhere in the bowels of the plane? I couldn't physically drag the young woman kicking and screaming to the cockpit. Nor did I have the endurance to secure her hand for five hours of flight. Sooner, rather than later, I would need assistance. But did I really have that option? If I had to involve the crew to save this woman from killing herself, most likely I would be ruining any opportunity I had to get Oliver Kane. The crew would probably hold her captive until an emergency landing could be arranged. An alternative I didn't want to pursue.

"You're doing this against my will," she said in a louder voice.

I glanced at the heavyset man sitting across the aisle from me. He was nervously biting his nails while viewing the tragic drama of Japanese planes dropping clusters of bombs on unsuspecting American ships in the Pearl Harbor bay. The man was unaware of the real-life drama several feet away from him.

The young woman emitted more low grunts as she tried again to pry her hand from my grasp. I had zero desire to get involved in her troubled life. But I couldn't just let her kill herself. The flight attendant had said it was difficult to ascertain the inner troubles of a person, especially a stranger. But if anyone should have caught on to the significance of this woman's actions, it should have been me. All the signs pointed to suicide. My passion to eliminate Oliver Kane had obstructed my view. A race in time I was still determined to win, but not at the immediate expense of this young person's life.

"Please. Don't." Her plea oozed with urgency. "Don't turn me in. I just want all the torment and hurt to go away. What you're doing isn't fair. Can't you understand that?"

A layer of sweat developed between our hands. This time she used her free hand as leverage to try to pull away from my grasp. What words could I offer to this young woman that would change her mind? She had asked me if I could understand wanting to die. More than she'd ever know. When I buried my daughter, I also included my will to live. But something kept stopping me from pulling the ultimate trigger and made me wait for a signal, like the message that came to me in Louis' office yesterday morning. What had prompted this young lady to go for the pills?

"Would you believe me if I said I understand how you feel?" I asked.

"Hell no," she snapped. "You don't know me. If you don't let go of my hand I'll—"

"You'll what? Yell for the attendant. We both know that's not going to happen."

"You're hurting my wrist," she said. Her features twisted into a suffering mask. "Please. Let me go."

I released some of the pressure. Much of her strength had returned. She was a lot stronger than I'd thought. My weight shifted in the seat. Better, but I still wasn't comfortable. No doubt if I released her hand, she'd shove the pills into her mouth.

"You were right about one thing, though," I said, keeping my volume down. "If someone had told me they understood what I was going through, I wouldn't have bought it either. Here's what I meant: I'm aware of what it is like to want to leave a hopeless world."

"Yeah, right," she exclaimed. "Like you're the world's greatest suicide authority."

"You'll just have to take my word for it."

"Every time I take a man for his word, I get screwed." Her throat produced an ugly chortle. "Let go of my hand. Now."

"I can't."

"What do you mean you can't?" she said. "Look, if you think you're doing a heroic thing here, you're not. I have good reason for wanting to take the pills. You, sir, will have to take *my* word for it."

"*Touché.*" She was quick. Her vibrant dark blue eyes revealed a wide range of emotions from embittered to innocent, with anger the most prevalent. But something she had said earlier remained in my head. What right did I have to prevent her from killing herself? I didn't have the right. Yet I'd be wrong if I did nothing and let it happen.

"I can't let go of your hand," I said in a calm voice. "I need you to stay alive."

"Just my luck," she groused. "I'm the only person on this plane that doesn't care if we crash or get hijacked. So who sits next to me? Reverend Do-Gooder."

Reverend Do-Gooder? The clever moniker she'd given me didn't fit a man intending to commit murder.

"I don't question whether or not your reasons for wanting to take your life are genuine. However, from a moral standpoint, I can't just sit here and allow a bright, attractive, and obviously troubled young lady to take her own life. Can't fault me for that. I bet you'd feel the same way if you were sitting in my seat."

"You'd lose that bet, mister." She turned and stared at the drawing of the young girl.

"I've got a good reason for needing you to stay alive," I said. "Self-interest. If I report you to the airlines or let you swallow those pills, there's a good chance this plane will make an emergency landing to get you to a hospital or a psychiatric facility. Even the morgue." A cramp developed in my hand until I readjusted the pressure. "For what it's worth, I've got a life-and-death appointment in Boston this morning. Any delay of this flight will terminate that meeting. I'm just being honest with you."

"That's pretty damn selfish of you," she responded.

"So is killing yourself."

I massaged my forehead, making my tired eyes open and close slowly. A quirk of fate had made us partners in the idea of death.

But she could never know that.

Damn. The little cowboy was heading down the aisle towards me while playing with his rope necktie. He had his boots and cowboy hat back on. Would he recognize my face in the dim light? My butt scooted down into the seat. Nice move, Mo. Sitting an inch lower wasn't going to make me invisible. The cowboy's lips puckered. Was he whistling or about to say something? He strolled past me without saying a word.

"Jesus," she groaned. "The final indignity. I can't even kill myself."

I studied her troubled eyes. Why would this woman attempt suicide on a plane? Why not in a restroom at San Francisco International? Or the privacy of a hotel room?

"What's your angle?" she asked. "Why haven't you taken the pills away from me?"

"I've been waiting for you to give me the pills on your own accord." I also didn't want to create a scene trying to force her hand open, which I wasn't sure I could do. "Will you give me the pills please?"

She motioned with her head at the movie screen. Ben Affleck was in a military uniform locked in an embrace with a pretty brunette nurse. With my attention diverted by the movie, the young woman tugged hard to release her hand. I managed to hang on. She seemed to be getting stronger by the minute. Or maybe I was losing strength.

"You've got as much chance of my giving up these pills as I have of being kissed by a hunk movie star," she said, peering at our coupled hands. "So I'm your prisoner until the plane lands. Then you'll let me go. Or rat me out to the crew. You don't give a diddly-shit about me. It's all about you and your alleged life-or-death meeting. Men don't change when they get elderly, do they?

Elderly? Even when Louis told me I had a heart condition, I never considered myself old. Katie used to say that I was the bomb. But now, to this distressed young woman, I was just an ancient old fart with an agenda.

"Sorry, miss. Age has nothing to do with my holding you prisoner."

If I garnered enough strength to hold this woman hostage for most of the cross-country flight, I'd have to turn her over to the flight crew. She'd still be alive and I'd be on target to complete my mission.

"You're all bastards," she growled. "It's in your genes. Just leave me alone. Let me do what I need to do."

"I can't change being old or being a man. You're correct about me using you, though. How's that for honesty?"

"Use me in what way?" she said, drawing back. Her eyes blinked their surprise.

"Time is an incredibly big issue for me. Having said that, maybe we can cut a deal. In essence, help each other. But you're going to have to trust me."

"Oh, sure," she said. "Men always want me to trust them. And they're always eager to help me – right out of my clothes. Is that what you want, a quickie mile-high-club visit to the restroom? Then will you let me have my pills?"

My head jerked towards the aisle. Standing a few feet away from me was the cowboy. He'd tilted his hat back. His legs were spread and bent at the knee. Both hands dangled at his hips like he was in position to draw on me.

"I see y'all like 'em young and skanky, huh, dad? Is she the reason we had to wait so long in line for the boarding agent?"

His words slapped me angry. This guy had no right to throw his vindictive venom at the young woman. Or any female. I felt her body stiffen. What was buzzing in her mind right now? Jeez, I didn't even know her name.

"I'm a little hard of hearing." I cupped my free hand behind my ear. "Would you please repeat what you said?"

Lines of annoyance wrinkled his face into a sneer. He leaned in closer. Too close.

"I said, y'all like 'em—"

My left hand snatched the cowboy's tie strings, bringing him within inches of my face. He looked like he was whispering something into my ear. The young woman shifted with my movement. I gave the bolo tie a hard twist, cutting off his air supply. He lost his balance and went down to one knee. A pain centered in my chest, but I couldn't let go. The cowboy tried to yank my hand away. I twisted harder. He stopped struggling.

"This young lady happens to be a friend of mine," I announced through tight lips.

Another quarter turn on the tie made the cowboy's eyelids flutter like he might pass out. He tried to speak, but only made gagging sounds. My grip eased.

"Your comments were out of line, rude, and insulting." I could smell liquor on his breath. His verbal attack had been powered by eighty-proof courage. "I've got half a mind to notify the flight crew about your harassing behavior. Is that what you want?"

"No," he groaned. His face glowed red even in the semidarkness.

"Perhaps there's something you'd like to say to this young lady, then?"

"Sor', ma'am," he choked out. "Please 'cept my 'pology. I was outta line."

The fiery hate that emanated from the woman's eyes probably could have melted the cowboy's silver star tie clasp. I released his bolo strings. He reeled back gasping for air.

The portly passenger sitting across from me tapped the cowboy's arm then instructed him to the move out his view of the movie screen. The cowboy pushed the man's hand away and stumbled forward. Portly Man ripped off his earphones and looked at me. I responded by pointing an index finger to my temple, making circle motions. He nodded and returned the earphones to his head.

The exertion had winded me. Short breaths didn't provide my system with enough oxygen. I ventured a deeper breath. At least the pain was gone. My fingers touched a tender chest. The discomfort I felt now was more like a cramp.

"See what I mean?" she moaned. "It never stops."

"This had nothing to do with you," I said. "That jerk was mad at me. We had a small confrontation back at the gate. He took it out on you because you are sitting next to me. His tirade was meant only to hurt me, not you. I'm sorry, but it wasn't your fault."

"Men have always taken it out on me." Her shoulders sagged.

"And why not? I probably deserve it." She gazed up with softened features. "I have to admit, though, no man ever defended me like you did. Even if you did it just to show that creep up."

"Listen, he shouldn't talk to you or any other woman that way." Breathing was easier for me now, but I felt fatigued. "My friends call me Mo. And your name is?"

"Not important," she answered in a passive tone.

She was right. I shouldn't have asked. Her name wasn't important. But she was.

"You know those bumper stickers that say "Shit Happens?" she said. "Had to be coined about my life."

"Is that a sketch of you when you were a little girl?" I asked, gesturing with my head. "Or is that your daughter? It's a nice drawing. The artist did a fine job."

"I drew this sketch of my daughter," she said, her tone indignant.

Her hand tensed and pulled. I managed to hold on, but the next time she'd be free. My ploy to change the young woman's negative mindset hadn't worked. She glanced at the drawing again, shaking her head.

"Look, you don't have to tell me a damn thing about yourself," I said. "But I can't understand why you'd ever want to leave someone that precious. It doesn't make sense."

"My daughter would be better off without me."

"I have a hard time believing that."

"You don't know what my life's been like," the woman said. "Or what's awaiting me. I don't want her to end up like me. She'll have a better chance if I'm not around."

The young woman's words had been difficult for me to stomach, but her act wasn't martyrdom. Her self-image, or lack of one, had blinded her vision and muddled her thinking. Right now, I understood a lot more than she did.

"My daughter was needlessly killed five and half years ago," I said. "I've never gotten over her death. Never understood why she had to die. The void of not having my wife, then my daughter in my life has been an empty cavern of despair. But there's a difference between you and me. I can never get my Katie back." I took a semi-deep breath. Then another. "Katie would have been about your age if she had lived. I noticed you in the airport waiting area because, from a distance, you looked so much like her."

I looked towards the movie screen to regain composure. Affleck was piloting a wounded English fighter plane straight down into the ocean. This young woman was doing the same thing with her life.

"I'm sorry about your daughter," she said, straightening the sketch on the tray. "My name is Mary."

"How do you think your daughter will feel if you kill yourself, Mary? And who do you think she's going to blame?"

"Blame?" she said, squinting at me. "What do you mean?"

Mary had said she didn't care about anybody or anything. But she spoke of love for her daughter. So much so that she was willing to sacrifice herself. She was taking the easy way out, though. Killing herself wasn't going to help her daughter. It would only damage her little girl for life. Why didn't she realize that?

"Your daughter's going to spend the rest of her days thinking she's responsible for your death. That's the way the real world works. Is that what you want?"

"No, of course not," she said. "But you don't understand. I can't undo the damage I've already done to her. To myself. This is the best way out, for me and for Rachel."

"Earlier, you asked me what I wanted from you. I want you to appreciate how important you are to your daughter. She's not better off without you. You may see yourself as a failure in some way, but you're not a failure to your daughter. She needs her mother to love and guide her, to lay down a foundation and set parameters, to always be there for her."

"I-I can't." Mary gulped for air. "You don't get it. If I can't make the right decisions for myself, how can I for my daughter? You make it sound so easy. Well, it's not. At least it's not for me. Why can't you understand—"

The plane vibrated, then took a sudden dive like an elevator with a broken cable. Screams and shouts clamored throughout the cabin. Another acute pain hit my chest with twice the intensity of the one a few minutes earlier. I released Mary's hand and reached blindly for the briefcase on the floor. I needed my pills. Where the hell was the case?

The plane stopped its fall, leveling off with a hop. The jolt lifted us into the air, bringing on another piercing stab to my heart. My seatbelt had saved me from hitting my head on the ceiling. Oxygen masks dropped from above. Cabin lights came on. If I didn't get a pill into my system right away, I wasn't going to survive this flight.

"Ladies and gentlemen, this is Captain Rupp. We've just experienced wind shear, causing the plane to drop. Everything's under control. Our attendants will be coming by to check with everyone. We ask that you remain seated and keep your seatbelts fastened. Please inform the attendant if you've been injured or if any damage has occurred."

Mary had her water bottle in one hand, looking at a palm full of pills. How could I stop her? I couldn't even help myself.

Chapter Seventeen

A nimated voices filled the plane's cabin like a packed restaurant during lunch hour. Burning pain continued to fire up my chest, extending down to my left arm. A plastic mask pressed hard against my sweaty skin as if someone was trying to smother me. Yet, the streams of cool air surged through my nose, inflating a flat brain.

When I opened my eyes, Mary's blurred face hovered inches away. Her hand held the oxygen mask over my nose. My tie had been loosened and the top button of my shirt opened. The air benefitted my breathing, but deep breaths promoted pain in my chest. I pushed the mask away, but grasped her hand.

"Mo," Mary cried out. "Tell me, what's wrong?"

My mouth opened to speak. Nothing came out. The tissue in my throat was as dry as a desert floor. I pulled her closer to me.

"My heart," I managed to choke out, freeing Mary's hand. "Pills. Briefcase,"

She moved away. I chanced several heavy breaths. If Mary yelled for help instead of going for my pills, I'd be better off not taking my meds and let nature take its course.

Something hard smashed into my shin. The briefcase. Mary set the case on my tray. Two metallic clicks sounded. The pills jiggled inside the prescription glass bottle.

"Frigging tops," Mary grunted out in an anxious voice. The vial shook in her hand, either from nerves or the tension she was forcing on the lid. "I. Can't. Get. It. To..." The top popped off. "How many pills, Mo? How many pills do I give you?"

"Half pill." Another pain pierced my chest. "Hurry."

"Shit," she groaned, peering into the bottle. "It looks like they're all whole. Shit."

Mary emptied the vial into her trembling hand. Her fingers

sifted through the white pills. Finally she picked out a half tablet, holding it between her thumbnail and forefinger. Her concerned eyes begged for direction. I pulled Mary's fingers to my mouth and pushed the potent pill past my lips and under my tongue. My heart was either going to burst from too much medication, or I was stealing a few more hours of life.

She placed her water bottle in my hand. I sent the bottle back to her. Water wasn't necessary. Damn it. Come on pill. If my heart didn't do me in, the suspense might.

"I'll get you some help," Mary said. "Maybe there's a doctor on board."

"No," I gasped. My grip encircled her slim wrist. "Just wait. A doctor can't help."

Mary's soft fingers intertwined with mine. The same hand that earlier had held her yellow pills. The vial was lying on her tray. Empty. What had she done with the pills?

"Ma'am, please try to remain calm." The flight attendant's voice carried from behind us. "Air-current drops happen all the time. Please relax. Everything is going to be fine."

Clearly the attendant wasn't referring to me or my condition. My arteries hadn't yet lit up with the electrifying surge I was expecting. Had I gone to the vial once too often?

"Color's coming back to your face," Mary gushed, touching my cheek with her fingertips. "The pill's working. You're going to be all right, Mo. Please be all right."

I attempted a smile. Having color in my cheeks didn't mean the pill was performing its magic. Pain was still prevalent, but not as intense. Yet the heaviness in my chest wouldn't go away. Was this the next stage? Louis, my friend and doctor probably couldn't answer that question any better than I could.

Mary dabbed my forehead dry with her sweater sleeve. Her eyes were moist and shiny. Was she scared because she cared? Or was she blaming herself for my attack? Perhaps she was affected by a little of both.

"Sir?" The flight attendant touched my shoulder. "Did you have another dizzy spell?"

"Dizzy spell?" Mary said, looking up at the attendant with a puzzled expression.

"The dizziness comes and goes." The admission was true, but misleading. My fingers sent Mary a squeeze message. She remained silent. "I'm okay. We're both fine."

"Boy, those spells must be horrible," the attendant said. "You're flushed, perspiring." She smiled at Mary. "Well, you look like you're in good hands. Oh, my. You dropped your pills onto the floor. Let me help you pick them up."

"I'll get them." Mary's hand reached out to stop the attendant. "Take care of the other passengers. Somebody may need your help. As you said, he's in good hands."

Mary glared at me as soon as the attendant moved on. Then she unhooked her seatbelt and bent forward to pick up her pills. Thank God she hadn't swallowed them. But that didn't mean she wouldn't. When she sat up her left palm was filled with her yellow and my white tablets. She reattached her seatbelt.

"Put the pills in here, Mary." I lifted my empty vial from the tray. The discomfort in my chest had leveled off, but hadn't disappeared. "Please."

"No," she fired back. "Dizzy spell my ass. You were bullshitting me. You said the pills were for your heart."

"You're right. I lied." I turned the container label around for her to read. "But not to you, Mary. I stretched the truth to the flight attendant."

"I don't get it," she said, studying the label. "Why didn't you tell the flight attendant about your heart? Aren't they trained by the airlines to assist passengers with various types of conditions or emergencies? An intelligent man like you would know that. What's really going on that you're not telling me, Mo."

If I had a hat, I'd tip it to Mary to acknowledge her astute summation. In addition, she'd just turned the tables on me, earning my admiration. I smiled and placed my hand on her forearm.

"Mary, do you remember when I said that I couldn't afford any delays? That was the truth. I had another attack earlier in the boarding area. When I boarded, the flight attendant greeted me then questioned me about my health. She wouldn't have let me board this plane knowing I was having heart pain. I would have missed my meeting. So I told her that I suffered from dizziness."

"This important meeting of yours," she said. "Are you seeing a heart specialist?"

"In a sense. Only this man breaks hearts. He doesn't repair them."

I winced when a smarting stab hit my chest. Mary unbuttoned the next button on my shirt. Her eyes widened when she noted the red scar on my chest.

"You're still hurting, Mo. You need a doctor."

"Most of the pain has gone. You've heard about our California earthquakes, haven't you? What I'm experiencing now is like the aftershock." I took time for a few shallow breaths. "By the way, thank you for coming to my aid. But you lied also."

"What the hell are you talking about?" she said. "I didn't lie to you."

"Mary, you told me you didn't care about anybody or anything. But you came to my rescue. Saved my life." I moved the pill bottle closer to her, prompting her to disconnect our eye contact. "Mary, I need you to keep talking to me. It takes my mind off what's going on in my chest. And will you please put the pills in the vial?"

Mary opened her fingers and stared at the white and yellow tablets piled in her palm. I couldn't physically stop her now from downing the pills. And she knew it.

"Come on, Mary. Please put the pills into the bottle. Not for me. But for you. And especially for your daughter, Rachel. And someday for your grandchildren."

Mary gazed at me then shook her head. She lifted the water bottle from the tray. For God's sake, no. I looked into the aisle for the flight attendant.

"You're still sweating." She handed me the water. "Maybe this will cool you down."

I refused the water again. Mary took the vial from my fingers. The pills clinked into the container. Relief flowed through my body like medicine.

"Giving you the pills doesn't solve my problems, you know?" she said.

"Maybe not. But you did the right thing."

"Did you mean it?" She squared her shoulders. "About Rachel blaming herself."

"With all sincerity, yes. You love your daughter too much to have her think she caused her mother's death." I took a breath. "But now this isn't just about Rachel, Mary. You wouldn't want to go through life with the burden of thinking my heart attack was your fault. Which, of course, it wasn't."

"Jesus. How the hell did you know that?" she asked.

"Elderly insights."

"You're not elderly, Mo." Mary's blue eyes scanned my face. "You're handsome. Distinguished looking. Kind of like Michael Douglas." The curve of a smile showed. "When I first saw you in the airport, I thought you looked like a man who would smell good. And you do. That alone makes you different than any man I've ever known." She touched my forehead. "You need to trim your eyebrows, though."

My body shook. God, it hurt to laugh. Katie used to say the same thing to me.

Mary's view shifted past me. Her features narrowed into a fierce expression. My head turned in time to catch the flirting sailor from the boarding area. And his wink.

"Men are attracted to me," Mary said. "All the wrong men." She traced a fingernail on the drawing of her daughter. "I got pregnant with Rachel at seventeen. I didn't really love Larry, but I married him anyway. I quickly learned he wasn't right in the head. Jealousy triggered his monster temper. He'd beat me when he got liquored up. And I'd let him take his aggressions out on me so he wouldn't go after Rachel."

"Why didn't you kick him out? Send him packing? Or just take Rachel and leave."

"I was afraid to." Mary wiped her chin with the heel of her hand. "Larry got drunk one night and killed a man after a bar fight. Actually, he ran the guy over with his truck in the parking lot after they fought in the bar. He was convicted of manslaughter."

"So I take it Larry went to prison?" I said.

"A six-year sentence."

"Problem solved."

"You would think so," Mary said. "After the sentencing, Larry swore he'd kill me and Rachel if I divorced him or didn't take him back when he got out. Larry never wanted Rachel. Not when I was pregnant and definitely not after she was born. Hell, he doesn't really want me either. He just doesn't want anyone else to have me."

Patches of sweat stuck to my white shirt. I didn't doubt Mary one iota when she said Larry would kill her and Rachel. A black on white headline floated in my head, "Another Oliver Kane Client Exonerated – Mother & Daughter Murderer Goes Free." If Larry had been wealthy, he would have been a prototypical Kane client. Free to run over someone else after a bar fight or on the road. And free to hurt Mary and her daughter.

What the hell was I doing? My mind was so ingrained with Oliver Kane that I'd incorporated him into Mary's life story, too. Except the longer she talked, the less likely we'd have trouble with the flight crew. And the longer she'd stay alive.

"How long ago did Larry go to prison?" I asked.

"It's been over four years," she said in a loud whisper. Then her fingers flew to her head like they'd been magnetized. "For God's sake, this is insane. You've just had a heart attack and I'm giving you an account of my life's shitty history. You look like you're your burning up. You should be in a hospital getting medical attention."

Mary placed the back of her hand on my forehead. She pushed off the armrest, inched forward in her seat, and raised a hand for the flight attendant. I clutched her forearm.

"The pill creates a flushing surge through my veins and arteries." Our eyes locked together. "Just keep talking, Mary. Please. It's good for both of us."

"This must be the crazy row," she said, shrugging her shoulders. "At least you're not going to charge a fee for listening to me babble. Do you actually want to hear more?"

"Absolutely." I placed my hand on top of her hand to keep the physical connection. "What happened after Larry went to prison?"

"I divorced him. Thought six years was enough time for me to get my act together. Rachel and I could disappear from Larry and Boston for a better life somewhere else." Mary exhaled a loud sigh. "It was tough trying to support the two of us. Every time I found a decent job, something would go wrong. Then I met an older man who seemed real nice. Until I realized he was more interested in Rachel than in me – if you know what I mean. I caught him standing naked by her bed one night as she slept. For whatever reason, I attract the bad ones. Who knows, maybe if I'd had a strong father figure like you, my life would've been different. Too bad we couldn't have met earlier."

I gave her a weak nod. A trace of guilt burned within me. I wasn't Mary's father. Nor was I her friend. In a sense, I was like all the rest of the men she'd met — using Mary until I didn't need her anymore. Granted, I would have helped her had we met under different circumstances. But not now. Not with the limited time I had left. I looked up at the cabin ceiling. Why did You put Mary and me together when I can't help her?

"I found a great job as a waitress," Mary said. "Then the new manager hits on me with his words and hands. I flat turned him down. Next thing I know, I'm out of a job."

"Did you go to the manager's supervisor?" I asked. "Perhaps there were other sexual harassment accusations against this guy."

"Damn right I ratted him out," she said. "Who do you think they believed? Me? Or a married, bible-banging employee who'd been with the chain for over ten years?" She pounded a thumb against her chest. "Maybe, the next time the scumbag gets his horns up, the complaint won't fall on deaf ears."

I smiled. She had fought to keep her job. And to protect the next victim. How ironic.

"I started working for an office temp agency," Mary said. "You know, to upgrade my work environment and to . . . well, hopefully, demonstrate what I could do. I have some talents. But I've never been given the opportunity to showcase them."

My heart, or what was left of it, went out to her. She was a fighter. Rather than accept all the bad choices and unlucky breaks, she had the gumption to change her lot in life. What the hell drove her to attempt suicide?

"What kind of abilities are you talking about?" I asked.

"Believe it or not, I sketched that picture of Rachel by memory at the airport. I'm not trained, but I am an artist. I can draw anything. My creativity comes naturally. No one's ever taken me seriously. I guess my lack of schooling and . . ." She peered at my pill bottle. Her expression turned dark. "What the hell? It doesn't really matter anymore."

Cabin lights dimmed again and *Pearl Harbor* continued. Mary switched on her overhead light then turned it off. Did the dark suit her better? The window once again had become her focal point. Not a good sign.

I relocated the vial of co-mingled pills to my shirt pocket. This much I knew: Mary was clearly terrified to land in Boston. Something hidden in her psyche held the answer as to why. I nudged her elbow, unsure she even felt it.

"You know what?" Mary said, turning back to me. "Some people aren't meant to be happy in this world." Her voice was flat, less animated. "It took me a long time to realize that I'm one of them. I guess I'm not a quick learner."

"I don't believe that, Mary."

"You might as well hear the rest of it." Her voice quivered. "I hooked on with a big marketing agency in Boston as a receptionist. Really liked the job, even though the work was menial." She peered down at Rachel's picture. "One day, Mr. Wonderful walks in. Zack. He's on loan from the agency's San Francisco branch for a month. I mean he's smart, gorgeous, sweet, stable, even owns a house there. Most of all, he's smitten with me. Treats me like a princess. Buys presents for Rachel. Doesn't even rush me for sex. Then he proposed to me before he had to go back to California. He wanted to adopt Rachel and send her to private schools. Have more children. He didn't want me to go back to work. Just wanted me to stay at home and be a housewife. I couldn't believe that my break in life had finally arrived. And it couldn't have come at a more perfect time."

Mary's thumb wiped at tears trickling down her cheek. A

dark, brooding expression lined her face, as if she was replaying the next horrifying scene in her mind. I couldn't imagine where this story was going, except that something happened between Mary and Zack.

"Honestly, Mo, I'd never been so happy before in my life," she said, in a cheerless tone. "Even Rachel was excited. Zack had arranged for me to go to San Francisco. To help him put the wedding together. Get acclimated with The City. I quit my job. Moved Rachel in with my mother. Then I flew to the west coast to be with him."

The sailor walked past us again. Mary was oblivious to his flirt hit this time. Her mind was back with Zack.

"So there I was at Zack's beautiful house. In this glorious city. A whole new world was opening up to me. Zack went back to work. I started to unpack. Instead of hanging up my negligee in his bedroom closet, I put it on. We hadn't been intimate yet. I wanted to surprise him. A leather overnight bag in the closet caught my eye. I don't know why I opened it up. Maybe I was looking for old love letters." She snapped out a cold laugh. "That's exactly what I found, along with pictures and videos. Very graphic, vile pictures. My Mr. Wonderful had been wonderful to many other people – all men."

Whoa. I hadn't expected that. And clearly she hadn't either.

"He deceived me from the very beginning," she said. "In this day and age, I still can't comprehend why Zack did it. I mean, most of the people I know don't care if you're straight, gay, or bisexual. You know, I had an inkling that he might not be straight. Then again, some guys are just shy when it comes to sex." Her expression turned vacant, sick. "I totally lost it, Mo. Vomited right there in the closet. Zack just wanted to use Rachel and me as camouflage. He didn't love us. We were just his pawns for show."

"What did you do?" A sour feeling gripped my stomach.

Mary looked at me then turned away. Her upper torso rocked, making me dizzy. I grabbed her shoulder to stop the movement and pulled her to me.

"What happened, Mary?"

"I tore that negligee off, dressed, and found a carpenter's

staple gun in the garage and nailed every freakin' picture, letter, and video to his bedroom wall. I know I should have just left the house, but I felt violated. So I waited for the son of a bitch to come home so I could confront him."

With a backhand Mary knocked the water bottle to the floor. She made no attempt to pick it up. Fortunately the top had been on it. Her fingers clenched into a tiny fist and pounded the armrest.

"When Zack finally came home, he saw all the porn stuff on the bedroom wall. He still wouldn't admit that he was gay or bisexual. If he had informed me in the beginning, it wouldn't have bothered me. Instead of apologizing for deceiving and using me, he said that I was lucky he chose me. Who else would offer me the good life like he could?"

"What happened to Zack, Mary?"

"I shot him, Mo. Don't you think I had every right to shoot Zack?"

"Did you kill him?" I blurted out. "Did you kill that man?" I stared at her, astounded.

Jesus. Who was I to judge what she did? And why she did it. Mary had been betrayed. She had as much right in her eyes to kill Zack as I had to kill Oliver Kane.

CHAPTER EIGHTEEN

Light flickered from the TV screens in the darkened cabin. Mary sat in silence staring at me with a blank expression. If she'd murdered Zack, the police were probably looking for her. I removed the phone implanted in the seat in front of us. San Francisco's Chief of Police was a longtime friend of mine. Perhaps a good word from me might help Mary . . .

"I didn't kill Zack," she whispered. "At least I don't think I did."

I returned the phone to its seat back base. A sense of relief eased me into the chair. Fatigue spread through my body as if it was functioning on an undersized engine.

"What exactly did you do to Zack, Mary?" I said in a weak voice.

"I used the staple gun to shoot him in the face and groin, places where it would hurt him the most." Her features contorted into an ugly mask. "There was blood everywhere. He was screaming in pain, holding a body part with each hand. I had to get out of there. I grabbed my purse off the bed. Zack's bottle of prescription sleeping pills was on the nightstand, standing out like forbidden fruit. He couldn't sleep without them. I snatched his pills and ran out of the house. When I got outside, I could still hear his sissy wails from the sidewalk."

I gave Mary an understanding nod. Although Zack deserved every retaliatory staple she had fired at him, I was more than pleased to learn he was probably still amongst the living. How interesting. The idea of killing a bad seed like Oliver Kane was palatable to my moral principles, but the thought of Mary murdering someone didn't taste the same.

My eyelids closed. Did Mary even realize she may have dodged a disastrous bullet? If Zack's squeaky-clean image was his primary concern, having his name advertised on a police report was the last thing he would want. My eyes popped open. What if Mary had gone back into the house to hurt him more?

"Mary, where did you go once you were on the sidewalk?"

"I realized all of the clothes I'd brought with me, basically my whole wardrobe, were still in Zack's house. So I headed back up the stairs, but stopped before I hit the landing." She pointed at the vial of pills bulging from my shirt pocket. "It then dawned on me that I had everything I needed. Wouldn't you have felt the same way, Mo?"

I looked away from her. After Katie died, I lost all semblance of hopefulness. Nothing in life seemed right. But the session in Louis' office yesterday made me realize hope was still inside me, waiting to be drawn out. The release had been triggered by the reality of dying, giving me a sense of urgent purpose to put Oliver Kane out of commission. What could I do to extract the hope hiding in Mary?

"I can't say I would have felt any different than you," I said, turning to face Mary. "But there's a missing variable in your question. I don't have a dear daughter with me anymore. You do. And that dear little girl needs her mother."

"Exactly what I considered in the boarding area at the airport," she said. "I had the pill bottle in my hand. I needed my hurt to go away by never waking up again. But then I decided to get on the plane for Rachel's sake, not mine."

"Having realized that, did you then consider how fortunate you were?"

"Oh, yeah, life would be rosy again," she shot back. Her arms flew up, knocking the purse from her lap. The bag landed on the floor with a thud, joining the bottled water. Her eyes flashed at me. "I'm a real fortune cookie. I can't believe you said that."

I smiled. She was agitated with me, taking her away from the gloomy present and horrible past. A temporary fix, allowing me an opportunity to pry open her hope chest.

"I wasn't slighting your traumatic experience, Mary." My fingers re-buttoned my shirt to fight a sudden chill. "I used the word "fortunate" in the sense of: What do you think your life would have been like had you married Zack?"

Mary's head shot back as if my words had slapped her across the face. She didn't answer me. I would have loved to have had the ability to peek into her brain just then.

Lights lit up the cabin. Passengers around us removed their headsets. *Pearl Harbor* had come to an end. Heads twisted, arms stretched, and legs stirred. Mary and I had to be more careful now not to draw attention to ourselves.

A roll of my wrist exposed the face of my watch. 2:34 a.m. Boston time. Two hours and a few minutes change before we landed.

"Consider this scenario," I said. "You would have been Zack's prisoner. That's why he didn't want you to work. And why he wanted Rachel to go to private schools." Her eyes were still questioning me. "Don't you see, Mary? Control is more of an issue here than Zack's sexuality or corporate image. He intended for you and Rachel to be totally dependent on him. Money. The house. Rachel's education. A lifestyle you'd be reluctant to give up for Rachel's sake. He would have had complete control of your lives. Ultimately, being married to Zack had the potential to be more painful than the beatings you received from your ex-husband."

Mary gasped. She peered down at the floor then up at the ceiling. Something I had just said must have stabbed the hub of her fear.

"Earlier," I said, touching her forearm, "you told me the timing of Zack's proposal couldn't have been better. What else aren't you telling me, Mary? What frightens you about going back to Boston?"

Mary retrieved her purse and water bottle from the floor. Her hands did a tug-of-war on the purse straps. When my Katie was in a quandary, she used to tug on strands of her hair.

"I called mother before the plane took off," Mary said in a low, lifeless voice. "Mother was in a panic. She had just heard Larry was getting out on early parole from prison. Next week. There's nothing I can do about it. If I live in Boston, he'll find me. I don't even have a bed to sleep in, but he'd still find me."

"Surely you could stay at your mother's house?"

"Mother lives in the tenements with another lady. It's not even Mother's place." Mary eyed the drawing of her daughter. "There's hardly room for Rachel. If I moved in, I'd be putting all of them in jeopardy." She shook her head. "Maybe if I'd had the knowledge about Larry's parole beforehand, I wouldn't have let my temper get the best of me. I would have stayed with Zack, even under false pretenses."

"Okay, I get it now. Why don't you and Rachel move to another city or state?"

"Yeah, right," she exclaimed. "With what? I don't have any money. Or a job." Her eyes fixed on me. "Rachel will be safe if I don't go near her. Even safer if I'm dead."

"Contact the police, Mary. Tell them what's going on."

"What're they going to do?" she said. "Put Larry back in jail on my say so? The cops can't do a thing until Larry breaks the law. By then, it'll be too late."

"Good point."

"Don't you see, Mo?" she said. "There's no way out. I should just take the pills."

Now it all made sense. Mary looked even more despondent than the pathetic person I first saw on the plane. Rachel's picture trembled in her fingers. In Mary's mind, her inability to protect Rachel had her trapped.

"You said you could draw anything." I made a wiggling hand motion like I was signaling a waiter for a check signature. "And that you're creative. I need to know the extent of your creative talents."

"What?" Mary's face creased in confusion. "Christ, Mo. Why would you ask me that question? I wouldn't have said I'm an artist if I didn't mean it. I never should have told you. It's not like I can draw myself out of this mess."

"Perhaps you can." I offered Mary the pen from my shirt pocket. "I already know that you're a talented artist from your sketch of Rachel. What I don't know is how creative you are. Show me."

"Show you?" Mary snapped, ignoring my pen. "Show you what? Honest to God, Mo. That pill must have gone to your head. I'm in no mood to. . .oh, screw it." She extracted a sharp-pointed sketching pen and drawing pad from her purse. "I'll show you that I wasn't bullshitting you. What do you want me to draw?"

"Virginia, an associate of mine, now owns an advertising agency in San Francisco. One of her flourishing accounts, Bent Metal Winery in Grass Valley, is expanding into a different demographic and market by creating a new label called Bear Moon Wine."

"Bear Moon Wine?" she repeated, tapping the pen tip into the

107

tray. "Are you jerking my chain, Mo?"

"Listen to me, Mary," I said, ignoring her turbo temper, a trigger that ignited the fire inside her. "The Bear Moon Wine account is real. That's b-e-a-r. A successful ad campaign could be worth millions of dollars. You need to concentrate, okay?"

Mary sighed. She bit down on the pen's top. Then she nodded to me.

"All right. Let's try this." My tone was no different than when I had a heart-to-heart with Katie. "The concept is to target less sophisticated wine drinkers, young adults like yourself, both genders, with several tasty, light wines. The goal is to take a slice away from the wine cooler and beer market pie."

Mary nodded and jotted down some notes. Lately, when Virginia came to the house to discuss business, and to mooch a Mrs. Green dinner, she'd bug me to come up with a Bear Moon Wine strategy, with no results.

"Think gimmicky, unusual, out of the box," I suggested. "A new label design, changes in traditional packaging or the bottle, a character, or a catchy slogan. A great project for an artist with a creative mind, don't you think?"

"How many types of wine are they offering?" she asked. "And is it pricey?"

"Excellent questions, Mary. To begin with, they're coming out with two types at less than ten dollars a bottle. The wine's quality is exceptionally good for that price point."

Mary nodded. The pen in her hand began sketching as if it had a mind of its own. The tip of her tongue sneaked out from the corner of her mouth, which I doubt she even realized. Mary was passionate about her talents, yet I wasn't expecting anything professional. Hell, most of the talented graphic artists I'd worked with over the years had trouble creating extemporaneously. A risking idea at best, but to her credit, she'd taken on the challenge like a tenacious trooper. The creative endorphins in her troubled head had been ignited. The very same scheme Virginia had tried when she challenged me to come up with a unique campaign for the Bear Moon account.

I felt cramped. My knees almost touched Bruno's damp, wadded up info bulging from the seat pocket in front of me. Shifting my weight again didn't help. Some third-world countries should use riding coach as a method of torture – especially for a tall person.

My shoes inched back across the carpet towards me. I could still visualize the streets from the airport to downtown Boston. But the routes to Kane Tower were the least of my worries. My last two attacks had done irreparable damage. I wouldn't know if I could still drive until I got behind a steering wheel. My reactions were running in slow motion. Even walking off the plane without assistance was in question. How the hell was I going to get to the airport rental car area?

The virgin white sheet on Mary's tray was now covered with artistic straight and curvy black lines. I waved for our flight attendant, interacting with a passenger six rows ahead. She wasn't acknowledging my hand signal. I tried to lift myself out of the chair, with slow success. If I can't stand up, I can't walk. Or drive. Or kill Oliver Kane.

"Whoa." The elevation from rising to my feet hit me as soon as I stood. My hand grabbed for the seat in front before I lost my balance.

"Hey," the man in the seat in front of me shrieked, twisting around. He held the spot on his head that I'd just whacked with my hand.

"Sorry." I doubt my feeble smile made him feel better.

The attendant charged down the aisle towards me. At the same time, Mary pulled on my sleeve for me to sit back down. My butt hit the chair cushion and bounced. I may have lost a hell of a lot more than my balance. I no longer had the strength to navigate any kind of distance on my own. I would need assistance to get off this plane.

"Sir," the flight attendant said in a stern tone. "I'm going to insist that you please stay seated with your seatbelt on until the plane lands." She glanced in Mary's direction, then back to me. "We're still dealing with effects from the wind shear drop. If you need anything, please ask. I'll be more than happy to get it for you."

"Miss, I apologize. I'm still a bit dizzy. I was coming to you with a request."

The pen in Mary's hand dropped onto the tray. She glared at me. Did I just squander the ounce of trust I had earned from her?

"I'm not sure how far I can walk." I placed my palm over Mary's hand. "Would it be possible for you to arrange a wheelchair for me? And someone to push."

"No problem, sir," the attendant said. "I'll call ahead to have a wheelchair and attendant waiting for you when we land. We'll make sure to get you off the plane first."

Mary's hand squirmed under my grasp. Her cheeks revealed touches of crimson. The trust hadn't returned. Knowing a smidgen of Mary's history, I couldn't blame her.

"First off the plane would be great. I'm on a real tight time frame. Thank you, miss."

The attendant left for the back of the plane. Mary slid her hand from mine, intensifying her angry stare.

"What are you up to, Mo?" Mary pointed her pen at my chest. "Do you really need a wheelchair? Or is this some kind of ploy to rat me out to the crew once we get up front?"

"I'm not going to turn you in, Mary." My head nestled back into the headrest. "I've got other plans for you." Closing my stinging eyes was blissful. "We'll talk about my intentions after you finish your Bear Moon Wine presentation."

CHAPTER NINETEEN

I was hanging in the air, hovering like a helicopter or kite with no strings attached. Swollen white clouds splotched an endless sky. Hints of a breeze fanned my face. Being this far off the ground, I should see some semblance of land. What happened to the plane or the passengers? A whirling vortex appeared. The damn thing made me dizzy. I was being drawn to the enticing opening. An alluring soft voice called out to me.

"Wake up, Mo."

Mary's voice. Yet I couldn't see her. The vortex and clouds had disappeared, replaced by a sheet of darkness.

"Mo, wakeup," Mary urged.

My eyelids refused to lift. Mary kept nudging me, hurting my arm. The rest of my body remained rigid, unwilling to move.

"I'm sorry, Mo, but it's late. It's four-eighteen already. We're going to be landing soon. I finished my drawing for the Bear Moon Wine account."

I opened my eyes. The plane shook and bounced like a San Francisco tremor. Our window patch remained pitch black. Most of the passengers closest to us were sleeping or reading. This time Mary pulled my arm, annoying me all the more. But that wasn't as irritating as being blinded by a tiny light beam shining in my face. My fingertips pressed hard to stimulate my temples. A hard sniff proved ineffective in clearing sinuses leading to my brain. Falling asleep had been a mistake.

"Okay, show me what you've created," I said, squinting at the artwork on her tray.

Mary handed me her drawing without saying a word. A large moon with deep craters overlooked a dense, flourishing vineyard. Potent moonbeams were charging grapes on vines into vibrant maturity. Nice touch. Two bear-faced pillars arched together over a cave-like entryway. A sign said, "Welcome to the den of BEAR MOON VINYARDS." She'd misspelled vineyards. But clever just the same.

"This is just one variation." Her voice was quick and high. "I've got several other Bear Moon label ideas in mind."

Mary leaned towards my tray. She placed the tip of her pen inside the moon and linked a continuous line from one crater to another like connect the dots.

"The craters on the moon depict the shape of a Bear's face," she said.

"Well I'll be damned. You really are talented, Mary."

"There's more."

Mary's words gushed out even faster. Her face glowed with pleasure. She turned the sheet over to show another drawing.

"This could be a label behind the front label that's seen through an empty bottle. I believe a young adult wine drinker would appreciate this message after the wine has been drank." She closed one eye and made a funny face. "Or is it drunk?"

"Consumed," I offered, taking in the second drawing.

The label inside the bottle showed a bear on all fours, his bare behind facing me with his shorts down around his back paws. The bear had his head turned so I could see a sheepish, toothy smile. The caption in the moon background said, "When you're down to bare bottom, it's time to buy more Bear Moon Wine."

Unsophisticated, but clever. And with some tweaking, right on the mark.

"The bear," Mary continued, "could be wearing different shorts with other slogans for each type of wine. You know, make the bottles collectibles." The excitement in her voice faded. Her eyebrows knitted together. "You don't like it."

"Like it?" My head couldn't stop shaking. "Are you kidding? You're everything you said you were. And more. I just gave you a difficult production challenge. Most pros don't perform as well or as quickly as you just did. You have raw artistic talent. And a creative freshness. A gift. Unrefined, but a gift just the same."

"For real?" she asked.

"I'm not lying to you, if that's what you're asking."

"A lot of good that's going to do me." She jammed the pen back into her purse. "It's too late. Nothing can help me now."

I looked at the bear's furry behind and toothy grin and laughed out loud. I'd only met a handful of artists who could portray humor in their artwork like Mary just did.

"Perhaps there is a way out for you after all, Mary."

I swiped my credit card through the airline phone receiver. Mary's face was frozen into a skeptical mask. She had no idea who I was calling, but her distrust gene must have been operating in high gear. I punched in the numbers and waited for a connection.

A second ring went unanswered. Then a weak hello greeted me from the other end. I'd forgotten it was one-thirty a.m. in San Francisco.

"Virginia, I'm sorry. Waking you up couldn't be avoided."

"Mo," Virginia choked out. "Where are you, Boss? Are you okay? Is something wrong?"

Her voice gave me goose bumps. I could visualize Virginia rubbing sleep away from her amber-colored eyes, then smoothing short, brown bangs. Her features were ordinary at best, but she'd always been a beautiful young woman to me.

"I'm as good as I'll ever be, Virginia," I said. "Believe me this just couldn't wait. I'm on a plane sitting next to a brilliant young lady who has nailed your Bear Moon Wine campaign. Her name is Mary. Hold on for a sec." My hand cupped the receiver. "What's your last name, Mary?"

"McGrath."

"Her name is Mary McGrath. Before I give Mary the phone to pitch the concept she came up with, I want you to think back to that raw, scared, and incredibly talented young lady who walked into my office thirteen years ago." I took a needed breath. "Here's Mary, Virginia. I think you're going to like her and what she has to offer."

I pressed the phone into Mary's trembling hand. She inhaled and exhaled a deep breath the way a baseball hitter would before stepping into the batter's box. Mary's manner with Virginia was shy at first, then the exuberant passion she had for her creation took over. Too bad Virginia couldn't see the way Mary's hand accented the timbre in her animated voice. A seed of optimism had transformed Mary into a different person. Hope itself wasn't a strategy, but without hope she'd be back to her lonely island of despair.

Mary was too wrapped up in her presentation to notice I was smiling at her. Since I had been witness to her mood swings that fell faster than the Dow Jones average on one bad report, how long would her high spirits last? Probably until she was stabbed by the next crisis.

I craned my neck towards first class. Soon the pilot would start his descent to Logan Airport. The flight attendant had promised to have a wheelchair and attendant waiting for me once we landed. I'd save what little strength I had left being pushed to the car rental agency. But what about Mary? The longer I kept her with me, the safer she'd be.

Mary replaced the phone and sat poised like a cat that had just purchased a canary ranch. Her beaming eyes and squirming body language reminded me of my Katie as a little girl when she had to go to the bathroom or had something important to tell us.

"Oh, Mo," she gushed. "Please promise me that you're for real. And that Virginia's not your co-conspirator in some kind of evil plot to use me."

"I take it Virginia liked your Bear Moon Wine pitch."

"Every bit as much as you did." Mary squeezed my hand so hard it hurt. "Virginia asked me about my history. I didn't lie. I told her I didn't have much education or experience. She said that if Morgan Proffitt likes me, then I have to be good. Virginia made it sound like you're some kind of advertising god."

"We have a mutual respect for each other," I said.

Virginia's status in the ad biz game had vaulted to upper tier. She advanced my agency into the millennium with old-fashioned wisdom and New Age thinking. Conversely, I'd become a dinosaur in my own business. As one star lost its luster, another nova glowed ultra bright.

"This is the most exciting thing that's ever happened to me," Mary said. "Or is it? I thought the same thing about Zack." She studied my eyes. "I'm a slow learner in life. Knock Mary down. Then wait for her to get back up so you can knock her down again. Is this going to be another Zack story? Because if it is, just shove me out the door without a parachute."

"I'm real, Mary. So is Virginia. That much I can promise you."

But there were no givens in life either. I had no doubt Virginia would provide Mary an opportunity, similar to the way I had taken Virginia under my wing. Maybe the same way Virginia would have handled Katie. My daughter had the schooling, background, and a father who owned the business. Mary has the gift, but she still had to earn it.

"Virginia wants to see me right away," Mary said in an anxious voice. "She gave me her contact information, but I don't have money to fly Rachel and me back to San Francisco. Or a place for us to stay. Or even clothes. How am I supposed to meet with Virginia? She's going to hire someone else." Her hand went limp. "Then rip off my ideas."

From past wounds, Mary looked at scenarios in a different way. However, in this case, her instincts were correct. Many of the sharks in the ad business weren't as honest and credible as Virginia.

"Advertising is an extremely cutthroat industry, Mary. But integrity is Virginia's middle name. I can assure you that she's not going to steal your creative concept. Having said that, for some reason fate has put us together. I'm not sure why. But it seems to me we're at a stage where we can help each other."

"My God, Mo. You've done enough for me already."

"Please hear me out." I reached for my money clip. "At this moment, I can't think of two people who need each other more. You need backing, financing, and a place for you and Rachel to stay. Something I can provide. When you get to San Francisco, have Virginia introduce you to Mrs. Green. I believe that will be a match made in heaven."

"Mrs. Green," she repeated. "But how can I help you?"

"I want to hire you."

"Hire me to do what?"

"I'm going to need your assistance. Specifically your youth, strength, and most of all, your trust." My fingers kneaded the hundreds. "By the way, this offer of employment has nothing to do with the conversation you just had with Virginia. That's between the two of you. If Virginia offers you a position, and I believe there's a very good chance of that happening, it will be because you're talented and you will have earned it."

"I'll help you anyway I can," Mary said. "But you don't have to hire me. Friends don't do that. Whether you realize it or not, you're probably the best friend I've ever had." She rubbed the back of my hand. "And I don't even know you."

I had trouble swallowing. But this wasn't the time for maudlin thoughts.

"Let's get something straight here," I said. "What I'm offering you is strictly a business deal. I need you. You need me. Nothing more. Once our commitment to each other has been satisfied, that's it. No attachments. I'm sorry, but everything – including you – comes second to my meeting. Do we have an understanding?"

Mary gazed at the floor. Her torso went into a rocking motion again. Then she lifted her head, straightened her shoulders, and stared me down like a boxer in center ring before the bout.

"You're the most honest person I've ever met," she said. "Yes, we have an understanding, not that I particularly like the way you presented it." She arched her eyebrows. "You still don't have to pay me."

"How long will it take us to get to the car rental area using a wheelchair?"

"Getting a rental car at Logan Airport is a two-part process," she said. "At this hour it should take less than ten minutes to get to the arrival shuttle service area, which is right past baggage pickup. You'll have a good head start. The car rentals are off site. But the shuttles run pretty much non-stop."

"What do you mean by head start?"

"The rental car agencies don't open until six-thirty a.m." She studied my face. "What? Is something wrong?"

Was something wrong? Nothing except the key ingredient to my recipe for killing Oliver Kane was now missing, like taking the apple out of apple pie. I never considered the car rentals would be closed when we landed. Renting a car at 6:30 was pointless. Kane would be long gone. On the phone I'd dealt with him from the strength of being one step ahead with my dollars and knowledge. What the hell was I going to do for a car?

"I know you're not feeling well," Mary said. "But you have the look of a person who just swallowed something sour."

"Mary, did you drive a car to Logan airport?"

"Yes, but remember we're talking about Boston," she said. "I can't promise my car will still be there. Why?"

I lightened half my money clip of hundreds into Mary's hand, five thousand dollars, give or take a few hundred. The mass of green she was gawking at must have represented wealth beyond comprehension.

"Not only do I want to hire your services, I also want to buy your car."

"My car?" Mary ogled the bills in her hand then she laughed. "Some businessman you are, Morgan Proffitt. My car's not worth the registration fee. It's a piece of crap. Breaks down all the time. Why don't you just hail a cab at the airport?"

"A cab doesn't suit my needs. The money in your hand should be enough to purchase your car, two plane tickets to San Francisco, a new wardrobe, and a coming-home present for Rachel."

"You can borrow my car," she said, pushing the money back into my hand.

My attempt to force the money back to Mary failed, revealing a fact of life. Mary was now stronger than I was. I had to conserve my strength. I dropped the hundreds onto her lap. Her fingers went to gather the bills.

"Listen, Mary, whether you realize it or not, the amount of cash I just gave you isn't enough. Wish I could give you more. But it's imperative that I make my appointment on time and have a car at my disposal. You agreed to help me. And to trust me. Are you reneging on our agreement already?"

Mary's cheeks reddened. I couldn't blame her for being over-whelmed. A couple of hours before, she had nowhere to go and was about to end her life. Now she was holding a handful of hundreds and perhaps a new lease on life.

"It's too much," she said, waving the bills like a fan. "This doesn't make sense. The only people I've known who carry this much cash are drug dealers. My ex-husband Larry being one of them. Are you hustling me, Mo? Are these bills counterfeit?"

At another time in my life I would have laughed at Mary's question. But her sad response was a heartbreaker, conditioned by years of being around the wrong people. Her ability to completely trust someone may never return after what she'd been through.

"The money's genuine." I reached behind me for my back pocket. "I'll give you my wallet as collateral if that makes you feel more comfortable."

"Don't," she said, halting my arm with her hand. "Honestly, I wasn't trying to be rude or ungrateful." She stared at the money before stuffing the wad into her purse. "Thank you for your generosity. Someday I'll pay you back. I promise. But, what if Virginia doesn't offer me a job?"

"Then someone else will. I wouldn't have called Virginia if I didn't believe in you, Mary." The plane bounced again. We eyed each other, waiting for a drop that didn't happen. "Where did you park your, uh, my car?"

"I left it at the extended-stay parking lot," she said. "We can take a shuttle together. Or I can go to the lot by myself. Then deliver the car to you at arrivals. From there, I can take a bus or a taxi to where Mother lives."

4:29 a.m. by my watch. An hour and a half to get to Kane. If Mary delivered the car to me at the arrival area, I'd be better off time wise. An uneasy, know-better feeling enveloped me. The same anguish I experienced when I delivered Katie to the airport to catch her flight back to college by herself. A decision that has haunted my soul ever since.

CHAPTER TWENTY

T wo cabin bells sounded. Mary and I looked up at the same time at the blinking red Fasten Seatbelt sign. It was 4:31 a.m. Less than ninety minutes to land, pick up Mary's car, and drive to Kane Tower. Somewhere within that time frame I'd have to part ways with Mary. My meeting with Oliver Kane had to be one-on-one.

"Folks," the captain announced, "we've gained back most of the lost time due to the delay in San Francisco. Currently the weather in Boston is fifty-three degrees and you can look forward to clear skies for the whole day. We will be landing at Logan Airport in about twenty minutes."

"How far does your mother live from the airport?" I said, turning to Mary.

"Not far. I saw you studying maps. Where is your appointment?"

"At an office building on High Street in Boston's financial district. How long should it take me to drive from the airport to downtown?"

"That depends," she said. "Fifteen minutes, maybe. Then again, traffic is always a bitch in or around Boston. It could take more than an hour if there's roadwork, an accident, or a tunnel collapses."

Did she say a tunnel collapse? As long as we avoided the delays Mary mentioned I was in good shape time wise. The last leg of my journey would begin as soon as we landed. I'd made it this far, which was the good news. My strength, however, was waning at an alarming rate. I peeked up at the cabin ceiling. Two hours. Make that three. Just give me three more hours.

The overhead compartment still held my suit jacket. I unfastened the seatbelt and placed both hands on the armrests to propel myself up to a standing position. Mary's arm blocked me like a railroad crossing arm.

"Where do you think you're going?" she said.

"I have to get my coat. I want to be ready to go as soon as the plane stops rolling."

"You forgot I'm on the payroll. Relax, boss. I'll get it for you."

Mary scooted past me. Virginia was the only person who ever called me boss. A coincidence? The compartment door clicked open and slammed shut. She held the coat out for me to slip an arm through the sleeve. The plane took a sudden dip. She lost her balance and ended up sitting on my lap while still holding the coat. Mary was thin, but her weight was heavy on me.

"Really, Mr. Proffitt," Mary said, after a giggle. "I'm not that kind of employee."

Mary helped me with my jacket and returned to her seat. I stored the vial of our pills in my coat's front pocket and smiled. Mary was caught up in her prospective new life and the hope-carrots I'd dangled before her. But that was only a short-term repair at best. I was concerned, no I was goddamned fearful about what would happen to Mary after we parted. Would the newfound belief in herself and a man named Morgan Proffitt assist her through the next crisis?

The cabin vibrated when the plane started its downward pattern. More bells sounded. Early morning Boston sparkled through the minuscule window.

Mary's expression had turned serious. She white-knuckled the straps of her purse with both hands. Everything she valued, besides her daughter Rachel, was in that bag.

The plane's descent took place in quick stages. Runway lights closed in on us. The tires kissed the landing strip, followed by scrunching brake sounds. My heart pounded faster as the plane slowed at a gradual rate. A sense of excitement generated through my body, reminding me of the tense seconds before an opening kickoff of a big game.

"I'll need your arm as a crutch to get off this plane, Mary. And your legs as a tow."

Mary nodded. The nose of the plane headed for the airport at taxi speed. She unfastened her seatbelt before the plane came to a complete stop and leaned forward clutching her purse, ready to make her move.

"Folks, could I have your attention please," our flight attendant announced over the intercom. "Will you please remain seated until we can accommodate one of the passengers in need of special assistance? Thank you. We appreciate your cooperation."

I disconnected my seatbelt. The people around us stirred in anticipation, eager to get off the plane. But not as anxious as I was. Five hours ago, getting on this flight had meant everything to me. Now, all that mattered was departing as quickly as I could.

The plane came to a stop at 4:39, an hour and twenty-one minutes before I was to meet with Oliver Kane. Mary was the first person into the aisle, but not before stomping on my foot with her heel. Her urgency to help me was worth the pain. I hoisted my body up using the armrest and the crook of her arm. Being dependent on Mary didn't grate on my male ego. I was way beyond that. I couldn't accomplish my mission, or at least part of it, without her assistance. An eerie thought entered my head. By helping me, even in an innocent way, would Mary also be abetting me in a crime? I couldn't let that happen.

We entered the aisle way. The passengers heeded the flight attendant's instructions and remained seated, with the exception of a couple who scooted through the doorway. Weary faces peered up at us as we passed. Mary surged forward pulling me with her. She was supplying the power, yet I was having trouble keeping up with her.

A vinyl satchel extended out in Mary's path. She broke stride, making me bump into her. The little cowboy followed his bag. Undaunted, Mary charged ahead. Her momentum and a sharp elbow sent the cowboy flying back to his seat. Yee-haw.

Our flight attendant stood at the entryway smiling. She pointed to the open cabin door. A plump young female airline employee awaited us while holding the back handles of a wheelchair. The shiny metal chair was a scaled-down blue seat on four wheels, but my ride looked like a Rolls Royce to me.

"Sir, our wheelchair agent will push you to your next airport destination," the flight attendant said. "Good luck. I hope your dizziness goes away soon."

I plopped down onto a vinyl seat that had no cushion or give.

Even though I hadn't been standing long, it was nice to get off my feet. My briefcase rested on my lap. The agent turned the chair to the jetway that connected the plane to the airport. Her pushing ability was hampered by the slight uphill grade and her too many extra pounds. She wheezed in my ear. The chair made a sudden stop. I twisted around. Mary's hand gripped one of the handles.

"I'm responsible for this gentleman," Mary said in a stern voice. She commandeered the other handle. "We're in a big hurry. Get outta my way. I'm taking over."

"B-but, you can't do that," the agent argued. "Pushing's my job."

The chair surged forward. Mary was in control, no longer the lifeless person I'd first met. Under her command we navigated through the jetway with ease. The wheelchair agent's feet bouncing on the floor sounded behind us.

Our speed picked up once we entered the airport. We were on Mary's turf now. She veered to the left, moving faster than a herd of people racing in the same direction. The sound of the complaining agent became more distant.

4:48 a.m. No one seemed to notice me in the wheelchair. In a short period of time, I'd have to summon up the strength to climb behind a steering wheel and drive.

"This is Terminal C," Mary said, leaning close to my ear. We breezed past a lineup of glass kiosks showcasing territorial artifacts. "Up ahead, outside, is arrival pickup."

Looking through the glass about twenty yards before us, daylight hadn't made its debut yet. A few scattered travelers were positioned outside, waiting for their transportation. To our right, passengers stood anxiously around a baggage carousel. We didn't have any luggage to worry about.

"What do you want to do, Mo?" Mary asked. "We can take the shuttle together to the long-term parking lot. Or I can leave you out front then deliver the car."

A good question. If I joined Mary, she wouldn't have to bring the car back to me. On the other hand, my condition would slow down the process. She'd make much better time by herself.

"You go ahead, Mary. But please hurry back. We don't have much time left."

Electronic doors opened. Mary guided me outside to the nearest bench. A blast of wind chill penetrated my body. I locked the wheelchair brakes on both sides. She helped me out of the chair and onto the bench's plastic slats. A sad expression creased her face.

"Bye, Mo." Mary placed a soft hand on my cheek. "Don't worry. I'll deliver the car to you as fast as I can."

Mary sped off towards a shuttle bus I assumed was designated for long-term parking. Her purse hung from her shoulder, bouncing and swinging. She looked like a young businesswoman rushing to her next destination. Except her business was now my business. Come on, Mary, crank it into passing gear. If she missed this shuttle, how long would she have to wait for the next one? I wasn't even close to being on the road yet.

The bus door folded shut like a fan. Mary was still in a full sprint. The chassis lifted. Damn. She wasn't going to make it. The brake release sounded, announcing the bus's departure. Mary slammed into the accordion door with pounding fists. She shouted to the driver. Brake lights lit up. The bus body lowered, and the door opened.

Mary made her way to a window seat towards the back. She peered at me with the same unhappy expression as before and waved. Maybe she was winded. Or was something wrong? The shuttle jerked forward. Moments later, Mary and the bus were out of sight. An anxious pang stabbed my gut. What if Mary didn't return?

CHAPTER TWENTY-ONE

I could see my breath without saying a word. Captain Rupp had said it was fifty-three at Logan Airport, but it felt several degrees lower. The briefcase rested on my lap like a useless blanket. My joints were locked stiff, similar to the brakes on the wheelchair the perplexed, plump agent had reclaimed. The plastic slats underneath me were unforgiving, but not as uncomfortable as the pervasive feeling of being in a desperate hurry and having to wait.

A few passengers from my flight had retrieved their luggage and were off to their next destination. But here I sat, waiting like a wallflower hoping for a last-dance ride with Mary. I uncovered the face of my watch. Two minutes past five a.m.

A sudden patch of heat adhered to my face – a sticky unpleasant warmth. The same know-better feeling I'd experienced earlier had resurfaced. Was Mary in some serious trouble? For five years I'd been punishing myself for conceding too easily to Katie's solo trip back to school. If I'd gone with her like I'd planned, most likely she'd be alive today. Did I just make the same disastrous mistake with Mary?

My fingertips stroked tender chest tissue. What if something happened that changed her upbeat frame of mind back to unable to cope? The pills she had clutched so desperately when we were on the plane were still in my pocket. But she could have more pills in her car. Hell, she could even have a gun or a knife.

"Ya all right, pal?" a man with a heavy Boston accent asked.

A chubby airport security trooper studied my face. His head leaned close to me, perhaps to see if I was still alive. He had a reddish-brown mustache, glasses, belly hangover, light-blue stripe down his pants, and a silly hat that reminded me of a Frisbee with a bubble in it. Damned if he didn't looked like a bear in a ranger uniform. His meaty hand tapped on my shoulder, unintentionally hurting me.

"I'm okay," I muttered.

"Sir, ya look like a thin sheet of ice ready to crack apawt. I'll help ya back into the airpowt where it's nice and wawm."

"No thanks," I said. "Listen, my friend went to get her car at long-term parking. She's been gone close to fifteen minutes. I'm concerned. How long should it take her to pick me up?"

"She should have been here by now." The trooper adjusted his hat with both hands. "I'll give ya friend a few more minutes. If ya still sitting here when I come back, we'll go hunt for her. Sure you don't want to go inside?"

"Thank you, trooper, but I'd rather wait out here."

The trooper waddled to the next arrival area. His slow gait would allow me a few extra minutes before I'd have to deal with him again. Hopefully, I wouldn't be sitting here when he came back. I peered down at the cold cement. Did I get conned by a sharp and troubled young lady? Where the hell was Mary?

I looked up shaking my head, refusing to believe Mary would betray me. A cabdriver wearing a Boston Red Sox hat rolled down his window. He was positioned at the end of the line of green and white taxis, no doubt waiting for the dispatcher to give him an assignment. His cigarette smoke floated out of the cab's open window, dissipating into the early morning air.

I checked my watch again. Time wise, I couldn't sit here much longer. Should I take the shuttle or a taxi to extended parking? But then what? I had no idea of the make or model of Mary's car. Plus Mary and I might miss each other in the process. What if she didn't return? I hadn't planned for that. My whole plan had hinged on having a car I could drive. A car to use as the ultimate weapon of destruction of a man whose legal sword carved up driving laws at the expense of innocent lives. Being run over by a ton of moving metal or dying in massive accident would be a fitting way for Oliver Kane to leave the living. But that wouldn't happen unless I was behind a car's steering wheel.

I couldn't wait any longer for Mary. My hands pushed down on the slats to help me stand. If anyone had been watching, I probably looked like a man whose parts had worn out. I waved to the dispatcher. Damn. He either didn't see me or he was ignoring my existence. I looked at the cab closest to me. Smoke elevated from the cabbie's cigarette butt lying in the street. The dark-blue bill of his hat had been tilted to cover his face. He was grabbing an early-morning nap until his turn came up.

The distance across the cement walkway to the cab was about thirty feet, but it seemed like miles. My head screamed instructions to speed forward, but my legs wouldn't obey.

"Cabbie," I shouted, raising a hand and inching towards him. My voice didn't ring loud enough. Wake up, man. You're about to experience a fare to remember. "Cabbie."

A sharp horn blast came from an old brown Dodge Colt parked in the Arrival Pickup lane. The car was missing patches of paint from the hood and roof. The cabbie's head jerked up. He sidled his hat back to a normal position and scowled at his side mirror.

Twin oblong headlights coupled with a bashed in front bumper gave the Dodge a Siamese cat look. Another beep sounded. This time it was longer, more annoying. The cabbie twisted his head around to get a better view. The driver inside the darkened Colt was waving, but not at the cabbie. The hand signal was meant for someone standing behind me, except I was the only person in the general vicinity. The door clanked open, sounding like scraping metal. The driver waved again. The driver was Mary.

"Mo," she yelled, running towards me. Her features were locked in hard. "Don't move. I'll help you."

My chattering lips cracked into a thankful smile. Tears blurred my vision. Thank God Mary was all right and hadn't deserted me.

5:08 by my watch. Adrenaline pumped spirit into my veins. We were back on course.

"Sorry it took me so long." Mary affixed woven red mittens to my arm. "The freakin' car wouldn't start. Happens all the time." She took one of my exposed hands and tried to rub life back into the frozen skin with her gloves. "Jesus, Mo, you don't look so good. You're shivering like an out of tune car."

"Not used to your New England weather. Get me into the car. We need to hurry"

"Bet you were worried I wasn't coming back," she said,

launching her arm through my arm and leading me past the last cab.

"Never doubted you for a second," I puffed out.

Mary snuggled closer to my shoulder. Walking took my breath away, even with Mary's aid. As we approached her car, she steered me toward the driver's side. My shoes stopped moving as if they were glued to the cement.

"Change of plans, Mary. Can you drive part of the way until I thaw out?"

If Mary agreed, I could conserve what little strength I had left. We'd make better time. And most of all, I could get her home safely to her daughter Rachel.

"Sure, I'll drive, Mo. Anything you want." Mary parked me beside the passenger door. "Wait here. I can only open your door from the inside."

A section of the side molding hung on for dear life. The tires were without tread. The rims had no hubcaps. Dark, sickly exhaust poured from the back end. This vehicle wouldn't have a chance against one of San Francisco's hills. Mary had overstated the worth of her car. The Hartmann briefcase in my hand had more dollar value than the vehicle I'd just purchased. Some weapon.

Mary hustled to the driver's side. Once inside, she leaned towards me and pushed open the door with a grunt. She wiped a mess of paraphernalia off the seat to the floor. Paper wrappers, soda cans, children's clothes, a naked doll, and God knows what else decorated a worn blanket covering the backseat. I made a slow descent down into the passenger seat, noting for the first time a curvy crack that ran from one side of the windshield to the other. Oliver Kane was never going to get into this piece of crap car. But at this point, I had no other choice besides hijacking another vehicle.

"I hope this car has a heater." I wrapped my shivering arms across my chest.

"Of course the car has a heater," Mary said. "But it doesn't work. Sorry, Mo." She rubbed her mittens together. "I understand how important your meeting is to you. Anytime you want me to stop driving and get out, just say the word."

"Do we have enough time for you to drive to your mother's house?" I asked. "And for me to make my appointment downtown by six o'clock?"

"Like I said before, traffic can be the pits around here." Mary winked at me. "But it's early. Most of the heavy congestion hasn't started yet. With me as your driver, and a little luck, you should be able to make it no sweat."

"Then get us the hell out of here," I said. "And drive like there's no tomorrow."

Mary's confidence about our chances warmed me. Except, what did she mean when she said, "With me as your driver?" I didn't even think to ask her if she had a driver's license. What if we got stopped by a cop for speeding or reckless driving?

"You do have a license and proper registration, don't you? I asked.

"Of course," she said. "Put your seatbelt on, Mo. If Rachel was here, she'd tell you that the little brown bus doesn't move until everyone has their seatbelt buckled."

"Damn it, Mary," I said, reaching blindly for the belt. "You're wasting what's left of our precious time. Please hurry."

Strapping a safety belt across my achy chest seemed pointless, but Mary needed to focus on driving and nothing else. She jock-eyed the gearshift into first gear. I couldn't remember the last time I'd driven a stick. She manually released the parking brake, let the clutch out, and jammed her foot down on the gas pedal.

The engine coughed like an asthmatic. The car lurched forward sending me towards the cracked windshield until the seatbelt restrained my motion. The engine coughed again then died, strad-dling two lanes.

"Not again, damn it." Mary beat the steering wheel with her fist. "I was afraid this might happen. See what my life is like, Mo. Whenever something good happens to me, like meeting you, I should know by now that it's a prelude to the bad-news cloud hang-ing over my head ready to pour all over me."

"Stop it," I growled. "This isn't the time to panic. Or to feel sorry for yourself." Damn. I wish I knew something about engines to guide Mary out of this. "Okay. When your car stalls like this, how do you usually get it started again?"

"I pray," she said.

Shit. Time to panic.

CHAPTER TWENTY-TWO

Mary turned the ignition key back and forth. The engine wouldn't turn over. Her car was blocking both of the arrival pickup lanes at Terminal C. The dashboard clock had only one hand, forcing me to push up my sleeve. It was 5:11 a.m. Forty-nine minutes to get to Kane Tower.

A blue SUV inched its front end close enough to sniff the Colt's back bumper. A heavy-handed horn protested our idle presence. Mary's panicky eyes focused on the rearview mirror. She rolled down her window. The Dodge engine wasn't giving a hint of restarting, prompting a deep-voiced harangue of insults from the driver behind us. Bean Town's reputation for having an abundance of rude drivers was more than hearsay.

"Pump the gas pedal up and down, Mary." My right foot pantomimed pushing an invisible accelerator to the floor.

"Won't that flood the engine with gas?"

"Probably. But we don't have time for this baby to make up its own mind. Give it some juice and say your prayers."

The cabbie with the Red Sox hat tossed a spent match out the window. He offered an amused smile through a puff of smoke. The jerk took great delight in our plight.

Pungent gas odor seeped into the car. Mary worked the ignition and gas pedal at the same time. Another horn trumpeted from behind the SUV, prompting the SUV driver to respond in kind. Mary had been right. The engine was flooded, but it didn't matter. Her battery lugged into a death rattle, then quit. Mary's foot kept pumping, trying to resuscitate her dead car. This was getting uglier by the second.

"Stop, Mary." I slapped the dashboard. "It's over. If you had a gun we could put your car out of its misery. And at the same time I could wipe that goddamn smile off that cabdriver's face."

The words came out as if my lips had a brain. Pressure could make a person do and say ridiculous things. The smug cabdriver wasn't important. Exiting this damn airport was all I should be thinking about.

"There's a gun in the glove compartment," Mary said, still twist clicking the ignition and waiting for a miracle that wasn't going to happen. "Not that the gun would do you any good. It's not loaded. Hell, the stupid thing doesn't even have a firing pin. There's no way I'd keep a loaded weapon around because of Rachel. The gun's just for show, just in case. But if you want to get your jollies by fake shooting this car, be my guest."

A plethora of junk, including petrified French fries, fell onto my lap when I twisted the glove compartment latch and opened the door. My hand swam blindly inside until I felt the subtle coldness of the pistol's metal. I had no idea what kind of gun I was holding, but it looked meaner than hell. Desperate measures for a desperate man. In a moment the gun bulged in my pocket next to the vial of pills.

"I'll need your help to get out of the car, Mary."

"Get you out of the car? I'm blocking both lanes. We can't just leave my car here."

"The car's not going anywhere whether we sit in it or not," I said, struggling to open the door. "Now, are you going to help me?"

Mary coiled from the car clutching her purse. With her assistance, I was able to stand. My briefcase banged into the broken side molding when I lost my balance. I draped an arm over Mary's shoulder for stability. We moved away from the car. A whistle shrilled like an alarm. The roly-poly airport trooper had a gloved finger pointed at us.

"Yo, what the hell ya doin'?" the trooper yelled. "Ya can't leave yoah cahr there."

"You tell 'em, lard-ass," the SUV driver bellowed, then honked again.

"What're we going to do?" Mary looked back at the trudging trooper.

"Hey," I shouted, waving at the cabdriver in the Boston hat. "Carl Yastrzemski. Red Sox, number eight. The last batter in both leagues to hit for the Triple Crown."

The cabbie's face widened into an acknowledging grin. He nodded as if I'd just given him the passwords to a secret fraternity. His engine sparked to life.

"We're going to hire that green and white cab," I said.

"You told me a cab wouldn't help you."

"Change of plans. Right now a cab is the only chance we've got."

Mary peered back at her car, scrunching up her nose. A double toot from the trooper's whistle turned her head. She attached her arm around my waist and pushed me forward.

"What's the fare to downtown High Street?" I asked the cabdriver.

"Twenty-five bucks, chief," the cabbie answered. He tilted his hat back and aimed the cigarette in his mouth at the dispatch station. "But you gotta go through dispatch before I can take you."

"Don't have time," I said. "Get me there before 6:00 a.m. and I'll pay you ten times the normal fare."

The cabbie worked his gum overtime, making the cigarette bounce up and down like a tollgate. He glanced at the dispatcher then turned his attention to the trooper. Another whistle blast sounded. The trooper's lumbering pace had increased to a fast walk.

"I'm going to ram that brown piece of tin shit off the road if you don't move it," the SUV driver shouted.

"Get in, chief." The cabbie spit the cigarette out onto the street and switched off the dispatch radio. His slender torso rose into driving position. "I'll take care of Tony, my dispatcher buddy, later. Easiest two hundred and fifty bucks I ever made, minus twenty-five for Tony. That's if there're no accidents in the tunnel."

Mary scooted onto the backseat first, pitching her purse to the floor. She clutched my arm and pulled me in. I was welcomed by waves of warmth from the fanned heater.

The cab shot away from the curb like a bullet. Our bodies bounced back into the seat from the momentum, before bumping together when the driver faded into a turn. Mary's elbow connected with the hard metal of her gun stored in my coat pocket. She gave me a questioning look with narrowed, disapproving eyes.

"Just for show, just in case," I whispered. "Please trust me and play along."

Different sections of the airport were in states of disrepair and construction, like a major remodel. I couldn't remember ever seeing San Francisco International this torn up. The cabbie ignored the fifteen-mile-per-hour speed limit. He honked, braked, and swerved to miss a man in a crosswalk.

"It's up to us drivers to put pedestrians in their place around here," he said, peering into the rearview mirror. The cab leaned into a looping curve like it was on automatic pilot. "Where on High Street do you wanna go, Chief?"

"Are you familiar with the Kane Tower building?"

"You kidding me?" he said, ogling Mary in the rearview mirror. The indention in his thin cheeks made his large nose more prominent. "Everyone here knows where Kane Tower's located. Oliver Kane, the attorney, owns that building. Where're you from?"

"Logan Airport," I answered.

"Never heard that one before," he said in a sarcastic tone. He snapped his gum.

The cabbie's name was Benny, according to the license posted on the passenger visor. For Mary's sake, the less Benny knew, the better off she'd be. Mary didn't notice she was constantly being observed. By all accounts, Benny was trying to figure out our relationship. Was I Mary's old man? Or just a dirty old man?

"You and your daughter must be meeting with Oliver Kane himself if this ride's worth two hundred and fifty clams to you."

Nice try, Benny. He blew a pink bubble, waiting for my reaction. The bubble popped and he was still answerless.

Mary's lips parted to speak. Then she bit down on her tongue and looked away. Her eyes had widened when the cabbie mentioned Oliver Kane's name. Perhaps she had connected some of the dots regarding the person I would be meeting with. Was Mary wondering if she had made the same mistake again by trusting the wrong person? What was this crazy old man going to do next? Wish I could respond with an immediate answer that would satisfy both of us.

"You know, chief," Benny said, "Oliver Kane's my kind of guy. Best there is at busting the system's balls." He dug a finger into his ear. "You know, screw the system before the system screws you. I bet Oliver Kane could sue Logan Airport for towing your Dodge Colt away, and win a judgment you could retire on."

Mary flinched, as if she'd caught a sudden chill. Benny had reminded Mary that her car was probably in the process of being impounded. Whether she realized it or not, they'd be doing her a great favor.

"I gotta tell ya," Benny said lowering his voice. "Kane's one dude I wouldn't want pissed at me. Know what I mean? One of my buddies told me about a guy who tried to fuck, uh, get even with Kane. Next day they found the guy dead in a city park." Benny hacked out a smoker's cough. "Suicide my ass. Kane's like a legal loan shark. But if you get yourself in some deep shit while under the influence, Kane's the man."

As much as I tried not to respond to Benny's observations, his words made me cringe. Benny's eyes shifted from Mary to me then to the road. Kane was an idol to him. Yeah, and the Boston Strangler was a great humanitarian too. Any ounce of respect I may have had for Benny evaporated like steam in the wind.

The cab headed into another big loop. My jaw clamped shut in lieu of telling Benny the truth about his hero Oliver Kane. Benny, like most of the New England population, believed Kane was wealthy enough to own a high rise in downtown Boston. On the contrary, Bruno had forwarded information that said Kane paid for the right to put his name on the building. Kind of like a vanity license plate, only a hell of lot more expensive. If Kane was as deep in the red as Bruno indicated, he'd done a great job of keeping it out of public knowledge. But the high-profile attorney was so desperate for my cash that he had agreed to be a passenger in an unfamiliar client's car without knowing anything about the case. I'd soon discover how far my promised money would carry me.

Benny barely missed sideswiping a car. Mary's fingers latched onto my leg above the knee for balance. Her touch penetrated like a stab.

The loop led to a ramp bending into a curve. The cab didn't

slow down. Mary's other hand stretched to the side door to avoid sliding. We still hadn't left the airport.

Benny played bumper tag then darted in and out of lanes like a maniac just to gain a one-car advantage. Was this the way he usually drove? Or was he nervous about getting me to Kane Tower before the six a.m. deadline? 5:15 a.m. on the dashboard clock. I'd been under the impression we had plenty of time. Maybe we didn't.

"Are we going to make my deadline, driver?" I asked.

"Right now, we're still in good shape, chief."

"Then back off with the stunt driving. We both have a lot to lose if you get into an accident."

"It's like I told ya, chief." Benny's glare dominated the rear-view mirror. "The Ted will make us or break us. Always does."

"What the hell's The Ted?" I asked.

"Who's the greatest Red Sox hitter of all time," Benny quizzed, touching the bright red B on the front of his hat.

"Ted Williams, The Splendid Splinter," I answered. "Lifetime .344 batting average."

"There you go." He pointed to a road sign alerting drivers to the tollbooth for the Ted Williams Tunnel up ahead. "Around here, we abbreviate names of highways, bridges, and tunnels. For once they honored someone while he was still alive."

Ted Williams had a picture-perfect, symmetric swing from the left side of the plate. Wish I could say the same about my out-of-sync scheme to eliminate Oliver Kane. The strategy I'd pieced together had fallen apart. I didn't have a car at my disposal to use as a weapon. Precious seconds were ticking away, and Benny was as useful as a toothache.

"You're lucky, chief." Benny notched down his speed at the tollbooth approach.

"You never would've made it through The Ted if you was driving your own car. The tunnel's not open to all traffic—just taxis, buses, and commercial vehicles. They would've made you go back and take the Sumner Tunnel route to town."

I nodded to him. The other route I'd memorized from Bruno's map. If my memory served me right, I still could have made it downtown to Kane Tower by taking the Sumner Tunnel. But I'd never given a thought to road restrictions, one of the many oversights in a haphazard plan. Irreplaceable minutes would have been lost if I had to double back to the airport. Benny had said I was lucky. Perhaps my luck was being provided by a higher power.

While Benny waited to pay the toll, I noticed a small rip in the ceiling fabric above Mary's head. She had the same faraway expression I'd first witnessed at the airport. Was she playing along? Or had she lapsed back into her dark world of wanting to commit suicide again? Soon, I'd have to disassociate myself from Mary before she became my partner in crime.

The cab dipped down into the Ted Williams Tunnel. Benny skillfully maneuvered in between traffic. The long tunnel was wider than I'd anticipated. He braked hard, reacting to a bank of illuminated taillights in front of us. Traffic moved at a sluggish, more controlled pace. The slower we traveled, the faster my unsteady heart pounded.

5:17 a.m. and counting. Kane Tower was probably less than three miles away, but it might as well be thirty miles. Was there an end to this damn tunnel? I wished my hands had control of the steering wheel and my fate.

"You've got the look of a man who'd just let an easy ground ball go through his legs to lose the World Series," Benny said. "What we've got here is a tad more traffic than usual. But don't worry, chief. For the Ted, this is like doing seventy on a freeway."

A pickup truck cut into our lane without signaling. Benny's heavy brake foot vaulted us forward. He wrestled with the steering wheel. The truck hadn't missed hitting the cab by much. Careful what you wish for, Mo. If I'd been behind the wheel, I couldn't have reacted in time to avert an accident with that truck.

"Fuckin' chowder head," Benny yelled, flipping the truck driver the finger and the Italian, bent-arm lift thing between honks. "You get your license at Dunkin' Donuts?"

Mary took hold of my right hand. I squeezed back. A burning sensation spread from my chest to my throat. Pain snaked into my upper arm. I could expect an attack from the least little bit of excitement.

We passed a crippled cab with steam rising from its open hood, the cause of The Ted's congestion. Benny sent his cab dangerously close to the truck's back-bumper. Boston sport? Or had our driver lost control? I needed to rid myself of Benny as soon as possible. But where would I find another vehicle?

The pain in my arm diminished, but the burning remained. Benny screamed out more obscenities. Mary touched my cheek. Her fingertips glistened from my sweat.

"You're burning up," she whispered, rolling down the window. "You need a doctor. No meeting is worth dying over."

"If you marched by the beat of my heart," I whispered back, drawing her close to my lips, "you'd realize why that's not possible. Do you know how to get to Kane Tower?"

"Yes, of course," she said. "Pretty hard to miss."

"Once we get out of the tunnel it's going to get weird. Really weird. For your own protection, please play along. I know what I'm doing."

A bold statement that couldn't be further from the truth. Mary shook her head. If I knew what I was doing, she'd be safe at her mother's house. And Kane would be dead.

"Jesus Christ," Benny said, lifting the collar to his jacket. "It's colder than a witch's...You all right back there, chief?"

"Yeah," I answered. "Just a little car sick."

Benny bunched his shoulders into his neck and leaned forward. But his speed stayed the same. Wouldn't most cabdrivers pull over? Greed was conquering Benny's apprehension of what I might do to the inside of his cab.

The road's grade sloped upward. Lanes veered to the right. In a matter of seconds we were out of the tunnel and in the open air again. Nighttime was thinking about disappearing, but daylight hadn't taken effect yet. Katie used to call predawn and post dusk, "dark-lite." My eyes searched shadows the streetlights failed to illuminate. The outline of Boston's tall downtown buildings came into view. We weren't far from Kane Tower.

Benny stopped at a traffic light with the left turn indicator clicking out rhythmic beats. A bay smell of fish and sea critters drifted into the cab. Mary shivered, but the cold air invigorated me. The street that led to downtown was flat and open.

The light changed to green. Benny headed into his turn. An unlit side road up ahead to the right caught my eye. I slipped Mary's gun from my pocket.

"We're in good shape now, chief," Benny said. "Once we go over Fort Point Channel, we'll be on High Street in a few minutes."

"Driver, I'm going to be sick. Turn onto that side road and pull over," I ordered.

"Don't want to stop now, Chief. We're almost downtown. Just hang in there."

"Hang this, driver," I said, pointing the gun at Mary's head. "If you don't pull over, I'm going to shoot this young woman then you."

CHAPTER TWENTY-THREE

Mary's gun weighed heavy in my hand. Cabdriver Benny sped from the main road onto the deserted side street with his body hunched forward inches from the steering wheel. A nice trick, since his eyes were glued to the rearview mirror. I would have reacted the same way as Benny if someone held a pistol on me. He didn't know the gun was missing a firing pin and was bullet-less. Or was the gun really broken? Benny could be in some big trouble if Mary had lied to me.

The cab skidded to a stop in front of an abandoned factory. A haze of dirt floated upward in the headlight beams. The building was encircled by a temporary-looking chain-link fence and a valley of wild dry weeds. A dark, lonely place to commit a crime.

Benny kept the engine running. He raised his arms like a prisoner and turned to face me. A hostage I didn't know what to do with. My forefinger sneaked from the trigger to the trigger guard. I had no desire to hurt or kill anyone, with exception of Oliver Kane. Thirty-eight minutes before the 6:00 a.m. deadline. Time was running out.

"How far away are we from Kane Tower?" I asked Benny.

"Maybe five minutes if you hit the lights right. Look, Chief, I ain't got much dough on me. You can have my credit cards, but they're maxed out."

"I don't need your money. But I do want you to release the trunk latch."

"The trunk?" He squinted. "Why the fuck do you want me to open my trunk?"

The gun barrel shifted its aim from Mary's temple to the wrinkled spot between Benny's eyes. I drew back the hammer, pretending I was serious about shooting him. His Adam's apple poked in and out several times as he stared at the barrel. I was playing a game of Double Jeopardy Russian roulette. If he put me to the test, it would be the same as firing a loaded gun into my own head. I'd be easy prey for Benny.

Benny's large Adam's apple projected out again. His head finally tilted back. A few seconds later the trunk popped open behind me. Benny's white flag. Thank God.

"Do what you're told and you'll live through this experience." Jesus, I sounded like a heavy in a B movie. "So will the young lady. My intention isn't to hurt either one of you if I don't have to. But time is of the essence. Do I make myself clear?"

Benny blinked his understanding. Mary's glare contrasted with Benny's expression. She was confused and probably upset. I'd told her it could get weird. Didn't she realize I was only holding her hostage for show to keep her from getting into trouble? What if Mary didn't believe in me anymore? Would she sabotage my mission?

"Give me your cell phone, driver. Then slide over to the passenger seat. At all times, I want you to keep facing me with your mouth shut. Don't give me cause to shoot you."

Benny's hand inched towards the inside of his coat, then abruptly changed course for an outside pocket. He passed his cell phone to me. I dropped it into the pocket next to the pill bottle. His phone might come in handy. I wasn't sure my cell phone was still in working order after busting apart on the San Francisco Airport floor. But a criminal mastermind I'm not. Benny's hand had first headed inside his coat. A pocket that could be harboring a gun of his own? He could have killed me with one trigger squeeze. Or worse. Benny could have shot Mary.

"Driver, carefully empty out all of your pockets. Then give the contents to the young lady." Did I sound serious enough?

"Thought you didn't want my dough," he said.

"I'm about to change my mind if you keep flapping your lips."

He handed Mary his wallet, pen, pocketknife, loose change, and two condoms. His cheeks reddened when she smirked.

"I sometimes barter the cab fare with some of Beantown's pavement queens," he said, shrugging his shoulders.

"Now, show me what you have hidden in your inside coat

pocket." I nudged the gun at him. "Slowly. Very slowly."

Benny's hand disappeared inside his coat. His fingers reemerged holding a small pistol by the barrel. Mary gasped in surprise. The gun looked like a toy, but in all probability it was loaded and deadly. He placed the weapon in my open hand, handle first. I stored Mary's gun next to Benny's cell phone. My pocket bulged, but the gun was concealed. He leaned back with a wrinkled, scared expression, confirming my suspicions his gun was lodging bullets. I had his full attention now. How close had Benny been to changing his mind and shooting me?

"Get out of the cab," I ordered. "Both of you."

Frowning, Mary slid from the backseat to stand next to Benny on the road's shoulder. No doubt she was wondering why I'd involved her and myself in such a desperate act.

I didn't have time to explain a plan riddled with recklessness. Nor was I looking for Mary's approval. Or a way to justify my actions. I was only trying to protect her.

The seemingly easy task of extracting my body from the backseat had taken my breath away. Moist sea air penetrated my skin. The last remains of night and the cab's frame shielded Benny and Mary from being seen by traffic on the road leading to downtown. I leaned against the cab's cold, slick surface for support. Standing was difficult for me. Walking more than a few feet at a time was now out of the question.

"Miss, give the driver back his pocket paraphernalia," I said. "With the exception of his knife. Then go to the back of the cab and tell me what he has stored in the trunk."

She moved to the rear without a word of rebuttal. Benny inched his body closer to me. I aimed the gun at his feet.

"Sit down and take off your shoes and socks, driver."

"My socks and shoes?" Benny repeated. He did a little two step dance. "Ah, man. It's cold out, chief. Why do you want me to take off my—"

"You're too young to be so forgetful." I pushed Benny's gun forward, targeting his head this time. He flinched. What if the gun had a hair-trigger? My finger jumped to the guard again. "One more

141

question and you won't have a place to store that bad memory."

Benny crumbled to the dirt into a sitting position. He unlaced his high-top, black Converse All Star basketball shoes – the same sneaker brand I had worn in high school. The trunk flew open, diverting my attention to the rear of the cab. Mary was hidden from my view. Benny rose to his haunches, ready to spring again. My finger jumped off the guard to the trigger by instinct. Benny plopped back down. Good God, I almost shot him.

My cell phone rang out, answering the question I had about its condition. A Boston number glowed in green letters. The call could only be from one person. A loud nearby boat-horn blast went off just as I answered.

"Bruno here, Mr. Proffitt. So you made it to Boston. I know that Fort Channel boat horn like my own doorbell. Where are you meeting Kane?"

An earsplitting screech blasted from the cell phone. Loud enough to make Benny look up, and for me drop my hand with the phone to my side, the ringing still in my head. When I sent the phone back to my ear, the line was dead. The odds were my phone had been the one to crap out. Why did Bruno ask where I was meeting with Kane?

"All right," Benny grumbled. "My shoes and socks are off."

"Roll up both socks into one tight ball and stuff it into your mouth."

"My mouth. Jesus. Why—"

Benny caught himself. He combined heels and toes of both socks and rolled them into a large round cloth ball. The orb filled his mouth with room to spare. No surprise there.

"All I can find in the trunk," Mary called out, "is jumper cables, a spare tire, *Penthouse* magazines, and a toolbox."

"Is there electrical tape in the box?" I asked.

"If shiny black tape is electrical, then yes," she answered.

"Bring me the tape and cables."

The vibration from Mary slamming down the trunk made me lose my balance and slide towards the hood. I grabbed the side mirror before I fell. Pain centered in my chest, before shooting down my arm into my fingers. Once again my heart was rebelling against any hard physical movement I made. My clumsiness hadn't gone unnoticed. Mary rushed to me carrying the cables and tape. Benny's skinny body was in launch mode again, ready to attack.

"Relax, both of you." I jiggled the gun at Benny.

My thumb and trigger finger had gone numb. Benny didn't know what my problem was. He only knew something was wrong with me. His eyes shifted back and forth from the gun to my face. I couldn't hold onto the gun and this facade much longer.

"Miss, tie the driver's hands behind his back with the tape."

Mary put her hands on her hips and mouthed the word "why."

"Hurry, damn it. Then tie his ankles together and put a strip of tape over his mouth."

Damn. It was 5:29 a.m. already by my watch. What if Kane's watch ran a couple of minutes fast?

Mary used Benny's knife to cut off a last piece of tape and sealed his mouth. She stood up with another raised eyelid expression. I peeled five hundred dollars from my money clip and handed the bills to her.

"Roll the cabbie through the weeds until you hit the fence. Then tie him to a chain link with the jumper cables." My eyes stayed closed for an extra beat to combat a wave of dizziness. "I doubled the fee I promised the driver for his time and trouble. If he cooperates, put the money in his shirt pocket. If he resists you, bring me back his shirt and pants."

Benny emitted muffled moans with each roll. I slipped his gun into my coat's other pocket to balance the weight then fell ass-first onto the front passenger seat. Another smack attack of pain hit my chest. As much as I needed the air, I managed not to breathe too hard while I assessed the damage. My short breaths were getting shorter. I was literally running out of time.

CHAPTER TWENTY-FOUR

I sat in the cab's passenger seat with my shoes planted on the roadside's packed dirt. Benny's muffled cries sounded from the chain link fence. I swung my feet back into the cab. Then I removed the cabbie license from the visor and stuffed it into the glove compartment. I wasn't stealing Benny's cab. Instead, I was just renting a ride at an exorbitant rate for a short period of time.

The fatigue in my limbs didn't buffer the constant discomfort in my chest. My eyes closed for a few beats to contend with dizziness. I forced them open when Mary emerged through the thick weeds and charged at me holding Benny's pointy knife in her hand. She stopped a foot away from where I was sitting.

"Are you out of your freakin' mind?" Mary shrieked, closing the blade into the handle.

"Keep the decibels down," I whispered. "I don't want the cabbie to hear us. He thinks we're strangers. Let's keep it that way."

"For criminy sakes, Mo," she ranted in an emphatic murmur. "Do you have any idea what you just did? Sure as shit we're going to jail for armed robbery. If that's not spicy enough for you, add a pinch of murder for flavor if no one finds the driver."

"Mary, as far as the police are concerned, I'm the only person who's in trouble here. You're my hostage. I held you against your will and forced you to be my accomplice. And I'll make sure they find Benny soon."

"Accomplice? Police?" She pointed a finger at me. "What're you going to do? Rob a bank? Blow up a building? Murder someone?"

"The only business you need to be concerned about is driving us out of here as fast as you can." My hand latched onto her finger. "Please hurry."

"Damn right, I'll drive," she said, "'cause you're in no condition."

Mary retrieved her purse from the backseat before sliding in behind the wheel. After adjusting Benny's rearview mirror, she jammed the gearshift into drive, turning the cab in a half-circle with squealing tires towards the road to downtown Boston.

"And I'll hurry too," Mary continued, "straight to the hospital where you belong."

"No hospital. You said your mother doesn't live far from the airport. Promise me you'll drive to your mother's house. That's very important. You'll be with Rachel. You'll be safe there until you go back to San Francisco. There's still enough time if you drive fast. Promise me, Mary."

"All right, damn it. I promise. But please let me drive you to Kane Tower first."

"Out of the question."

"With all my heart, Mo, I want to trust you. Believe in you." She exhaled a long breath. "Haven't I gone along with everything you've asked of me? At the very least, don't you think I deserve to know what you're planning on doing and why?"

"Of course you deserve answers." My hand clutched the dashboard when she made a sudden lane change without slowing down. "But the less you know about my intentions, the better off you'll be. You've gone through some terrible things in your life. I don't want this experience added to the list."

We raced past Boston's World Trade building. Mary had more of a lead foot than Benny, but she handled herself well behind the wheel. A small bridge arching over dark water came into view. She traversed the bridge in seconds as the outskirts of downtown Boston unfolded. A turn under an elevated highway sent me into the door.

"Don't get me wrong, Mo. I so appreciate the fact that you're trying to look out for my interests. No one has ever protected me like you have." She swiped a quick glance at me. "Then, you are planning on doing something bad."

"From another perspective, I'm going to eliminate a legal social problem."

"What the hell is that supposed to mean," she fired back, slowing the cab's speed.

"Just keep driving."

The map in my head and my sense of direction disintegrated when Mary turned off the street that went into downtown Boston. She was heading to the left after a series of turns. I had no idea if we were going north, south, east, or west. At least traffic was sparse. Mary sent the cab into more turns that left my brain soaring. I was more disoriented than ever. A shortcut. Or was she trying to confuse me?

"You don't seem like the type of man who'd willingly do something against the law." She pointed her finger at me again. "I don't know what to do, Mo. You're weakening by the minute. I should be taking you to the hospital. You rescued me on the plane. Shouldn't I be doing the same for you?"

"You already have, Mary. You've become my lifeblood."

Mary's assessment of my health had been correct. I was fading fast. My breathing was tired. But this was the fourth quarter and I had run out of time outs. I wished there was enough time left for me to help Mary push her demons aside. Why couldn't I have met this distraught young lady at a different time and under different circumstances? I had a strong urge to put my arm around her. To embrace Mary the way I used to hold a young Katie when she was troubled by one of life's mysteries. I wanted to tell her in a soft, confident voice that someday she'd see through all of her blurry confusion if she would just give herself a chance. But Mary needed more help than my sage advice and a job from Virginia. I resisted the urge to lift my eyes to the ceiling. Are You listening?

We continued on a street outlined with commercial buildings. The further we traveled, the more "mom and pop" the businesses became. I hadn't seen a house yet.

Mary made an unexpected sharp left turn. She then veered right into an area of tall, brown-brick buildings that looked alike. She stayed on the narrow road that twisted between the structures before stopping at an illuminated entranceway. A broken plastic tricycle lay injured on a tiny patch of lawn. Two huge overflowing garbage dumpsters bordered the grass. The drapes in a ground floor window moved. Light flickered on and off through holes in the fabric as if someone was watching TV in the dark.

It was 5:34. I didn't know how to get to High Street and Kane

Tower from here. Time was running out. Mary shoved the gearshift into park, leaving the engine running and the headlights beaming on the building's orange front door. She closed her eyes and leaned her forehead against the steering wheel.

"What's going to happen to you, Mo?" she asked in a childlike voice.

My shoulders hitched into my neck. I knew my appearance was sickly, but she feared looking at me for another reason. Mary didn't know how to say goodbye. Neither did I.

"Please let me take you to the hospital." Mary said. "There're several close by."

"Not enough time. Nor would it help. How do I get to Kane Tower from here?"

"The fastest route," she said, gesturing with her head to the right, "is also the longest. But if I give you shortcuts, you'll get lost. Boston's nothing but one-way streets, with no rhyme or reason. And then there's the—"

"Damn it, Mary. It's five-thirty five. I'm almost out of time. Please. The fastest way to Kane Tower."

"Sorry. Follow this road until you hit Mystic Street and turn right. Turn right again onto Washington Street. Follow Washington all the way into downtown to Summer Street. Washington's really long. A right on Summer will take you to High Street.

"Right on Washington," I repeated. "Right on Summer to get High. Got it. How many minutes should it take me?"

"No more than ten minutes at this hour."

Easy enough directions to remember. Now the bigger question. Was I physically capable of following the directions if I was behind the wheel?

"Another favor, please." I removed Benny's cell phone from my coat pocket and handed it to Mary. "After I leave, wait a couple of hours, then use this phone to call the police and tell them where to find the cab driver."

"Sure, Mo. But—"

"Mommy! Mommy!" a young girl wearing pajamas shouted. She jumped from the concrete block stoop. Her neck-length auburn hair bounced up and down as she streaked across the lawn.

Mary was out of the car kneeling down to one knee. Rachel flew into her mother's arms. Wild mother and daughter rants of joyful questions and unabashed love wove together. How I used to love Katie's enthusiastic greetings when she was Rachel's age. And how I hated it when she got older and felt too dignified to act like that.

Mary lifted Rachel and carried her to the driver's-side window. I used the steering wheel as leverage to slide myself into the driver's seat. That seemingly small task sent a line of pain to my jaw and took my breath away. I thanked the automotive gods for inventing power windows. An aromatic smell of burning leaves found my nose.

"I have so much to tell you, sweetheart," Mary said, hugging Rachel again.

"Did you get a new car, Mommy? Are we going to drive to San Frisco in it?"

"No, Rachel. My friend Mr. Proffitt borrowed this car to get me home safely from the airport to be with you. But we're going to San Francisco as soon as possible."

"Hi, Rachel." It even hurt me to smile. "On the airplane, your Mom told me how special you are. And how lucky she is to have you as her daughter."

Rachel tucked her head into the crook of Mary's neck, turning shy all of a sudden. Katie used to do the same thing. Mary turned to me, her eyes blinking tears. I dug into my pants pocket and placed the silver hippo key ring that Katie had given me into Rachel's tiny hand.

"What's this?" Rachel said.

"A present for you, Rachel," I said. "The Hippo's name is Hope. Hope's special, just like you. Keep Hope close to you at all times so she can remind you and your mother to always believe in yourselves and to never give up."

"Thank you," Rachel gushed, jiggling the chain. "I like her." She struggled away from Mary's grasp. "I'm going to show Grandma."

Rachel scampered away around the cab, only to fall down on

the lawn. She jumped up like she was on a trampoline and made her way to the front door. How I wished my body had the same resiliency as hers. I threw the gearshift into drive. Mary leaned into the cab and planted a soft kiss on my cheek. She wiped away the evidence with her thumb.

"Please reconsider what you're planning on doing," Mary said. "Is that why you saved my life? To justify taking away someone else's life?" Mary took a step back chewing on her lip. "I saw your expression when the cabdriver practically wet himself talking about Oliver Kane. Somewhere there's a connection between Kane and your daughter. Don't do it, Mo. You're too good a man to stoop to that level. It'll make you the same as Oliver Kane."

My foot left the brake. The cab rolled forward on its own. If our roles had been switched, I would have said the same thing to Mary. She didn't try to hide the sadness registered on her face. A new future awaited Mary and Rachel. Under Virginia's tutelage, and Mrs. Green's TLC, the female McGraths could thrive in San Francisco.

"Mo," she shouted, cupping her hands around her mouth and nose.

I jerked the cab to a stop in the middle of the street. The motion sent my chest into the steering wheel, magnifying the soreness. Mary's form had shrunk in the side mirror. My responses were slow and uncoordinated. I shouldn't be driving, but there was no other choice. It was 5:38. Still enough time to get to Kane Tower if I didn't get lost.

"Watch out for the Big Dig," Mary announced.

My foot punched down on the accelerator. Amid the smell of smoke and burning rubber, the cab swerved from one side of the street to the other. The steering wheel challenged me to hold on. I missed hitting parked cars by micrometers. Tension made me hold the wheel tight. I aimed the cab to the center of the street, a safer way for me to drive until another car came my way.

"What the hell is the Big Dig?"

CHAPTER TWENTY-FIVE

Twenty-one minutes to get to Kane Tower. The street I was following twisted through a maze of tenement housing, making each curve seem like I'd been there before. Where the hell was Mystic Street?

Most of the residents in this dark neighborhood were still asleep. I glanced at the rearview mirror hoping to catch one last view of Mary. She was out of sight. Yet the concerned expression on her face lingered with me.

The Mystic Street sign came into view. Hard to believe that twenty hours ago I was in Louis' examination room being told my heart could stop beating at any moment. Louis would probably have a heart attack if he knew where I was. What I'd done. And what I intended to do. The cab rolled through the stop sign and turned right. So much had happened since I'd left Louis' office, none more important than meeting Mary.

From out of nowhere, reflective white stripes danced before me.

"Watch out," I screamed.

A jogger clad in a dark running suit had jumped back after venturing into the street without looking. Before I could hit the brakes or sound the horn, the cab buzzed past him. God, that was close. The runner was still alive only because he could react in time to check his momentum. My foot crept back to the accelerator, but not as heavy.

As if on cue, pain socked my chest. I held my breath waiting for the next jolt. I should pull over. Slow reactions impaired my driving, similar to someone under the influence of drugs or alcohol. The potential of losing control of the cab, running a red light, missing one of the streets Mary had cited, or smashing into something or somebody rose with each additional mile per hour I traveled.

I blew out an anxious breath. Who the hell was I kidding? I couldn't stop now. Not when I was this close to Oliver Kane. I arched up an eyebrow. Just give me forty-five more minutes. Then I'm all Yours.

Washington Street appeared on a green-and-white road sign. I made a right turn into light traffic, mostly commercial vehicles. My foot compensated for lost speed by pressing down harder on the gas. Driving at the speed limit hindered my chances of making the six a.m. deadline. The speedometer jumped to the right. I switched lanes to pass a slow moving van. If my fingers gripped the steering wheel any tighter, I'd never be able to uncurl them.

"Whoa!"

My foot hopped to the brake pedal before the cab rammed a blue-and-white police patrol car. No wonder traffic was moving so slowly. I sent the speedometer needle down to the speed limit, not by choice.

Nips of cold air propelled through the open side windows. Washington Street seemed endless. What was the name of the street I should turn onto after Washington? It had something to do with seasons. Come on, Mo, concentrate. Summer. Turn onto Summer Street. I'd lost most of my physical prowess and patience. My brain was all I had left.

The light up ahead turned from yellow to red. The patrol car turned right onto a side street without bothering to stop. The cab's front end filled most of a crosswalk when I came to a stop. A string of traffic passed before me. There was no damn cross-street sign. Mary had said Washington was lengthy. I hadn't been driving long enough for this to be Summer Street. Or had I? My eyes zoned in on the red traffic signal.

"Come on, damn it. Boston could change seasons by the time this light turns green."

The unique shapes of illuminated skyscrapers formed like distant mountains. Somewhere in that commercial jungle was the financial district and Kane Tower. It was 5:42 a.m. Stopping at all lights was a luxury I could no longer afford.

Green light. The accelerator received the brunt of my irritation. Too late to go back and retrace my steps. My gut told me Summer Street was up ahead.

The buildings on Washington Street became taller, an indicator the financial district wasn't far away. Berkeley Street caught my eye. The town of Berkeley was only a few miles from San Francisco, a city still sleeping in the midst of early Tuesday morning. Boston was in the throes of waking up. Pay attention, Mo. San Francisco didn't matter. Boston and its screwed up streets were my only concern now.

Another street sign appeared up ahead to the right. My foot eased off the gas. Herald Street. How close was I to Summer Street?

At 5:47 the cab shot past a hospital. One of the nearby medical facilities Mary referred to earlier? If I didn't find Summer Street soon I'd have to pull over and call Kane. A stoplight up ahead turned red. I sped through the intersection and the red light without hesitation.

Washington Street asphalt turned into red brick. Scents of cooking entered the cab, making my troubled stomach rumble. Chinese food this early in the morning? The street seemed to narrow, sidewalks were closer.

What the devil is going on up ahead? I braked to a stop.

Delivery trucks had the entire street blocked. The cab couldn't get by. To amplify my frustration, a Summer Street sign sat tall on a sidewalk pole at the end of the block. No time to wait for the trucks to move. I was close to Kane Tower. Close enough to jump out of the cab and run. The mind was willing, but the body wasn't. Nor would it do me any good. Without the cab, my meeting with Kane was useless.

I steered left into a one-lane alley. The tires squealed from the speed of my turn. I had no idea if I was driving against traffic. I slowed down in anticipation then turned right. Summer Street should be one short block away. Wrong again. The street sign said Winter Street. Goddamn New England humor?

I had no choice but to turn right onto Winter Street. Brick paved the street and sidewalks. Fruit and vegetable venders tended their outside product stalls. If winter didn't turn into summer, or at least spring, I'd have to pull over and call Kane. A call I was desperate not to make. Another sign appeared. I roared through an intersection onto Summer Street. Yes.

The early morning isolation of a major downtown metropolis

enveloped the cab. Glass and stone buildings became denser and taller, like a forest. I'd only seen a few cars and no pedestrians – a good sign. The less traffic, foot or otherwise, the better off we all were.

Less than eight minutes left. Kane Tower could only be a few blocks away. Enough time to follow the red-brick road to High Street. The sole of my shoe felt like it was glued to the accelerator. The faster I traveled, the more rapid my heartbeat. But the heaviness and pain in my chest were barely noticeable, as if a switch had been turned off.

The cab zoomed past streets I didn't care about. The next intersection could be High Street, but there was no sign. I stopped in the middle of the intersection, craning my neck out the window. This had to be High Street. Mary never did tell me which way to turn. On my left, the towering buildings on both sides of the street reminded me of the financial district in downtown San Francisco. The buildings weren't as tall on the right. I turned left. A sign confirmed that I was on High Street. I was so close to Kane my nose itched. Even numbered addresses and Kane Tower were on my right.

"Damn it, no." Both feet stomped on the brake pedal. Way to celebrate too early, Mo. After only one block, another sign warned "Do Not Enter." High Street had become a one-way street – the opposite direction to what I needed. Another blue-and-white Boston police car was parked at a curb, daring me to go straight. I turned left onto Federal Street. My luck had just turned to shit.

Federal Street looked no different from the other streets. At least there was no traffic. Up ahead to the right, a street intersected Federal. But the damn street was barricaded. The person managing Public Works must have had a degree in torment. A large sign said something about "The Big Dig," the very thing Mary had warned me about. The street was torn up like the aftermath of a bomb explosion. I was in a Goddamn Big Dig maze moving farther and farther away from High Street.

5:54. Six minutes to get to Kane Tower. The speedometer needle stretched past fifty, way too fast for city streets and a damaged driver. A sign on my right said Franklin Street. But another sign on my left read "No Right Turn." Son of a bitch. Franklin was a one-way street that ran in the same direction as High Street. How much farther did I dare travel away from Kane Tower? Screw it.

I turned onto Franklin Street without braking. The cab drifted into a slide with the tires screaming for mercy. My shoulder bashed into the door from the momentum of my wild, illegal turn. I pulled the wheel hard clockwise with all my strength and hit the accelerator. The cab's side fender caromed off a sidewalk fire hydrant on the left side of the street before the vehicle straightened out in the center of both lanes. Fortunately the sturdy hydrant didn't blow. I could only pray that an unsuspecting driver wouldn't come barreling down Franklin from the opposite direction.

Up ahead to the left, a garbage truck parked at the curb. A wave of dizziness hit me, followed by nausea. Almost at Kane Tower. Don't pass out, Mo. I swallowed hard several times. And don't throw up either.

The lift on the garbage truck groaned into action. One of the garbage men ventured onto the street, not expecting a car traveling the wrong way. The cab roared straight at him. My hand punched the steering wheel horn and stayed there. The garbage man froze then scampered for safety, leaving the metal garbage container rolling and spilling trash onto the street.

The front bumper nicked a piece of the can then the cab blasted past Congress Street at 5:56. Part of Congress to my right was also torn up, compliments of the Big Dig. Was Kane Tower one or two blocks up on High Street? I'd lost track. Pearl Street was the next block. I remembered Pearl from Bruno's map.

"Damn it to hell!"

A postal truck had turned onto Franklin. The son of bitch was coming right at me. What the hell was he thinking? That I was a frigging mirage? Or was he playing chicken with me? Neither. A cell phone was scrunched into his ear and shoulder while he peered at a clipboard. He had no idea a cab streaked towards him.

I leaned on the cab's horn again, finally catching the driver's attention. His mouth fell open like he was an opera singer belting out an aria. The clipboard dropped from his hand. Who was going to make the first move? We could counter each other if we turned at the same time. I was having trouble controlling the cab at the speed

I was traveling. The mail truck was on the clock to move first.

The driver's brakes squealed while he frantically turned the steering wheel. The top-heavy truck went into a spin as if the tires were on slick ice. He did a great job of avoiding the cab, but now his truck was in danger of flipping over.

The cab sped through the Pearl Street intersection. Every fiber in me wanted to watch the truck's plight in the side mirror, but I didn't dare take my eyes from the windshield. My ears would tell me if he crashed or not. No sound was a good sound.

"Oliver Street," shot out of my mouth when I saw the next street sign. Two right turns and I should be on High Street. Except Oliver was a one-way street going in the wrong direction. How fitting.

What the hell? It hadn't stopped me before.

A sloppy turn onto Oliver put the cab in the middle of the street. This road was dark, quiet, and uninhabited. I notched down the speed for my next right turn. The High Street sign made my chest pound even harder. This time, one-way was the right way.

Kane Tower was three buildings down on the left. A man stood on the sidewalk under a street light's illumination, reading a news-paper. A rush of adrenaline cleared my head like nature's instant vitamin, but my heart was beating too fast. Squeezing pressure spread from my chest through my neck to my jaw and ear. A sensa-tion I'd never experienced. What happened to the calm demeanor I'd demonstrated when talking to Oliver Kane on the phone from the San Francisco airport?

The cab's left front tire bumped against the curb one building before Kane Tower. Less than two minutes left before the 6:00 a.m. deadline. The digital temperature numbers on an office complex registered fifty-one degrees then confirmed the correctness of the cab's clock.

My eyes watered when I stuck my head out the window into the penetrating wind. Short breaths, Mo. My lungs sucked in as much of the Boston air as they could handle. I could use a circuit breaker to harness the surge of electric energy running through my veins. Too late in the game to take a pill. My flushed skin broke into a sweat. I was so close. Too close to be stopped now.

The torso standing behind the paper was thicker than I'd anticipated. Kane must work out, something Bruno didn't indicate in his report. What would Kane's reaction be when he caught sight of a cab as his transportation and me as the driver? At this moment, he'd be an easy target. I could empty Benny's gun into the newspaper. Or I could just run the son of a bitch over right there on the brick sidewalk. Then back up and run over him again. He'd never know what hit him. But that wasn't the way I wanted this mission to end. Kane needed to know why he was being sentenced to die in my court. And for Mary's sake, his death must look like an accident.

The cab inched towards Kane Tower. The brakes squeaked to a stop next to a parking meter. Ten feet away from me was the man I was going to murder. His black leather gloves clutched the sides of a *Boston Herald* early edition. I could even read the two main headlines, "PRIME TIME – 9th VOTERS HOLD KEY TO MOAKLEY SUCCESSOR" and "JUDGE GIVES LESSON TO UNDERAGE DRINKERS." Must be a slow news day.

A quick horn toot announced my presence. The *Herald* remained in place, covering his face and most of the upper half of his camel-colored overcoat. His brown shoes sparkled in the cab's headlights. The bastard was trying to make me sweat, and he was doing one hell of good job of it too.

My fingers squeezed together on my lap to combat my anxiety. A Freedom Trail sign sitting high on a sidewalk pole caught my eye, a walking tour depicting the history of the American Revolution as it began in Boston. That was one route Kane wouldn't be taking again.

Wisps of morning breeze sucked in the center of the newspaper. Gloved hands stretched the ends to fix the dent in the paper. He cleared his throat. Finally, at six o'clock on the dot, he lowered his paper shield.

The man wasn't Oliver Kane.

CHAPTER TWENTY-SIX

The man wearing an unbuttoned overcoat folded his newspaper in half and lodged it under his armpit. He hitched up his coat collar and stared into the cab. One eyelid twitched up while the corner of his mouth sagged, revealing he was just as disappointed in me as I was in him.

With the window open, Boston's 6:00 a.m. chill cut right to my bones as I sat alone and dejected in the cab. Seconds earlier I had parked in front of Kane Tower and had felt euphoric. The revolvers rested on my lap. I had no recall of removing them from my pockets. They weighed like cannons. For a person who always had a strong dislike for guns, enough for me to never own one, here I sat armed for the big dance and with nobody to shoot. Where the hell was Oliver Kane?

I stared at the building's revolving glass door entry outlined in metal trim. Floodlights attached to the high-rise exterior shone down on different shades of brown stone and the tall, gold KANE TOWER letters. Two large, square planter boxes, doubling as cement benches, took up space in the courtyard walkway.

Overcoat Man wiped a leather finger under his nose. A toothpick shifted from one side of his mouth to the other without the use of hands. A tight-fitting, brown suit and a neck, size extra thick, suggested he was a body builder. His bulldog face looked like a clenched fist. He spit the toothpick onto the brick sidewalk. Where the hell was Kane?

A sedan in need of a new muffler sped past the cab. The exhaust pipe produced a series of white smoke puffs. The car seemed out of place in an area that generated billions of dollars.

"Is your name Morgan?" A slight New England accent seasoned his speech.

"What?" I blurted out. The guns fell from my lap onto the floorboard. Did he really say Morgan? Or was I imagining that he called my name? "What did you say?"

"I asked you if your name's Morgan," he replied, with an impatient edge.

"Yes." My enthusiastic response hurt my chest, but the pain was cushioned with optimism. "I'm Morgan."

The goon standing before me had to be an Oliver Kane employee. Did Kane send this guy to rough me up or steal the money I'd promised to deliver? I flinched when the goon's hand reached inside his overcoat. My hand reached down for a gun. He produced a cell phone and held it to his face like a walkie-talkie, a radiophone. His eyes peered up at Kane Tower offices. From this angle I couldn't see if anyone was standing at a seventh-floor window.

The phone in the man's hand beeped. A series of ringing coughs shook his big body while the goon waited for an answer. He wiped his nose again and spit on the brick.

"Yes," a voice drawled from the phone's speaker.

"Sir," the goon said, wrinkling his nose. "Mr. Morgan's here."

"Describe him to me, Rollie."

Was that Kane's voice? The scratchy quality of the speaker in the radiophone made it difficult for me to be sure. But it had to be Oliver Kane on the other end. Who else could it be?

"The dude's in his fifties," Rollie said, eyeballing me. "Wearing nice threads. He kind of looks like the Michael Douglas from *Wall Street*. Not *The Streets of San Francisco* Michael Douglas."

"What's Michael Douglas driving?" the voice asked.

"He's driving a cab," Rollie said. "But he don't look like no cab driver I ever seen."

"Have you inspected his vehicle?"

Rollie bent from the waist, cupping a glove over his eyebrows. He checked the dashboard and front seat then peeked through the side window at the backseat. Satisfied, he straightened up.

"Yeah, everything looks cool, Mr. Kane."

Yes. Oliver Kane was on the line. A stab of apprehension penetrated my gut. Why hadn't Bruno informed me that Kane had a bodyguard? A highly-improbable oversight for a detective as thorough as Bruno. My searching eyes drifted past Rollie's big body looking for more Kane bodyguards lurking in the shadows. What motive could Bruno possibly have had to hold back info about Kane's hired security? That wasn't the only question buzzing in my head. I still couldn't figure out why Bruno had called me, wanting to know where I was meeting Kane.

"Have you checked Mr. Morgan out?" Kane asked

"No, sir. I was waiting for your lead."

Rollie moved to my open window. Tobacco stink emanated from his clothing. What had Kane meant by "check out?" Did he want Rollie to see my driver's license? That could be a problem. When I told Kane on the phone from the airport my name was Morgan, he assumed Morgan was my last name. The name Proffitt would ring loud bells.

"Let me see some proof, pal, that your name's really Morgan," Rollie demanded.

Damn it. I reached for my wallet. The effort rewarded me with smack of chest pain. Rollie poked a hand through the window and clamped a hurting grip down on my wrist. He snatched the wallet from my fingers and searched for my ID.

"California driver's license," Rollie recited into the phone. "His name's Morgan, all right. Morgan...Uh—"

"Pro-feet," I said as loud as I could. "My last name's pro-nounced Pro-feet. It's French. People mispronounce my name all the time. That's why I go by Morgan."

"Sir, the last name's pronounced Pro-feet."

"Pro-feet," Kane repeated. "From California. He's come a long way for my advice."

"Get out," Rollie said, jerking the door open after he pushed the wallet back into my hand. "I need to pat you down. See if you're packing."

Packing? Like carrying a gun? Rollie would see the guns on the floor if I got out of the cab. He'd also notice how unsteady I was on my feet, two necessary reasons for me to remain seated. My shoes stepped on the pistols. I fought the urge to look down to see if they were fully covered. Rollie wouldn't take no for an answer. But

Kane had been receptive to my arguments earlier. And Kane was my only leverage over Rollie.

"I told you to get out of the cab," Rollie ordered, with phone still at his mouth.

"I heard you the first time," I snapped. "Tell Mr. Kane that I'm not about to be frisked in public like a common criminal. I've had quite enough of your goonish behavior. You've left a bruise on my wrist going after my wallet. Does your boss treat all his potential clients like this? Shut the door, Rollie. My deal with Mr. Kane is off."

"Sir, Mr. Mor...Ah, Pro-feet says he ain't about to—"

"I heard, melonhead," Kane growled. "Put Morgan on the phone. Talking through you is like talking to a fucking wall."

Rollie handed me the phone. The sneer on his lips might have to be surgically removed. I pressed the button Rollie had used. Careful, Mo. Showing weakness to Kane was like bleeding from an open wound in a shark tank.

"Morgan here, Mr. Kane." Words hurried from my mouth like I was out of breath. "I admit my decision to come to Boston to seek your counsel was rushed and desperate. Having said that, I'm not accustomed to doing business this way. Thus far it's been a god-damn indignity. You may be the best man for the job, but I'm not without options. In other words, Mr. Kane, you're skating on thin ice with hot skates."

"All right, Morgan, you've made your point. Rollie said you're driving a cab. Are you a cabdriver?"

"Your man Rollie astutely indicated I didn't look like a cab-driver." Rollie threw me an approving nod – a first. "I don't drive taxis for a living. Nor had picking you up in a cab been my first choice for transportation. In short, Logan Airport rental car agencies don't open until six-thirty a.m., and I didn't have time to charter a limo. Since the nature of our discussion is highly sensitive, I grossly overpaid a cabbie for the private use of his vehicle. As I told you before, money's not an object. Please accept my apology if a taxi doesn't meet with your approval. I can assure you the meter's not running."

"Real cute, Morgan," Kane droned sarcastically. "Certainly you can understand that a man in my position has enemies."

"Whether you have enemies or not doesn't concern me, Mr. Kane." Pain hit my shoulder. Was that punishment for the lie I just told? "I only hope you can appreciate my reluctance to deal with low-class thugs."

Rollie puffed out his chest in a defensive mode. His eyebrows met in the center, causing him to squint. The more I talked, the more it hurt, and the more ornery he looked.

"What Rollie lacks in tact," Kane said, "he more than makes up for by protecting me and my interests. And he's paid a considerable amount of money to do so. To show that I'm a reasonable man, Morgan, I'll meet you halfway. Since I don't know you, I must insist that Rollie do a weapons search. But you don't have to get out of the car."

"I didn't come all the way to Boston offering you a potential of fifty thousand in cash to be disrespected," I declared.

Rollie's eyes opened wider when he heard the amount of cash I'd offered Kane. He grinned. The slow gears operating in his head had just sped up.

"I'll agree to your search on one condition, Mr. Kane. Once Rollie informs you I don't have any concealed weapons on me, that's it. Then it's client-attorney confidential time on the way to the airport. No more games. No more Rollie. Just you and me. Do we have an understanding?"

The radiophone squawked as Kane mulled over my condition. Rollie's head shake told me I'd screwed up. Most people were wary of Kane. Rollie had probably never heard anyone speak to his boss the way I just did. Maybe I had gone too far in throwing a strong bully back at Kane. But wouldn't Kane be more suspicious if I'd agreed to his every demand?

"All right, Morgan, we have a deal," Kane said. "I'll be right down." The phone beeped then beeped again. "Rollie, once you do your search on Morgan, get my suitcases from the lobby and take them to the cab."

Kane's bodyguard knelt down in front of the open door with one knee planted on the brick. He proceeded to pat me down.

Foreplay wasn't Rollie's forte. He wasn't manhandling me the way he had earlier, but he was still rough. Most of my body had become sensitive and sore to touch like the day after a strenuous workout.

"Open the case," Rollie said, pointing to my briefcase on the passenger seat. "But don't reach inside."

Damn. The folder with information about Oliver Kane and pictures of his house, office, wife, and girlfriend would be dead giveaways. But what other choice did I have? Rollie threw me a hard look when I lifted the briefcase lid. Then he cussed under his breath. The phone tapped against his temple.

"The glove compartment," he barked. "What's in the glove compartment?"

"I don't know. This isn't my cab."

Rollie moved to the passenger side. Damn. He'd think I was dirty if Benny had another gun stored in the compartment. It would only agitate Rollie more if I tried to stop him. He ripped open the glove compartment door. His face brightened after he pulled out a stuffed manila envelope from under Benny's license. His fingers tore at the clasp.

"Maps." He tossed the envelope back into the compartment. "Freakin' maps."

I'll be damned. Rollie's mind was preoccupied with the hue of fifty thousand in cash, not a weapon. Kane may have more enemies than he thought. And I just dodged another bullet. From Rollie's angle, he should be able to see the guns under my shoes on the floor. But right now, a gun was the last thing he was looking for.

Rollie lifted his bulk to a standing position and performed a neck-cracking routine. Then he turned his back to me and stomped to the lobby. I fumbled for the guns on the floor, putting them in their respective pockets. My fingertips grazed the pill bottle. Constant spurts of pain had been escaping from my heart like a leaky faucet. I could think of only one positive to having chest pain. If I was feeling it, I was still alive.

"Hey, Pro-feet," Rollie bellowed, lugging two huge suitcases. "Pop the trunk."

I had no clue as to where the trunk release was. My fingers slid underneath the dash and stopped when they connected with a notched groove. I pulled the latch towards me. The cab's white hood popped open.

"Aw, man," Rollie groaned, dropping the designer cases onto the sidewalk. With two hands, he pushed the hood down before moving to the driver's side. He tugged a lever to the left of the steering wheel that clicked open the trunk. Then he shut my door. "And Mr. Kane thinks I'm dumb. I know how to open a friggin' trunk."

The cab's back chassis slumped down when Rollie threw the suitcases into the trunk. With the lid up, I couldn't see him. My shoulders notched into my neck, awaiting the shock and noise of the lid being slammed shut. Instead, muffled metal clanking sounds filtered into the cab. Rollie was rummaging through Benny's tool kit. The goon was still looking for the cash and maybe a gun. If I'd hidden the money in the trunk, would Rollie have pocketed the cash and not told Kane?

A rhythm of fast-paced, hard-soled shoes pounding on the brick-inlaid sidewalk prompted Rollie to bang the trunk down. A serious-faced Oliver Kane walked to the cab with an expression I could recognize and appreciate. He was a man on a mission.

Seeing Kane in person brought on another gush of adrenaline throughout my system. He was wearing a leather sports coat over a black turtleneck sweater. His briefcase swung at the side of his charcoal slacks. With his tanned features, slicked-back, dark hair, trim body, and confident stride, Oliver Kane looked like an animated *GQ* page.

Rollie was chewing on a new toothpick. As Kane approached, Rollie's shoulders straightened like a soldier in the presence of a general during inspection. Kane looked past Rollie then made eye contact with me for the first time. He studied my face as if he was reaching into his memory bank of mugs. I had been sitting in the audience during the Adam Harding prelim hearing. Could he recognize my face? Kane had piercing, blue eyes that seemed to look inside, then through me. He angrily allowed his briefcase to plummet onto the bricks.

"I've seen you before, Morgan," Kane said.

"We've never met, Mr. Kane." Not a lie, but obviously he did see me at the trial.

"Rollie, get that fucking toothpick out of your mouth," Kane snarled. "Makes you look even more like a punk." His eyes shifted to the backseat while Rollie spit the toothpick to the ground. "Where's my luggage?"

"I put your bags in the trunk, sir," Rollie answered.

"Didn't I tell you to bring my bags to the cab?" Kane said. "I never said anything about putting them into the trunk."

"Yeah, but if this dude's taking you to the—"

"I don't want to hear your damn excuses, Rollie." Kane picked up his briefcase. "When are you going to learn to do exactly what I say?"

"Sorry, Mr. Kane." Rollie looked down at the brick. "Won't happen again."

Rollie reached for the backseat door handle. Kane knocked Rollie's hand away with his briefcase, then turned his attention to me.

"Get my luggage out of the trunk, Rollie. I'm not going anywhere with Morgan until he shows me some money."

Rollie motioned for me to open the trunk latch again. Kane may be a poor poker player, but he was no fool. He just asked me to ante up fifty thousand dollars in cash for a game of showdown. Money I didn't have on me.

"Hold it, Rollie," I said. "Getting Mr. Kane's bags won't be necessary."

The money clip in my left palm was about a pound short. Benny's gun in my right hand compensated for the weight difference. Neither hand would satisfy Oliver Kane.

CHAPTER TWENTY-SEVEN

A glaring Oliver Kane stood on the brick sidewalk ten feet away waiting for my response to his money demand. He was an easy target. I was still sitting behind the cab's steering wheel. My hand inched Benny's gun across my thigh towards the open window.

Kane signaled to Rollie with a head nod. The bodyguard reached inside his overcoat. I'd bet fifty thousand dollars in cash that Rollie's premature trigger finger was petting a hibernating gun. He was unaware I was armed even after the rude frisk he'd given me earlier. For the love of Mike, Pete, and God, did I just corner myself into shooting two people?

"The money, Morgan," Kane demanded, his open palm stretched towards me. "No dough, no go."

"He's stalling, Mr. Kane," Rollie said, showing a portion of his revolver's bluish-gray surface. "I don't think he's got the scratch."

"Shut up, Rollie," Kane said, still looking at me. "What's it going to be, Morgan?"

Good question, Kane. At best, my reactions were slow. Plus I'd never fired a gun at anyone. Hell, I'd never fired a gun. If Rollie got a shot off before I could shoot Kane, I'd accomplished nothing. I sent Benny's gun back into my coat pocket holster. There had to be another way.

Rollie took two steps towards the cab. The money clip palmed in my left hand was fat with hundreds, around five thousand dollars worth. But the last of my cash represented only ten percent of what I'd promised Kane. The gray matter in Rollie's head may be a few ounces deficient, yet even he knew I was short the money. I could only hope Kane's state of mind had remained on tilt from being so far in the red. In that case, he'd still think of me as his potential ATM.

Another round of smarting pops emanated from my heart. My head twisted away from Kane with fast-blinking, moistened eyes.

Time was critical, but I was forced to wait for the hurt to finish its course. I blew out several short breaths, spread the bank notes like a magician fanning a deck of cards, then extended my fingers out the cab's window. The bills flapped in the breeze, hiding a shaky hand. Hostility radiated from Rollie's scowling eyes, but I had Kane's complete attention. A good start to the illusion of making five thousand dollars look like fifty thousand.

"We seem to have built up a mutual wall of distrust, Mr. Kane. And we don't have much time left to tear that wall down. Allow me to make the first overture of good faith. Here's an upfront down payment. You'll get the rest after we confer."

I shuffled the bills back into a neat pack. The bundle dropped into a free fall, slapping down onto the brick pavement. Bills flicked off the top of the pack, drifting high and low on the current's whim. Kane stood motionless, his eyes elevated in disbelief watching his cash fly off. He released his briefcase and darted to the money still on the ground. On the way, he swiped at a floating Franklin and missed. His black loafers skidded on the uneven brick before he was able to stomp on the remaining pile of hundreds.

"Don't just stand there, dipshit," Kane barked at Rollie. "Get my money. And I better not catch you rat-holing any bills in your pocket."

Rollie pushed his heavy body towards a hundred dollar bill bouncing in the air. He changed his mind when he noticed two bills traveling in close proximity to his right. His overcoat bottom flew up cape-like even though his motions were slow. The tantalizing green paper made him look foolish and uncoordinated, like he was chasing chickens with no boundaries. At the rate Rollie was going, he should be distracted for a while.

"Get in, Mr. Kane," I said. "The clock's ticking and we've got a lot to discuss."

Kane did a quick eye audit before pocketing the money. He glanced at the cab's front door and frowned. Why was he reluctant to join me? Kane should have forty-five thousand more reasons to jump in. Something was wrong.

Kane stooped to retrieve his briefcase. A loud thump, followed by a groan caused him to look back over his shoulder. Rollie was sprawled out on the sidewalk, stomach to brick after making an off-balance stab at a bill and coming up with air. Kane shook his head, not in empathy, but at Rollie's futility.

"I don't go anywhere in a car without Rollie." Kane produced a cell phone from his jacket. "But you're correct about running out of time."

My fingers squeezed the gearshift knob. I was screwed if Rollie joined us. The bodyguard may be a lowlife thug, but that doesn't make him worthy of a death sentence. Sorry Kane, but Rollie wasn't invited to your going away party.

The fact that Kane paid for protection was telling. As annoying as my attorney Robert Shecter was, he didn't need a bodyguard. Kane must have had threats or attempts made on his life. Was that the reason he was reluctant to get into the cab alone?

"This is Oliver Kane," he said into the phone. "Give me an update for American Flight 11, Boston to Los Angeles, 7:45 departure time. "No, I don't want to wait. Shit."

I could give Kane a faster, better update. The word departure would take on a new meaning for him. He was about to be grounded, permanently.

Kane cranked out a sharp whistle for Rollie's attention. He pointed a finger to several renegade hundreds trapped against a stone pillar. Rollie charged towards the building before the wind shifted. Kane peered down at his shoes while covering a vacant ear with his hand.

"Still on time," Kane said. "I'd thank you, but you made me wait too long." He flipped the phone shut in one motion.

"Obviously, time is an issue for both of us, Mr. Kane," I said raising my voice. "I want to make sure I get my money's worth in the limited time we have. Why don't you get into the cab while we wait for Rollie? It's more convenient for us to interact."

"You're slick, Morgan," Kane responded, with a tight-lipped smile. "I'll give you that much. You've pretty much called the shots, messing with the way I operate. Don't forget what I told you. I'm not a man to fuck with."

"I haven't forgotten, Mr. Kane. Not for one second. More than ever, you've convinced me that you're the man I want."

Kane squinted at Rollie as if he was watching a horror movie. Then he ran a forefinger across the scar splitting his eyebrow. He was obviously torn. Was that his decision-making gesture? Come on, damn it. Climb into my cab-web, said the anxious spider to the reluctant rider.

Sirens whined from a distance behind us. The rearview mirror showed nothing but an empty street. Rollie stood frozen next to a Kane Tower pillar with a handful of hundreds. Kane stared nervously down High Street then glared into the cab. The sirens grew louder, more threatening. Did Kane think I was working with the police, trying to set him up?

"For Christ sake, Rollie," Kane screamed. "Put the money away. Then get your ass out of view."

Illuminated red buttons on the tops of police cars appeared in the side and rearview mirrors. My right hand clutched the gearshift, ready to take the cab out of the restriction of park. Was the Boston SWAT team after us?

The oncoming rumble of engines and blaring sirens made the giant building-enclosed street feel like a stampede. Rollie had disappeared. I flicked off the emergency brake, turning the tires to aim at Kane. Kane stood several feet off the cab's left front bumper. He alternated his view between the street and the cab, backpedaling. He was vulnerable with no one to protect him. My foot held steady on the brake pedal. Would this be my last opportunity to take Kane out?

The crescendo of sirens formed earsplitting surround sound. When the gearshift connected with drive, I disengaged my foot from the brake. I had visions of the cab jumping the curb and pinning Kane against the building like a decal. Four blue-and-white police cars blasted single file past Kane Tower, close enough to feel their vibrations. My foot jumped back to the brake. The cab's front tires rested on the curb.

Kane followed the speeding police cars with his eyes until they disappeared. I snuck the gearshift into reverse sending the frame bouncing back onto the street. No doubt Kane had noted the cab's erratic movement. He marched at me with blue eyes blazing.

"For a second there," he said, "it looked like you were going to run me over."

"My apologies. Bit of a panic on my part. I thought the police cars were going to ram into the cab."

Kane ran his finger over his scar again. He turned his back to me and stared at the building entrance. His shoe stomped into the brick as if he was exterminating a giant bug. We were both wondering where Rollie had gone, and when was he coming back.

I could hear precious seconds ticking away in my head. Maybe Kane was hearing the same sound. He didn't want to miss his flight to Los Angeles. Why wouldn't he get into the cab?

"Perhaps I've made a mistake, Mr. Kane." My foot pushed down on the throttle, producing a roar from the engine. "Your unwillingness to conduct business is telling. I don't mind admitting that your untrusting nature is baffling to me. Please return my small cash retainer, and I'll be on my way."

I'd just thrown a huge bluff at him. He wiped a hand over his mouth then did the eyebrow thing again. If Kane called me, or even raised me back with a counter, the game was over. My hand reached for Benny's gun again.

Kane shot another fleeting look at the building entrance. His hand disappeared into the pocket housing the money I'd given him. I could hear and see his exhale. He ambled towards the cab. My finger notched into the trigger. His eyes stay fixed on me. Like in poker, was he looking for a "tell" expression that would identify my intentions?

He moved past the driver's door. My eyes shifted to the side mirror to follow him. Kane stopped. Then he opened the cab's rear door. I couldn't believe what I was seeing. My first fare was sitting in the backseat with his briefcase resting on his lap. A portion of his face appeared in the rearview mirror. The door remained open.

Four things registered to me at once. Up close, Oliver Kane had striking, electric eyes any mesmerist would dream of to induce a quick trance. He smelled as good and as expensive as Bruno had advertised. The scar running through his left eyebrow was more pronounced. And Kane's twitching body language said he was uncomfortable sitting in the cab.

I repositioned the rearview mirror to observe Kane's every move and reaction. My heart was pounding like jackhammer, intensifying the discomfort in my chest. Kane opened his briefcase. He flipped his gloves inside the case and removed a yellow legal pad. A gold pen came out next. His demeanor was all business. He used the top of his case as a desk, writing in the upper right-hand corner of the page. We were about to consult, albeit below-board. Yet he never considered any form of social warm-up like offering me his hand. Would he have done the same if I was sitting in his office?

"Could you please move to the front seat?" I asked. "I'd prefer that we communicate across from each other."

Kane extracted a small bag of Planter's Peanuts from his pocket. His teeth tore off the top of the bag. He spit the plastic onto the sidewalk then emptied all the peanuts into his hand without offering me any. He shook the nuts like dice then shot a cluster of them into his mouth from the top of his fist. The son of a bitch was stalling, biding time, and waiting for Rollie to appear.

"Again, Mr. Kane, I'd appreciate it if you'd sit up here with me. I also think it would be a good idea for you to close your door before some sleepy Starbucks-deficient pedestrian walks into it. I'd hate to start our business with a lawsuit."

"Around here," he said, "Dunkin' Donuts serves the best coffee."

The last of the peanuts went into his mouth. He wiped his hands together, chewing like a hungry cow. His upper body leaned out the cab to look longingly at the building's entrance. He pulled his head back in then followed the path of a Lexus motoring past us. If Boston's financial district was anything like San Francisco, we were minutes away from the start of the morning's normal craziness.

"The clear air is crisp, and the colors of fall are resplendent," Kane cited in a theatrical voice. His tongue ran over his lower lip to catch any remaining salt from the peanuts. "I read that once from a travel brochure describing a Boston September. Apropos, don't you think?"

"I couldn't care less, Mr. Kane. Why don't we cut out the crap and get to the point of why I requested this meeting with you? But I insist that you sit up front with—"

"The answer to your request is a vehement no," he snapped. "I never travel in the front seat." His shoulders dropped as he leaned back. "You know, nearly 600,000 people here are packed into a radius of forty-six square miles. Most of them know who I am. But I still don't know who you are. Quite frankly, I can't figure you out, Morgan." He underlined something on the pad then pointed the pen at me. "Are you out to get me? Or are you in so much trouble, I'm the only person who can save you?"

A tall, blue-suited young man wearing a backpack and running shoes walked fast towards the cab's open door reading a newspaper. Kane slammed the door shut before the man had a collision. The man was unaware that Kane had just done us both a big favor. Kane rolled his wrist to peek at his Rolex. Time was running out, for both of us.

"Mr. Kane, what if I told you that I killed a man with my car? At the time, I was sober as a teetotaler and in no way impaired by drugs. The act was premeditated. I simply wanted the bastard dead. With that knowledge, will you still take my case?"

"Of course," Kane offered, without changing expression. "The circumstances aren't what I specialize in, but I'll take the case for a quarter of a million dollars upfront and a half mil after I get you off." He smiled. "I give discounts for cash. That shouldn't be a problem for a man who says money is no object."

I acknowledged him with a nod. Another green-and-white taxi pulled up behind us. A nicely-dressed woman in a long, gray skirt lugged out a heavy case, the kind that had wheels. After paying the cabdriver, she rolled the bag behind her towards Kane Tower. The taxi coasted next to us and stopped. The driver peered into our cab, maybe looking for Benny. The grin on his face disappeared when he saw a man wearing a suit, and a face he didn't recognize sitting behind the wheel.

"I've admitted that I murdered this man on purpose." My left hand squeezed the steering wheel until the cab motored away. "What if I told you he wasn't the first person I'd killed with my car? And probably not my last. Do you still represent me?"

"Absolutely," Kane said in an indifferent tone. "With the rate you're going, Morgan, you should consider putting me on a monthly retainer." He smiled again. Then he readied his pen to the pad.

"Give me the particulars. Where did the last accident take place? How long ago? Were there any witnesses? What's the deceased person's name?"

"The murder took place in Boston this morning." My moment had arrived. I turned and aimed Benny's gun at Kane's face. Another strike of pain hit my chest. "The man's name is Oliver Kane."

"Who the fuck are you?" Kane demanded, his chin jutting out in defiance.

I pushed the short barrel closer to him. Kane flinched back into the seat. His confrontational expression had been replaced with fear.

"I'm the ice queen's father," I announced, pulling the trigger.

Chapter Twenty-Eight

Gun powder fouled the cab's air. Both of my ears were ringing to the same tune. The backseat bullet hole was a good six inches away from Kane's cheek, a lot closer than I had intended. Yet pulling the trigger on Benny's gun had been cathartic in a way I never could have imagined. So much so that I was pain free for the moment. Who knew?

The forearms that covered Kane's face lowered. He examined the small hole in the seatback then turned his concentration to the windshield. He was looking for Rollie or anyone else who could help him get out of the dilemma I'd created. Someone must have heard the shot, yet to my amazement not one person was in sight.

Kane made a sudden lunge for the door handle. I countered his move by pointing the gun at his hand. His body froze in a rigor mortis-like state, but his eyes questioned me.

"Allow me to counsel you, counselor," I said. "Don't go for the door again. Keep your hands on the briefcase where I can see them. Sending a bullet your way created an unbelievable high for me. Can you imagine how good I'd feel if I hit you?"

"Just who the hell are you?" Kane snarled, placing both hands flat on the case.

"I'm a man with a gun demanding that you move to the front passenger seat," I said. A seat often referred to as the death seat, but Kane probably knew that. "The deck is stacked against you, Kane, and I'm holding the only wild card in my hand."

"Look, I've told you before I can't sit up there." Kane removed the bills he'd stuffed into his coat pocket earlier and flipped the wad of hundreds onto the seat beside me. "Here, take your money back. You want legal advice. It's yours. Free. Pro bono. I'm sure we can find an agreeable solution to rectify whatever the problem is. Come on, Morgan. At the very least, I deserve a chance to defend myself."

Kane was conditioned to talk his way out of anything. He

173

could plead his case until he was tattoo-blue in the face. There was no chance he would convince me to change my mind about his involvement in Katie's and other deaths. His gift for circumventing the judicial system meant nothing now. He was out of his element here in my court.

"I'll give you an opportunity for a closing argument on one non-negotiable condition." I gathered and stowed the bills into the glove compartment without losing sight of Kane. "Move your shyster ass to the front seat."

"So I'm on trial here, is that it?" He touched his eyebrow scar.

"Your winning record for defending clients is undeniable. But let's see how good a lawyer you are when it's your life at stake. Keep in mind that every word, move, look, and sound you make will most likely be held against you."

Kane sniffed. His eyes shifted from the gun in my hand to the briefcase sitting across his lap. Like with Benny, I never considered that Kane could be carrying a failsafe weapon in case someone got past Rollie's protection.

"What if I refuse to partake in your kangaroo court?" he said, sticking out his chin again.

"Then, Oliver Kane, you leave me no choice but to be judge, jury, and executioner. It's your call. But make it now."

"You haven't even told me what crime you believe I committed," Kane said. "To my knowledge, I haven't hurt anyone. What you're doing is criminal and fucking insane."

"I can't debate your argument about my being crazy." I managed a smile. "Anyone who would freely shoot an unarmed person has to be demented in some way. But then again, anyone who would knowingly represent a guilty murderer, like your offer to me earlier, can't be right in the head either."

Scattered patches of financial district pedestrians, most with Dunkin' Donuts coffee cups in their hands, appeared out of nowhere, traveling both sidewalks. I was running out of time. Someone was bound to notice me pointing a gun at the man sitting in the backseat of this cab. And Rollie could return at any moment. Kane's eyes were zeroed in on the gun. If the son of bitch tested me, was I capable of shooting him?

"You still haven't answered my question," he pleaded. "What did I allegedly do?"

"I gave you your options. You've run out of time, Kane."

"Some friggin' options you've given me," he said, reaching for his briefcase. "All right, I'll move."

"Without the briefcase," I ordered. "Make no mistake, Kane. If you make a phony move or cry for help, you give me no choice but to pull the trigger."

Kane slid across the seat to his right. A finger touched his scar again. He shoved open the door. One foot touched down on the street, then the other. He was in no hurry. Once again his eyes searched for a means of escape. He stared at a woman cruising by on the brick sidewalk, swinging a large purse. She ignored him and his probable silent pleas. He lifted his body to a standing position. If he was going to run, now would be the time. He focused on the gun in my hand then the front passenger door. He scowled at the door as if it was an entrance to the electric chair. In a sense it was.

A city truck lumbered past us. Kane glanced at the building entrance and sucked in a deep breath. He threw open the front passenger door, shaking his head. What was it about cars, especially the front seat that traumatized this man? He lowered his body onto the cab's seat, leaving the door open. Sweat glistened on his once-tan complexion.

"I've met your condition." His voice dripped with anger. "Now, what do you want?"

"I want my daughter back."

"Okay," he said, with brightened features. "I'll help you."

"Too late, Kane." My finger twitched from the trigger guard to the trigger. I pushed the gun at him. "She's dead. And you're the person responsible."

"Me!" Kane recoiled. He lost his balance. His hand seized the dashboard to prevent falling out of the cab. "You're out of your mind. I never killed your daughter."

"Close the damn door, Kane."

"Morgan, you don't understand. If I close this door, I'll have a major panic attack. I just can't..."

Kane gazed at the windshield. A confident glint returned to his eyes. I stole a look at the building, confirming my suspicions. Rollie stood at the lobby entrance next to the grey-skirted woman with the briefcase on wheels. She aimed a finger at the cab with her mouth flapping like an auctioneer. She must have heard the gunshot and ran for help.

Rollie's legs spread. He drew his gun. The woman ran screaming into the lobby, leaving her bag at the door. With two hands, Rollie aimed the gun barrel at the cab and fired. A bullet caromed of the cab's roof, sounding like an exploding bomb.

"That dumbshit could have hit me," Kane cried, ducking down in the seat.

"How convenient would that be?" I said. "Oliver Kane and his client killed by his bodyguard. Wish I'd thought of that."

CHAPTER TWENTY-NINE

Rollie crouched into a shooter's stance again. Did he just send me a loud warning? Or was he a lousy marksman? Kane wasn't taking any chances, ducking his head underneath the cab's dashboard. I remained upright, holding Bennie's gun on Kane and waiting for Rollie to make the next move.

Kane's head crept up high enough to see what was happening. Maybe he couldn't stand the silence. His eyes widened with disbelief. So did mine.

Rollie turned to his left and dropped the gun onto the brick. He lifted both hands and placed them on top of his head. What the hell?

"Why did he drop his fucking gun?" Kane said, looking in disbelief at his bodyguard.

A tall, slender man with wavy, dark hair stepped from the shadows at the far right end of the Kane Tower building holding a gun aimed at Rollie. He was dressed in black clothing. I caught a glimpse of the man's features as he marched into the building's illumination. A face I'd seen twice before; on last night's flight in the newspaper photo of the disgruntled family, and the angry-looking fiancé leaving a courtroom after an Oliver Kane defeat. The same man who had sat behind me at Adam Harding's preliminary hearing. Now I knew why Bruno Santiago had no wife to go home to at night.

Rollie went down to his knees at Bruno's direction. The private detective moved close enough to kick away the gun lying on the brick. Bruno moved to stand behind Rollie the same way an assassin would. Then he nodded to me.

"It looked like you could use a little help," Bruno said. "This one's on me. Now get the hell out of here and execute what you came here to do."

My foot punched down on the gas pedal, sending the cab to the

177

middle of High Street, leaving tire marks on the road. Kane's brief-case and legal pad plummeted to the backseat floor. Momentum slammed the passenger door shut before Kane could jump out.

"Stop the car," Kane screamed. Both of his hands clutched the unattached safety belt like it was a rope hanging over a deep ravine. "For God's sake, pull over. Please. Stop."

Kane's shoes pounded into the floorboard. He uttered streams of unintelligible, groaning words. Why wouldn't he release the strap to buckle the seatbelt? Whatever his reason, I wasn't disputing the move. The seatbelt strap was as good as a set of handcuffs.

I resisted the urge to look back at Bruno. Obviously, Bruno knew Kane had a bodyguard, a major fact he didn't want to share with me. What other information had Bruno neglected to tell me?

Up ahead, on Kane's side of the street, the police cars that had raced past us earlier were parked at the curb. My foot left the accelerator. A security alarm screeched from one of the build-ings. Two males resembling back-alley, San Francisco vagrants had their wrists handcuffed behind their backs. None of Boston's finest noticed Kane ogling them or heard his screams of panic when we sped by. The upper half of Kane's body rocked on the seat. His eyes pleaded.

"I'm begging you," he said in a tortured tone. "Please stop the car."

I stayed at a few notches over twenty-five. Too fast for Kane to jump out, but not noticeably over the posted limit. His rocking motion quickened.

"I didn't kill your daughter," he shouted.

"Does the name Adam Harding ring any bells with you?"

"Harding," he repeated. "Harding was a client of mine until the twit did himself in."

"But not before Adam Harding killed a total of four people. One was my daughter, Katherine Proffitt, the ice queen as you referred to her at your big payday victory gig."

"How'd you find out about the party?" Kane said. "Okay, I may have made the ice queen crack. What do you think my comment will get you in a court of law?"

My brain screamed for me to empty the gun's bullets into Kane's heart. That was exactly what Bruno had wanted me to do – kill Oliver Kane. My finger jumped off the trigger. Bruno hadn't been neglectful when he didn't inform me about Kane having a bodyguard. Quite the opposite. Bruno had feared any knowledge of Rollie might deter me from going to Boston to complete my mission. After our phone connection had died earlier this morning, he'd guessed right about where my meeting with Kane would take place. Kane's evil had touched Bruno too, enough for him to involve himself by handling Rollie. But if Bruno had an axe to grind, why hadn't he killed Kane himself?

The cab drifted dangerously close to a parked car. Kane shrieked out a warning. I jerked the wheel hard to the left. Kane's body continued to rock back and forth, while his head swiveled from me, to the windshield, the passenger window, then back to me again. His movements made me dizzy. My left hand gripped the steering wheel tighter.

An insightful laugh grunted from my throat. Why should Bruno implicate himself by murdering Oliver Kane when he could maneuver a puppet named Proffitt to do the dirty deed for him, the single reason he took my case? And he received ten thousand dollars in cash to boot. He'd been waiting all this time for just the right circumstance. Bruno was many steps ahead of me and even sharper than I'd thought.

My finger switched back to the trigger. Being Bruno's fall guy should have bothered me, but it didn't. Bruno had correctly figured I was the loose cannon in this scenario – the only person who had nothing to lose. Why not use the dying amateur hit man?

Bruno was going to get his wish, but not yet. Kane thinks revenge is my motive. It wasn't, but I couldn't help but want him to experience the fear Katie had felt before she died. He needed to hear – although I doubt he'd understand – that I was taking his life to save the lives of other sons and daughters.

"Proffitt," Kane said nodding. "Morgan Proffitt. Proffitt Advertising. The countersuit. Your daughter was driving a car registered to your firm. Is that what this is all about? Hell, your insurance company couldn't wait to settle, paying us $250,000 before we went to court. You should consider yourself fortunate. Had the case gone before a jury, we could have received a judgment ten times that amount."

"This isn't about money, Kane. Money can't replace my daughter. Or the other innocent people who died because of Harding, your other clients, and you."

But Kane was right about the settlement. The countersuit had been about money. If the case had gone through the court system, and the jury sided with Harding, no telling how much the dollar award would have been. Why, then, had Kane been so willing to settle? Ethics? Or lack of them? Harding came from a wealthy family and didn't need the money. But Kane did. If Harding had lost the decision, Kane would have received nothing. Kane knew the insurance company would jump at a below-market settlement rather than chance a big payout. The countersuit wasn't about justice for Harding. The suit represented guaranteed money for Kane, somewhere close to ninety grand.

"Look, Proffitt, I understand your grief." Kane's voice lacked sincerity.

"Do you actually believe the crap that spews from your mouth?" I said. "If you understood my grief and the heartache of others, you wouldn't defend clients like Adam Harding. You represented Harding when he ran over and killed a man a year before he crashed into Katie. You knew full well that Harding's actions caused my daughter to lose control of her car. Yet you defended the miscreant anyway."

"What's done is done," Kane said, with a shrug of his shoulders. "There's nothing you or I can do to bring your daughter back. I'm not the bad guy here. I didn't kill her. The system killed your daughter."

"That's your defense? The system killed Katie?" The gun barrel bobbed up and down with each word. "You are the system, Kane. How many Adam Hardings have you represented? How many lives lost does that factor out to be? Then add the number of family members affected forever by their loss. How many more people are going to die because of the DUI Doctor's expertise? Your defense is overruled, counselor."

With each passing second, the gun I held on Kane felt like it was gaining weight. The urge to pull the trigger was like waiting to scratch an irritating itch. Would Kane leave the security of the unattached safety belt to make a move on me if I lowered the gun?

"This is utter madness, Proffitt," Kane said, staring at the gun barrel. "I didn't make up the DUI Doctor moniker. Some reporter labeled me with that tag."

A Congress Street sign came into view. If my memory served me right, Congress Street connected to the Ted Williams Tunnel somewhere along the line as a return route to Logan Airport. A sharp left turn created a momentary slide. Kane swung into the door, his face bunched together into an ugly expression.

"Where the fuck are you taking me?" he asked.

"Maybe to hell."

Congress Street turned into the straightaway I'd been looking for. Buildings sped past us at a faster rate. Kane's head rotated back and forth from the window to me.

"Let me remind you," he said, "that people are still considered innocent in this country before proven guilty. The Adam Hardings of this world have legal rights, guilty or not. And so do I."

"But that shouldn't give you the right to continue killing people."

"Be that as it may, Proffitt, legally speaking, I'm not responsible for the death of your daughter. Or anyone else's death for that matter." Kane jammed a thumb into his chest. "Instead of blaming me, go change the system. I was doing my job just like any other attorney would. Get over it, man."

Kane's words were more painful than any hurt I'd experienced in my chest. I couldn't hold back a guttural groan. How could anyone ever get over the needless loss of a child?

Tears blurred my vision until they propelled wet lines down my face. Kane leaned towards me, removing a hand from the seatbelt. My tears of grief may have given him confidence that I was vulnerable to an attack. I fired the gun, shattering his side window. His eyes flickered in shock. Jets of cold air from the open window smacked our faces. Kane inched away from me, gripping the seatbelt again with both hands. Beads of sweat formed on his forehead. He bit into his lower lip until blood trickled down his chin. His right hand released the seatbelt. He managed to throw the door open. The wind made his eyes squint and hair blow amok.

"Go ahead and jump," I hollered. "If the fall doesn't kill you, surely one of the cars behind us will." I produced a selfish chortle. "Wouldn't it be ironic if the person who ran over the DUI Doctor was high on drugs or booze? Jump. Now's your chance."

Kane drew back into the cab. He slammed the door. The cab raced past a sign for an upcoming overpass. My foot nudged down harder on the accelerator. Was there a reason why I should let this evil man live instead of crashing the cab into an overpass pier?

"You're not going to kill me, Proffitt." Kane eyeballed the dashboard speedometer. "Seeking revenge for a loved one is an enticing idea, but highly improbable for a moral man. Twice you've missed shooting me, probably on purpose. Besides, if I die, you die."

"Couple of holes in your theory." I swerved the cab off the road and onto a paved shoulder. "Hole number one, this isn't about revenge. By taking you out, I'll be saving other innocent people. Hole number two, my heart's damaged beyond repair. I'm as good as dead anyway. And so are you, Kane. You had your chance."

"Oh, Jesus," Kane screamed, bouncing up and down on the seat. "I don't want to die this way, Proffitt. Not in a car. Not in this seat. Please."

The gas pedal crept closer to the floorboard. Benny's cab sped towards the cement target like a locked-in missile. The overpass loomed larger by the second. Desperate, Kane threw a hand towards the steering wheel, which I batted away with the gun. A sharp pain hit my chest. Kane was afraid of dying. I was at peace.

"You're no better than Adam Harding if you kill me," he yelled. "No different than Oliver Kane."

From Kane's lips, his pleas rang hollow. Except Mary had said the same thing to me.

Chapter Thirty

The cab was on a collision course with tons of cement. A truck's frantic horn wasn't telling me anything I didn't know. Kane's legs were curled up on the seat. His hands squeezed life out of the safety belt strap. He readied himself for our impending crash with closed eyes, screaming like a man who knew he was going to die.

Kane's tortured cries should have been melodic to my ears. But I felt no joy. His assessment of me had been correct. I still wanted Kane dead in the worst way. Yet if I killed him, what consequences would my actions have on Mary? She'd know the truth even if I made the crash look like an accident. Was killing Oliver Kane more important than Mary's future?

Good Lord. I wasn't sent here to kill Kane. My mission had always been to save Mary. Why else were we seated next to each other on the plane? I was destined to be there for Mary, to capture her suicide pills before she released them into her mouth. Mary, not Oliver Kane, was the reason I'd been kept alive this long.

My foot jumped off the gas pedal. The gun dropped to the floorboard between the pedals and my feet. Both my hands were on the wheel now. I fought the urge to pound down on the brake, fearing the cab would spin out of control. A slight turn on the steering wheel aimed the cab's front end away from the overpass pier. We veered from the shoulder and sliced over two lanes, then past the solid white line dividing the street. Speeding traffic heading towards downtown now targeted the cab.

I twisted the wheel to the right. Oncoming cars swerved to avoid this green-and- white projectile. Horns sounded in unison. The cab slid back over the white line into an opening of moving metal trying to avoid us. A multiple-car collision that should have happened, somehow didn't. We were clear for now.

Kane's eyelids twitched open. He turned to look through the rear window at the overpass. White-knuckled fists held onto the belt strap like a lifeline. A weak, disbelieving smile formed on his lips. My shoe did a double tap on the brake pedal. The cab slowed to normal speed. A van passed us on the right as if we were idling. Remaining traffic hung back as if the cab was a plague on wheels.

Kane made no attempt to take control of the steering wheel. With Benny's gun lying on the floorboard, I was no longer armed. But I still had the upper hand as long as I was the driver. Kane was still fearful of releasing his hold on the seatbelt.

"You sick, sadistic bastard," Kane hissed, peering at a wet circle decorating his lap. The smell of urine permeated the cab then was blown away by the wind from the open window. Kane turned to me with a face contorted and creased. His knee knocked the dashboard. Then banged it again. "Is this what you wanted? To strip a man down to his soul. Are you satisfied now, Proffitt?"

Was I satisfied? Hell, yes. Not from humbling Kane, but for doing right for Mary. The value of Mary McGrath's life exceeded my desire to eliminate Kane. Had I killed him, I would have been a hypocrite, destroying every fragile fragment of belief Mary had in me. I doubted Kane had the capacity to understand the difference.

"Make no mistake, Kane," I said. "I came here to take your life. Not to humiliate you. You've done that all on your own."

"Then what stopped you?" he asked. "Are you afraid of dying with me?"

"Afraid, of dying with you?" I repeated in a calm voice. "In a sense. More like fearful of being linked with you." My head shook in disgust. "Not once have you accepted any responsibility for your actions. Nor have you shown one iota of remorse."

"Screw you and your pious hypocrisy, Proffitt." Kane stared at his watch face. "You'd be singing a different song if you needed my services. They all do."

"They?" I said. "I'm not one of them. I believe what you're doing is morally wrong."

A road sign for the Ted Williams Tunnel turnoff appeared on the right. I flicked the turn signal and drifted into the slow lane without losing speed. Kane eyed the speedometer, his shoe sounding out rhythmic beats on the floorboard carpet. He glanced at his watch again.

"Your little chicken shit circus act may have shaken me up a bit, but it isn't going to stop me. If you don't have the balls to pass go and collect the DUI Doctor, then release me."

"Exactly the plan, Kane."

How my priorities had changed. All I wanted to do now was deliver Kane to the airport. In one piece. Then be rid of him.

"Wish I could feel pity for you," I said, feeling conversational now. "But I don't. You hired a bodyguard for protection. Clearly, I'm not the only person who wants you terminated. I would have been doing society a favor by murdering you."

"Idle words from a man unwilling to back them up," Kane fired back. "What made you change your mind?"

"A soul," I said. "Something you're obviously missing. Someday a vigilante parent, spouse, sibling, son, or daughter will take justice into their hands by eliminating your legal lunacy for good. Each stranger you meet will be a potential assassin. And one day, when you least expect it, someone will accomplish what I didn't pull off. It's only a matter of when, where, and how. That shadow of fear will always be with you, Kane."

My shoe heel sent the gun sliding when I transferred from the accelerator to the brake. The car in front of us was traveling below the speed limit. Kane's body swung from the change in momentum. I switched lanes, advancing the cab's speed.

"I don't give a hot damn whether you or anyone else approves of what I do," Kane spat, "or how I do it." A smirk overtaking the corner of his mouth could have been mistaken for a smile. "I was once referred to as a necessary evil. Fitting, don't you think?"

This man relished the glamour and attention his role as a law maverick had brought him, especially from influential people. Similar to the way bad boys attracted some women. His handsome exterior and rebel image covered an ugly interior wart.

"I've created and cornered a market," he continued, "for a select populace who live by different standards than others. People unlike you. These individuals believe their status and money puts them above the law. Above other people. As long as I'm around, they don't have to play by societal or legal rules of punishment even if they damage valuable property or kill someone. At-fault offenders are my choice of client. Want to know why? Because they'll be in trouble again. More money and celebrity for me."

Kane's bravado had resurfaced, surpassing the sniveling pants pisser who had been sitting there minutes ago. He was more reprehensible than the people he represented. The bastard knew he was riding with a man who'd been seconds away from obliterating his life. But that didn't matter anymore. Kane had moved on.

A black Porsche tailgated the cab, flashing headlights on and off. The speedometer needle leaned a quarter inch past the speed limit. If I'd been doing eighty, the Porsche would still be on my bumper. I switched lanes again, allowing the Porsche to pass.

"Damn it," Kane shouted, gesturing his head at a Ted Williams Tunnel sign. "Take me to the airport. Now. There's still time for me to make my seven forty-five flight."

I didn't respond. Kane's fist pounded the dashboard. The bully was used to getting his own way.

"I promise you, Proffitt, if I'm not sitting on that plane before takeoff, I'll have you thrown in jail for the rest of your life. Then, after I sue you for everything you've got, I'll go after your family."

"Good luck, Kane. I have no family left thanks to you." He obviously didn't believe me when I told him I was dying. "And what are the laws regarding serving a dead man papers to appear in court?"

"I'm serious, Proffitt. One phone call on my part is all it will take. You'll never know what hit you if I don't make this flight. One phone call and you're just a memory."

"How the hell did you get this way?" I asked.

A tactic lawyers use is knowing the answer to the question asked. He sneered hostility at me, then twisted his head away. As it turned out, killing him would have been too merciful. I had a better way of getting at him.

"Let go of the seatbelt strap," I said.

"No fucking way."

"Were you sitting in the death seat when your drunken father crashed his car going the wrong way on a freeway?"

"You cocksucker. You have no right to talk about my father like that."

"Why did your mother commit suicide?" I asked. "Couldn't she live with the shame?"

"Don't you dare bring my mother into this." He pointed at the windshield. "Proffitt, the Ted. You're going to miss the Ted Williams Tunnel to the airport."

"How many other lives did your drunken father destroy from behind the wheel before he was sent away to prison?" I steered the cab into a curvy turnoff.

"If my father'd had me as his attorney," Kane said, "he wouldn't have gone to prison. He'd be alive today. So would my mother."

Kane daubed wet eyes with his sleeve. Tears he tasted were no different than the tears swallowed by those of us who'd lost loved ones because of his actions. How young had he been when the seed germinated in his head to circumvent the system at the expense of innocent people? Forty years of hatred and despair had rotted his soul to the core. The cause wasn't an excuse. Nor did it give him license to continue to legally murder people.

The cab dipped down into the tunnel. Bumper-to-bumper traffic greeted us. Kane stared at his other enemy. 7:08 a.m. on the cab's digital dashboard clock. Taillights from the car ahead of us blinked on and off like a Broadway sign. My foot responded accordingly. We moved a car length at a time. Kane growled like a cornered animal. He had less than forty minutes to catch his flight.

"For Chrissakes," he said, craning his head out the window. Then he turned back to face me. "We're not going to make it. Do something, man."

Traffic inched forward. Kane's teeth chewed on his lower lip again, reopening his wound. The delay was due to a fender bender and two arguing drivers, a rubbernecker's delight. Speed picked up once we passed the idled cars.

We looked at the dashboard clock at the same time. Kane's edgy body language told me we still had a chance to make his plane. Wet pants and all. But why was he so nervous about missing a flight? Perhaps Kane wasn't the only suitor vying for Tammy Jo Moore's voluptuous assets.

A blast of pain exploded in my chest, sending a cluster of hurt traveling down my shoulder and up into my jaw. My foot slipped off the gas pedal. Numbness spread into my left arm and hand. My heart felt like a pin cushion being poked over and over again. A low moan escaped my throat. My right hand clung to the steering wheel, fighting the inclination to cover my chest.

"What the hell are you doing?" Kane yelled.

The Ted was spinning. A ripple of acid bubbles rose from my stomach to my throat. The vehicle next to me honked. So did the car behind. The cab must be weaving. I stabbed for the brake pedal with no success. Every motion brought on more pain. How much longer could I hold onto the wheel?

"What's wrong with you, Proffitt?"

"My heart."

"Goddamn it, not now."

"Take the wheel," I ordered, through clenched teeth.

"No. No. I can't." He kicked my thigh with his shoe while still holding onto the strap. "You have to drive. I don't know how. We're almost out of the tunnel."

Kane needed a miracle to make his flight to L.A. The same kind of act of God that had placed me on the plane to save Mary. Except Kane was being guided by the devil's hands. And this tunnel foreshadowed no light at the end for me.

CHAPTER THIRTY-ONE

With my head sticking out the cab window, I choked in mouthfuls of tunnel exhaust like a roach caught in a can of Raid. I could visualize a last photo of former advertising magnate Morgan Proffitt dry heaving into the Ted Williams Tunnel. Perhaps a snapshot worthy of *Boston Herald* front-page status on a slow news day, but not a picture I wanted to be remembered by.

With my right hand on the wheel, I panted. Oliver Kane shouted encouragement to me. Kane's inspiring support did nothing to offset the paralysis freezing my upper left side. Nor would it get us to the airport any faster.

The pain in my chest had leveled off. Takes a licking and keeps on ticking – the old Timex commercial referring to their watches, not my heart. The ad never showed what happened after the watch stopped running. Negative advertising doesn't sell.

The steering wheel tugged at my fingers. I pulled my head back inside the cab to find two hands on the wheel. Kane was assisting me. His right hand still remained attached to the safety belt, stretching him out like a human Gumby. Kane's eyes fixed on the windshield, his lips and cheeks puckered. For the first time in his life he was steering a car. If possible, it seemed his anxiety level had gone up several degrees. He was breathing fast.

"What time is it, Proffitt?" he shouted, unable to take his eyes from the road. "Give me the time, damn it."

"Seven nineteen," I said, removing my hand from the wheel. "You still have twenty-one minutes before takeoff."

"Shit," Kane groused. "We could make the airport in time and I could still miss boarding my plane. This is your fault, Proffitt."

"Guilty," I pleaded.

Earlier I enjoyed harassing Kane, but now it gave me little solace. My right foot on the gas pedal supplied the power. Kane maneuvered the cab through the tunnel. We adjusted to each other's inadequacies. Steering with one hand was about as good as I was going to get from him. We made one hell of a dysfunctional team.

"We're almost out of the tunnel," he said in an anxious tone.

Kane nudged the wheel a fraction of an inch, then compensated by moving the same amount in the opposite direction. The cab drifted from one side of the lane to the other as if the driver was intoxicated. Now was probably not a good time to critique his driving.

My fingers rubbed tired, stinging eyes. Once I dropped Kane off at the terminal, his ultimate fate would be out of my hands. Pangs of mixed emotions pulled at me. For Mary, I was doing the right thing. But I still couldn't help feeling Kane deserved to die. Not for the people he'd victimized, but to shield future victims from his reprobate clients. In a sense, if Kane was involved in another killing, I'd be just as responsible because I let him live.

"Relax, Kane," I said. "At least you have the option to catch a later plane. It's not the end of the world if you miss your flight."

"Easy for you to say," he said. "You don't know what's waiting for me in L.A."

"Tammy Jo Moore is obviously attracted to dangerous men who represent themselves as having big bankrolls. Are Miss Moore's talents worth another divorce and digging yourself deeper in the red?"

"Jesus Christ, man," Kane blurted out. "Whoever gave you the specifics on me is good. Damn good. It had to be that guy who took care of Rollie back at Kane Tower. I want his name."

"And I want you to quit circumventing the law to defend miscreant drivers." I shook my head. "It looks like neither one of us is going to get what we want."

I tried to rub life back into my lifeless, left arm, to no avail. Bruno would be in some serious danger if Kane ever discovered his identity. No one knew that better than Bruno. Would it inspire Bruno to groom another assassin when he discovers Kane is still alive?

"I'll find out who you hired, Proffitt," Kane said. "Like I said, the guy's good, but not good enough. Here's what you don't know. I have a meeting this morning, L.A. time, with a Hollywood mogul and his movie director. They're interested in basing a character in their screenplay on me. There's another lawyer the director is considering, but he's nowhere near as flamboyant as I am. If I dazzle them with my rhetoric, and that's a given, I'll be hired as a consultant, reaping in beaucoup bucks. Plus, Tammy Jo gets a small part in the movie. A win-win. But it could all turn to shit if I miss this flight and my meeting."

"I get it now, Kane. If your meeting doesn't take place, perhaps Miss Moore will have second thoughts about joining you in Hawaii after you probably promised her a role in the movie. Pressure wise, that's a double-dip of shit."

Taillights lit up in front of us. My foot jabbed at the brake and missed. Kane stomped his shoe repeatedly, driving an imaginary brake to the floorboard.

"There's another scenario you haven't considered," I said, hitting the brake pedal this time. "Whether you make it to the meeting or not, you're a dead man. If not by me, then it's going to be someone else. Go ahead and hire a fleet of bodyguards. It won't do you any good. You saw how easily I got past Rollie, and I'm just an amateur. It'll happen again. You should consider replacing Rollie with a chiropractor to correct the stiff neck you're going to develop from looking over your shoulder."

Kane nodded, but not from buying into my warnings. Traffic ahead of us veered to the right. Soon we would be out of the tunnel and approaching the airport.

"You're an intelligent man, Proffitt. And a fool just the same. Kudos for evading my ring of protection. No one has ever gotten that close to me before. No one will ever get that close again." He turned to eye me for a second. "But consider this. If you'd had the gonads to kill me, Morgan Proffitt would've been labeled a demented killer. Oliver Kane would have become an innocent martyr. Dead, I'd be even more famous. Either way, I win."

"Enjoy your martyrdom straight to hell, Kane. I'd like to think you'll have enough time to flash on all the lives you helped destroy before you die. But that's probably wishful thinking on my part. Your day of demise is coming. Someone else will succeed and do the deed. Maybe as soon as today."

"So now you're Proffitt the prophet," he said, snorting a laugh. "I'm not impressed."

The cab moved up and out of The Ted. Daylight made us squint. With effort, I pulled down my visor. I was still feeling discomfort, but my heart pain hadn't returned. Nor had my strength. Or the use of my left side. The outskirts of the airport came into view.

"Up ahead, about a quarter of a mile," Kane said, straightening his upper body.

"You'll need to brake for a right turn. I just might make it if you'll push the frigging gas pedal down a little harder." He frowned at the daylight glare hiding the LED clock numbers. "What does the clock say?"

"Seven twenty-nine." Acid bubbled from my stomach to my throat again. I'd give anything for a Zantac right now. "What terminal, Kane?"

"B," he answered. "American Airlines. Turn right here."

Mary and I had used Terminal C. Logan was busy with cars, people, and construction. The layout of the airport terminals was different than San Francisco. I'd lost my sense of direction, but Kane was doing the steering. His tongue now ran sideways between his lips. He transferred his body weight.

"Take the wheel, Proffitt." he said, releasing the steering wheel.

He withdrew tickets from his inner coat pocket. My right hand instinctively clutched the wheel. Terminal B came into sight, then the American Airline sign.

"Boarding gate twenty-six," Kane mumbled, after thumbing through the packet. He captured the wheel again with the tickets still in his hand. "Slow down."

Spaces at the curb were filled. Cars and taxis had formed a disjointed second line. Kane curled his legs, readying to spring out of the cab. He stuffed the tickets back into his coat. My foot eased off the gas.

An airport cop signaled with his hand for me to squeeze into an open space. Kane threw open the door while we were still moving. The cab slipped in between two parked cars and stopped. It was 7:31 a.m., fourteen minutes left for Kane to board the plane. I could only hope that Kane would receive his just dues at the hands of someone who placed no value on human life. Someone just like himself.

"Where's my money?" he said, with his eyes on the open briefcase in back. "You still owe me fifty grand."

"You've got a good case, Kane." God, it hurt to laugh. "I've given you something far more valuable than money."

"Yeah, what's that?" he said.

"Your life."

"Very funny, Proffitt. As funny as a heart attack. I need the green. Hand it over."

Kane's eyes scanned my body. Then he lunged at me leading with curled fingers. I made no attempt to stop him, not that I could have with one weakly-functioning arm. The brunt of his force was absorbed by the door and my numb shoulder, but it still managed to knock the wind out of me. Kane grabbed two handfuls of my lapel before searching my pockets. He came up empty-handed. His once-vibrant blue eyes were reduced to slits.

"More tricks," he said. "What did you do with the cash?"

Feeble grunts leaked from my throat. I still couldn't breathe. I wouldn't have answered him even if I could.

"Screw it." Kane twisted around and dug his knees into the upholstery. He dragged his briefcase over the top of the seat, reached inside, and extracted a small plastic bag containing white powder.

My breathing returned in spurts. Kane's anxious words came out unintelligible. At the first sign of trouble at Kane Tower, he'd reached for his briefcase. He hadn't gone for a weapon as I'd suspected. In peril, Kane went for the security of his drug. Now, harried for time, Kane's drug stash was more important to him than the cash. He removed the loafer from his left foot. His eyes did a quick surveillance to see if anyone was watching. He stuffed the baggie inside the leather toe and shimmied his socked foot back into the shoe.

"Christ, I don't have time to check in my luggage," he said, gawking at the trunk.

The impatient cop motioned at me again. I acknowledged him with a nod, but made no attempt to move the cab. He blew on his whistle and signaled more vigorously.

Kane leapt from the cab and darted into the white-striped crosswalk, heading towards the entrance. He bounced into a dark-complexioned young man. The man lurched forward fighting to maintain his balance. Kane kept running without bothering to look back. He disappeared into the airport. The odds were he wouldn't make his flight, but I wouldn't bet against him.

The airport cop kept gesturing at me and blowing his damn whistle like I was a criminal. Maybe I was, for allowing Oliver Kane to live.

CHAPTER THIRTY-TWO

The Logan Airport traffic cop's whistle blew out beats to a song I'd become familiar with. Then he hollered at me. I couldn't decipher his words above the constant hum of traveler activity, not that it mattered. He was telling me to go away, among other things.

The cab's back door cranked open, startling me. In the rearview mirror I observed a man with a shock of wavy silver hair sliding a blue overnight bag onto the seat. He chucked a battered wood cane on top of the bag.

"Sorry, this taxi's not in service," I said. "Find another cab."

The old guy lowered his small frame onto the seat. He used two hands to close the door then scooted in tiny increments until he settled a bit north of center.

"Did you say something driver?" he asked, cupping a hand to his ear.

Pasty-white skin drooped under his chin. An age-spotted hand tightened the knot to his green tie. His blue coat hung loose. Brown pants finished off his hodgepodge outfit.

"Listen, I'm not a cabdriver...Oh, shit."

The cop marched at the cab tooting like a train whistle. What the hell was I supposed to say to him? I'm not a licensed cabdriver. I stole this taxi to kill a man and changed my mind. No harm – no foul. Yes, I'm aware that I look like Digger O'Dell's next customer for a grave plot.

I swung the cab back onto the road. Tires skidded behind us, followed by the blast of a horn. I was just another obnoxious Boston cabbie to the irate driver I'd just cut off. And to the befuddled airport cop the cab just whizzed by, I was one less pimple in a blemished job.

"I got mixed up," the old man said. "Thought I was at Arrival and ended up at Departure. Shits to get old. Aren't you going to ask me where I want to go?"

"I've already told you this cab's not on duty."

"What?"

Damn it. Talking to a hard-of-hearing person is like trying to communicate with a drunk while sober. Or negotiating with a ticked-off traffic cop.

The road directed us to Terminal C. Another cop motioned for me and other vehicles to keep moving. How could I unload my aged non-fare in the middle of the street? The poor old guy wouldn't stand a chance.

We traveled around airport parking. For some reason Terminal E came next. E was like a ghost terminal, exactly what I'd been looking for. Several pole signs warned me to keep moving. Nevertheless I snuggled the cab up to a red cement curb.

"Why are you stopping, driver?" the old man asked in a booming, craggy voice.

"I'm. Not. A. Cabdriver," I shouted back. "I'll pay you to take another cab."

"That's a good one." He chuckled. "A cabdriver offering to pay me not to be his fare."

"A hundred-dollars," I said. How interesting. When money was mentioned, he could hear me. "I'll give you a hundred dollar bill."

The old man laughed again. Then he went into a spasm of deep, phlegm coughs. Each hack sent a shock of hurt through me. His face turned no-parking-curb red. He removed a white handkerchief from his breast pocket and held it to his mouth until the jag ended.

"You okay?" I asked, after turning to face him. His watery eyes focused on my mouth as if he was lip reading.

"All in the way you look at it," he said, wiping his nose and mouth. "I'm dying. Got the big C. Just wanted to see my son and grandkids one last time. The daughter-in-law I could do without. They live near Fenway Park. Will you drive me?"

Fenway Park. The only major league ballpark I'd never experienced. His inspiration was worth much more than a C-note. My journey wasn't over yet.

"Think you could move up here with me?" I asked as loud as I could. The last time I uttered those words I had to back it up with a gun. "Easier for us to talk while I drive."

He cast a yellow-tinted smile. Each tiny movement was in slow motion. Wish I could help him, but he was in better shape than I was. He lifted his body from the cab and hooked the grips of his bag with the cane handle to slide it towards him.

A sharp pain hit my chest. I emptied the pill vial onto my lap. One white tablet went under my tongue. I swept the remaining yellow and white pills onto the floor. Warmth surged through my veins, creating a tingling sensation in my dead fingers.

A plane's engine roared overhead. It was 7:53 a.m. Assuming Oliver Kane was fortunate enough to board his flight on time, was that his plane en route to Los Angeles?

My new friend settled onto the front passenger seat. He connected his seatbelt and turned to me with moist gray eyes that had tiny flecks of red in the white parts. A hearing aid I hadn't noticed before was planted in his ear.

"My friends call me Mo," I said, offering him my only working hand.

"Paul," he said, grasping my fingers. "Most of my friends are dead."

"Did you say that your son lives by Fenway Park?"

"Right off Boylston Drive. A few blocks from the park."

"I hope you still know how to get there from here, Paul."

"With my eyes closed. Used to be my condo. Gave it to my son after my wife died."

Sweat adhered to my skin, compliments of the mighty white pill. My left side was still numb, but the hurt in my chest had subsided. I sent the cab back onto the terminal road. Paul bent forward and clicked on the radio. His crooked finger dialed around until the digital numbers stopped in the 800's. He turned up the sound louder than normal.

"Think I got the sports station. Don't see so good no more, Mo. Hope you don't mind if I listen to the radio. When I'm in town I love to hear what the Sox fans have to say."

"Don't mind at all," I said. "If Boston's sports-talk radio is anything like San Francisco's, the fans who call in are uninformed and like hearing themselves talk."

Paul chuckled. Another plane thundered above us. If Kane wasn't on the other plane a few minutes ago, he could be on that one.

My window was rolled down; Paul's was nonexistent, obliterated from the last bullet I'd fired at Kane. Paul hitched up the collar of his coat. I turned up the heat.

Paul relaxed back into his seat, listening to opinions spin from the sports jockeys. Wind made strands of his white hair flutter against his forehead. He closed his eyes.

"What's it like to see a game at Fenway Park?" I asked, leaning the cab into a curve.

"I forget which writer called Fenway Park a lyrical, little bandbox." Paul's eyelids lifted slowly. "There's no other ballpark like it. Left field Green Monster. Pesky's Pole in right field. Ted Williams spitting at the crowd. Curse of the Bambino suffered by fans and players alike. Fenway's got history and charm like an old whore who turned into a lady."

We finished the airport loop and headed towards The Ted. Mary and I had traveled the same route in what seemed like a century ago.

"Are the Red Sox playing here today?" I asked.

"Nope. They're on the road playing the Devil Rays in Tampa Bay tonight. How much longer you gonna be in town, Mo?"

"Not long."

Cars up ahead slowed down for the Ted Williams Tunnel tollbooth. All the lanes were bumper to bumper. The driver at the tollbooth in our lane seemed to be telling the toll taker his life story. Paul didn't mind the wait. He was enjoying a radio debate pitting Ted Williams against Joe DiMaggio. Time for me, however, was still an issue.

"Paul, do you have two bucks on you for the toll? I can't get to my money right now."

"Weren't you the guy offering me a hundred bucks?" Paul

laughed before going into a mild coughing fit. He offered me two shaky ones. "Here's your tip in advance."

My left forearm lay dormant on my lap when I reached across my body to pay the toll. The toll taker was half sitting on a stool listening to a small radio dialed into the same station. His money-grabbing hand wasn't willing to go past halfway for the bills. I couldn't extend any farther. We were at a tollbooth standoff.

"Ted Williams was twice the ballplayer Joe DiMaggio was," I said.

"You got that right, Pops," he replied, lifting his butt and snatching my money.

My little white lie to the toll taker behooved me. If we had been in New York, I would have said DiMaggio was better. Paul must have agreed with me because he didn't say anything. Or he didn't hear me.

The cab entered the tunnel. My heavy eyes stung. I forced them to stay open. My left shoe settled on the brake pedal while the right shoe worked the accelerator. Using both feet would give me a better chance to react, even though the driver behind us would see nothing but bright red brake lights. Traffic slowed to a near standstill. We inched forward. Ambulance lights flickered up ahead. Finally, we passed attendants lifting a person strapped to a stretcher into the back of the ambulance. Heart attack? For Paul's sake, I needed to hurry.

The sun nearly blinded me when we veered up and out of the tunnel. I tugged down the visor. Weather wise, it looked like the start of a fine New England day.

The abandoned property where Mary and I had left Benny the cabdriver came into view. The shaggy weeds were too tall for me to see if Benny was still tied to the fence.

It was 8:39. After crossing the Fort Point Channel Bridge and smelling those fishy, bay odors, we headed towards downtown. More Big Dig signs. Then Paul guided me to a highway. I purposely stayed in the slow lane, driving slower than the speed limit.

"The Big Dig is an understatement," he said raising his voice over the radio. "Before they finish, they'll have to start all over again. Maybe they'll call it The Big Re-Dig."

"We're interrupting regularly-scheduled programming," a deep-voiced radio announcer broke in, "to bring you a special news report. We've just been informed there's been an explosion in one of the World Trade Towers in New York City. Again there's been an explosion in New York City at one of the World Trade Towers. At this point in time, we have no confirmed information as to how the explosion happened. Or if there are any casualties. Stay tuned for a further report on the World Trade Center."

"Sons of bitches," Paul spit out. "It's happening again, like in '93. Probably the same A-rab group who tried to blow up a tower with a basement car bomb."

I peered at Paul, puzzled. What the hell was really happening? We rode in silence. Most likely, Paul was overreacting by insinuating that some group had exploded a bomb with the express intention of destruction and death. A mind-numbing thought.

"My best friend's daughter was in the '93 blast," Paul said in a shaky voice. "She wasn't one of the six that were killed. But she was never the same."

The radio repeated a sober musical riff several times, indicating more important news ahead. I turned up the sound even louder. The same announcer's voice came on.

"Once again we interrupt regular programming for a special news report. An explosion has occurred in one of the World Trade Center towers. The explosion took place at approximately eight forty-five Eastern Standard Time. We've been informed that smoke and flames are billowing out of a huge, gaping hole in one of the uppermost floors. The cause of the explosion is still unconfirmed. We repeat, there has been an explosion—"

"Take the next turnoff," Paul said in a morose tone. "Maybe I'm one of the lucky ones. I don't have much longer to put up with the insanity."

Paul seemed to know what was happening even if the news reporter didn't. The road from the turnoff led us onto Boylston Drive. Good thing. Paul had stopped talking. He had withdrawn into a mind cocoon. A state I was familiar with. We had to be close to his son's house. Was he too shook up to tell me when to stop?

We passed a Fenway Park directional sign. I notched down the cab's speed when we entered a neighborhood, dense with apartments or condos. Pedestrian traffic was sparse. It seemed like a nice area, especially compared to where Mary's mother lived.

"Good morning," the radio news voice said after the jingle. "But it's anything but a good morning. Folks, we're going to keep it here at news central for the time being."

"Left on Jersey Street," Paul said. "Then another left on Queensberry." After the cab completed two slow turns, he gestured with his head to a brown brick building with a red awning. "Just stop here."

Here meant the middle of the street. Parked cars and trees bordered both curbs. Paul unbuckled his seatbelt, and with an effort, shoved open the door.

"A major disaster has occurred," the radio voice said. "Here's what we know thus far. An airplane crashed into the World Trade Center at eight forty-five this morning. It has now been confirmed that the north tower was hit. Smoke and fire can be seen coming out of a major hole in one or more of the top floors."

Paul studied the cab's inactive meter. He turned his back to me and twisted his legs out of the cab. His shoes fell onto the pavement with a thud. He clutched his bag, rose slowly with the aid of his cane, and limped across the street to his son's condo building.

After Paul disappeared through the entryway, I accelerated. My attention turned to following signs to Fenway Park. Field lights atop tall standards came into view first as the cab approached from Yawkey Way. The outside of Fenway Park consisted of red brick and an ocean of green paint covering metal and wood. Fenway reminded me of a large minor league ballpark. "No Parking" signs on metal poles lined the sidewalk. Tarps covered vacant vending booths. Without the lights, Fenway could be mistaken for an old industrial business complex.

I knew Fenway was something more, though. Any true baseball fan would. History emanated from the stadium's pores.

The announcer didn't wait for a musical opening. He didn't have to. The urgency in his tone was his introduction.

"Folks, if you've just tuned in, an airplane crashed into the north tower of the World Trade Center in New York City. We've heard nothing regarding casualties. But we've just learned that the plane that hit the World Trade Center is a commercial jet liner."

I turned right onto Brookline Avenue. Then another right onto Lansdowne Street. Red and navy-blue Red Sox banners hung outside the stadium. The passenger side flanked the back of the left field, Green Monster wall. I could almost hear a raucous Fenway crowd cheer.

A sidewalk statue of Ted Williams appeared on Van Ness Street. Heavy tightness squeezed my heart. My breaths came out in pants. A piercing jolt of chest pain came next. My eyes watered. Both feet jammed the brake pedal down. The cab's momentum pushed the front tires over the curb and onto the sidewalk before coming to a jarring stop.

"It's nine-ten a.m. this eleventh day of September," the newsman said, distress oozing from his voice.

I managed to throw the gearshift into park. Tears leaked down my cheeks. I could hardly breathe.

"Folks, we've received an unconfirmed report about the plane that crashed into the north tower of the World Trade Center in New York City. It is thought to be an American Airlines commercial jet, Flight 11 that departed Boston's Logan Airport en route to Los Angeles."

"My God," I shrieked. "American Flight 11. That's Oliver Kane's plane."

I eased back into the seat, smiling. If Kane managed to board his flight on time, the son of a bitch got his just reward. My eyelids tumbled down then popped up. A sick, empty feeling supplanted my euphoric moment. I may have received what I'd wished for. But at what expense? Other people, good innocent people must have died in that crash.

Chest pain intensified with each heartbeat. My heart felt like it was ripping apart.

"Folks, it has now been confirmed. American Flight 11 that departed from Boston's Logan Airport this morning was the plane that crashed into the north tower of the World Trade Center in New York City. As of yet, there is no report of casualties. Why this flight, en route to Los Angeles, detoured to New York is a mystery."

I placed a hand over my failing heart. Fenway Park became a blur. Was it possible I hadn't had to travel all the way to Boston for Oliver Kane to die? Or did my intervention cause Kane to miss his flight? Nonetheless, if I hadn't been on the plane to Boston, Mary wouldn't have survived.

My breath caught. At long last, I would be with my wife and daughter again.

ACKNOWLEDGEMENTS

Heartfelt thanks to the following people for contributing, in a myriad of ways, to my novels, *The Ticker, Bum!,* and *Will to Kill.*

Debbie Aldred, Fred Aldred, Allison Anson, Bill Archibald, Bob Archibald, Julie Archibald, Kristol Archibald, Nancy Archibald, Frank Baldwin, Scott Benner, Elaine Blossom, Maria Bolleri, Robin Brooks, Judy Brown, Scott Brown, Bill Burns, Dennis Cacace, Carole, Sharyl Carter, Yvonne Chamorro, Whitney Cicero, Shiela Cockshott, Mary Ruth Conley, Charlotte Cook, Pat Cuendet, Brian Davis, Darryl Davis, Gary Davis, Joanne Davis, Helen Dolan, Carolyn Flohr, Margi Grant, Karen Griffiths, Laurel Anne Hill, Valerie Huber, Warren Joiner, Murray Kanefsky (MTK), Marie Kennedy, Becky Levine, Jenn Lindsey, Serena Ludovico, Laura Lujan, Karin Marshall, Mike Marshall, Allison Martindale, Alicia Mazzoni, Sharen McConnell, Lori McGrath, Tracy McNamara, Virginia Messer, M. J. S., Jeff Morena, Colleen Conley Navarro, Robbie Regan, Amy Rindskopf, Alicia Robertson, Debby Rose, Dr. Howard Rose, Laura Senderov, Jack Smallwood, Scott Smith, Steve Stahl, Kelli Jo Stratinsky, Gail Tesi, Catherine Teitelbaum, Elisabeth Tuck, Marge Tyree, Mike Tyree, James F. Whitehead, Vicki Williams, Donnalynn Zarzeczny, Joe Zukin.

Very special thanks to three literary angels who love Mexican food and selflessly gave their time, expertise, and support to my writing projects. Barbara G. Drotar (her novel, *Mama's Arms,* will soon make its debut) inspired *The Ticker* with her great true short story and encouragement. Jana McBurney-Lin (author of *My Half of the Sky & Blossoms and Bayonets*) has passionately read/critiqued all my manuscripts enough times to be considered a co-author, and Martha Clark Scala (published author and poet, picture artist, and contest winner extraordinaire) shared her wonderful common sense edits and wisdom.

My apologies, in advance, if I failed to mention a deserving person's name.

CPSIA information can be obtained
at www.ICGtesting.com
Printed in the USA
FFOW05n0751080414